MCCALL

By the Author

McCall

London

Innis Harbor

Last First Kiss

Wild Wales

Laying of Hands

Return to McCall

Visit us at www.boldstrokesbooks.com

McCall

by

Patricia Evans

2024

ISBN 13: 978-1-63679-769-4

THIS TRADE PAPERBACK ORIGINAL IS PUBLISHED BY
BOLD STROKES BOOKS, INC.
P.O. BOX 249
VALLEY FALLS, NY 12185

FIRST EDITION: JUNE 2024

CREDITS
EDITOR: STACIA SEAMAN
PRODUCTION DESIGN: STACIA SEAMAN
COVER DESIGN BY TAMMY SEIDICK

For my parents, Herschel Penn and Juanita Evans.

Chapter One

Sara Brighton's favorite time of day was the moment she left her restaurant, usually after midnight, and heard the door click shut behind her. The deafening clatter of plates and rushed voices fell away almost instantly, and within just a few seconds, only the cicadas stirred the silence. It was the same tonight as she started her walk toward the river in the heart of Savannah's downtown. Night blooming jasmine scented the air, and the live oaks dripping with Spanish moss formed a hazy canopy between her and the stars. The gothic iron fences lining Savannah's famous cemeteries were placed perilously close to the sidewalks, and every night she considered walking through them but didn't, the thought forgotten by the time she reached the river.

She unbuttoned her chef's coat as she walked and tucked it into her bag. Only one bar was worth visiting after midnight on River Street, Clary's, and in the ten years she'd owned her restaurant in Savannah, she could count on one hand the nights she skipped stopping in for a drink on her way home. Most of the downtown bars catered to tourists, but Clary's was the local dive bar where most of the queer community hung out, including the drag queens after the weekend shows at Club One. Sue, a Midwestern old-school lesbian of few words, usually covered the late shift at the bar. Tonight she'd poured Sara a double whiskey by the time she'd reached the barstool.

"It's about time you showed up," Sue said, sliding it down the bar toward her. "Drink up."

"How flattering," Sara said, catching the glass with a wink. "I didn't realize you were counting the minutes till you saw me."

Sue was definitely not her type, but flirting seemed to irritate her, so she made a point to do it every chance she got. Sue raised an eyebrow and nodded toward her glass.

"Yes, ma'am," Sara said, downing it in one swallow and handing the glass back to her. "What's the rush?"

"Your restaurant is on fire," Sue said, looking at her watch. "Has been for about fifteen minutes." Sara shot up from the barstool; she knew Sue wasn't joking. Sue didn't joke about anything.

"You might want to consider turning on your cell phone once in a while," she said. "Your night manager has been calling here trying to reach you since you left."

Sara reached for her wallet as she headed toward the door, but Sue shook her head and said it was on the house.

"I've already called you a cab to take you back," she said. "It's waiting outside."

Sara flew out the door and into the back of the cab, gave the driver the restaurant address, and pressed her head against the cold glass of the window to stop her head from spinning. The walk from the restaurant to River Street always took about thirty minutes, so the fire must have started right after she'd left. All the guests had left and the tables had been cleared by the time Sara left Kelsey, her night manager, to close the kitchen, so it was hard to imagine what could have started a fire so quickly.

As the cab pulled up to the restaurant, a surreal sea of flashing blue and red lights from the emergency vehicles surrounded it. Kelsey ran up to Sara as she stepped out of the cab and hugged her hard.

"Why didn't you answer your cell phone?" Tears were streaming down her face, and she looked both relieved and like she might hit her. "I thought I saw you leave but it started so quickly no one was really sure you weren't still in there."

"I'm fine," Sara said, holding Kelsey's shoulders and trying to calm her down. "But what the hell happened? She looked over at the ambulance beside the firetrucks but didn't see anyone being treated.

"The fire guys think it was a gas explosion," Kelsey said, using her sleeve to wipe the tears from her cheeks. "Mr. Corleone was installing a new gas stove next door after they closed and something went wrong."

Sara's restaurant shared a wall with Corleone's, Savannah's only authentic Italian restaurant. She owned the building and had leased the space to them for the last seven years. They'd mentioned they were installing new appliances to her last week, but she hadn't realized Mr. Corleone was planning to do the work himself.

"Was anyone injured in the explosion?"

Kelsey shook her head. "No, Mr. Corleone and his son were installing the stove after they closed the restaurant so they were the only ones there. They were blown back by the explosion, but other than a concussion and some bruises on Mr. Corleone, both of them are fine." She nodded toward the emergency vehicles. "Another ambulance took them to the hospital a few minutes ago, just to be sure."

They stood together for a minute, watching the water from the firehoses arch over the roof and fall into the building. Manic flames in shapeshifting colors burst out of the windows on both floors, the glass falling and shattering onto the sidewalk below.

"There goes the last ten years of my life," Sara said, the words instantly lost in the deafening wail of the sirens.

❖

Sara's parents had bought the building for her a decade ago as a thinly veiled ploy to keep their openly gay daughter as far from their conservative community as possible. Sara's decision to go to culinary school embarrassed them, and just before she graduated, her mother pulled her aside and reminded her it wasn't too late to make something of her life. Both her brother and sister had graduated at the top of their classes and went on to Ivy League universities, but Sara had always struggled with her schoolwork and barely managed to finish high school.

Luckily, her best friend enrolled in culinary school the summer after high school graduation and convinced Sara to come along, and she'd instantly loved it. After she graduated, she moved from Memphis to Savannah, where her parents offered to buy the building and equipment she needed to open her own small restaurant. It had turned out to be way more work than she'd imagined, but the restaurant slowly gained popularity in the Southern fine dining scene and was written up in *Food & Wine* magazine three years later with the coveted title of *Best New Restaurant of the South.*

After the fire, Sara spent a few weeks salvaging anything she could from the charred remnants of the restaurant, which wasn't much, and sorting through the paperwork for the insurance companies. When the settlement finally arrived and she'd sold the land where the building had been located, she realized she didn't have a clue what to do next. She'd put in too many hours at the restaurant over the years to have a girlfriend, and none of the occasional flings she'd had with tourists had lasted, not that she'd wanted them to. About a month after the fire, as Sara sat on her porch and watched the last of the fireflies fade into the violet evening light, the thought occurred to her that there might be a silver lining to the situation.

By the next day, she'd gone through her things, narrowed them down to only essentials, and given away what she couldn't fit in the back of her truck. She left a check for three months' rent for the landlord, which fulfilled her lease, and disconnected the utilities. It felt surreal that she so easily could dismantle the entire life she'd built over the last decade, but that quickly became a strange sense of freedom she'd forgotten even existed. Sara stuck her arm out the window of her truck as she drove out of town, feeling the wind slide smoothly over her hand.

The drive northwest took three days, but she finally reached Boise, Idaho, and stopped for lunch just outside the city before starting the two hour drive up the mountain to McCall. Sara sat on a rest stop picnic table and ate a sandwich she'd bought at a gas station, feeling fairly certain she'd lost her mind. Her plan, if she could even call it that, was to drive into the mountains to a tiny lake town she hadn't seen since she was fourteen. Her parents had sent Sara and her sister Jennifer to a camp in McCall, Idaho, every summer until she'd declared herself too old to have to go and her sister started lifeguarding at the pool in town. She'd never forgotten how beautiful Payette Lake was; the small town was centered around the lake and surrounded by mountains, with community docks where the locals parked when they drove their boats into town. But that's all she remembered about the place, which really wasn't enough to go on when uprooting your life, but she figured it was as good a reason as any other. The money from the insurance settlement was enough to buy some real estate and a few months to decide what to do with her now nonexistent career. As she ate the last of the regrettable chicken salad sandwich and tossed the wrapper into a trash bin, all she knew for sure was that she wanted something different.

When Sara finally reached McCall, she knew the first thing she had to do was find a place to live, and she'd spotted a handwritten notecard at a gas station on her way into town. It was written in pencil and taped onto the notice board with yellowed Scotch tape:

Small cabin available, suitable for a single man only, ask for Mary at the drugstore.

Sara pulled the card off the board and walked back outside to her truck, shading her eyes from the glaring sun. It was July, and she'd forgotten how bright the sun always seemed to be at higher elevations. Either that or she'd just been trapped in a steam-filled kitchen for the last decade.

A bell above the door clattered to life as Sara pushed open the glass door of the drugstore. It hadn't been hard to find. The population of McCall was just over two thousand people, so walking from one end of town to the other took five minutes. A plump older woman behind the counter looked her up and down as she came in.

"What can I help you with, dear?"

"I believe you may have a cabin for rent that I may be interested in," Sara said, "If this is your ad."

Sara held up the notecard and the woman put down her coffee and donned her glasses, leaning in to peer at the card as if it was written in a different language.

"Oh, that," she said finally. "I've been trying to get rid of my husband's old fishing cabin for ages. I'd almost forgotten about it, to be honest."

"Is it still available?" Sara noticed that she wore an apron covered in what looked like flour streaks and cinnamon dust.

"It's available," she said, smoothing her hands over her apron, "But I'd imagine a woman might want something a little less... rustic." She seemed to consider that for a moment, then stuck out her hand and introduced herself as Mary Parker. "But I'd be happy to show you if you'd like to take a look at it."

"I like rustic, actually," Sara said with a smile. "I don't need much."

That seemed to please Mary, and she grabbed a key from the cash register and motioned for Sara to follow. They walked back out into the bright sunlight and Mary locked the door behind them.

"Where are you parked?" Sara asked, nodding toward her vehicle. "I'd be happy to follow you there, if it's easier."

"Don't be silly. There's no sense in taking two cars; it's only a mile down the road," Mary said as she walked toward the curb. "You can ride with me."

She stopped at a cherry red scooter that sounded more like a Harley-Davidson when it roared to life. Sara didn't know a lot about motorcycles, but she was pretty sure that most scooters didn't leave the factory with engines like that.

"What are you waiting for?" She shaded her eyes and cocked her head to one side. "You're not one of those California people that needs a helmet, are you?"

Sara hopped on the scooter behind Mary and pulled her hair into a ponytail. "No, ma'am, I'm not."

As Mary revved the engine and pulled out onto Main Street, Sara smiled as the wind suddenly swept past her face. McCall was already getting interesting.

Mary pulled into a gravel drive about a mile later and cut the engine. "I hope I'm not wasting your time. The cabin is solid, nothing wrong with it, but my husband used it as a place to gut fish and drink beer until he passed away last year, so it's not fancy on the inside."

The deep blue lake sparkled in the afternoon sunlight just beyond the cabin. Pine straw covered the stone path to the porch, and as they walked to the door, Sara looked up into the treetops that were shifting and whispering as if they were trying to get a good look at her. Dry leaves littered the porch and wasp nests occupied every corner of the roof above, but a handmade porch swing shifted with the breeze and wind chimes tinkled just above the railing.

"If you go out the back, there's a deck that overlooks the lake, and a dock that comes with the cabin if you've got a boat," Mary said, looking over her shoulder at Sara and turning an old brass key in the lock.

When she opened the door, sunlight beamed into the main room of the cabin, illuminating the dust floating in the still air. An old leather couch sat across from the fireplace, and an antique trunk with leather straps served as the coffee table. A small kitchen with windows that overlooked the lake was just beyond the main living area, and above that was a loft with a sloping roofline on both sides and a large window on the back wall.

"There's a bathroom down the back hall, and the water and electricity are still hooked up. I never did get around to having them disconnected."

She opened one of the kitchen windows and a cool breeze from the lake swept into the cabin, lifting the edges of the white flour sack curtains. Mary nodded toward a vintage turquoise refrigerator that looked like it had seen better days.

"The appliances in the kitchen still work, and that monstrosity just won't quit, unfortunately."

Sara nodded and peered out the kitchen windows at the lake, shimmering in the late afternoon sunlight. A square ceramic farm sink with faucets made out of copper pipes sat just underneath them, and scarred oak countertops stretched out on either side.

"Where are you from, anyway?" Mary asked as she picked up a scattered pile of newspapers on the table. Mismatched chairs sat around the edges like disheveled children.

"I'm from Memphis, but I've lived in Savannah for about ten years." Sara looked around as she spoke, taking in the collection of old coffee cans next to the woodpile in the corner. "I owned a restaurant that burned down about a month ago, and I guess it kind of left me at loose ends."

"I'm sorry to hear that." Mary looked over at Sara with softer eyes. "It's hard when your whole life gets turned upside down."

"That's the truth," Sara said, smiling and running her hand over the cool edge of the ceramic sink. "But this place is perfect for me. I'll take it."

"Really?" Mary's brows pushed together and she looked over her glasses as if she was trying to determine if Sara was lying.

"I'd love to rent it if the offer's still open," Sara said, "But I'd understand if it's too soon. I know it was special to your husband."

Mary laughed, shaking her head. "Honestly, I'm dying to get

rid of it. The property taxes go up every year and I don't have any use for it." She looked around the room, taking it in. "I never spent any time here so I'm not sentimental about it. I've even thought about selling it, but not too many people looking for a lake house want to take on a place like this."

"If you're open to that," Sara said, "I'd love to get it appraised and consider that possibility."

Mary laughed and swatted at a fly that buzzed between them. "You may be nuts, kid," she said, sealing the deal with a handshake, "But I like your style."

Sara spent the rest of the day getting some essentials in town and a takeout pizza for dinner. She'd offered to stay at the bed and breakfast at the edge of town until she'd signed the lease and paid her rent, but Mary had just handed her the key and told her to drop the rent by the drugstore over the weekend. Sara didn't bother to unload her vehicle when she arrived home, just brought in the groceries and set them on the table before she walked out on the back deck. The sun was just setting over the lake, a fiery orange that sank slowly into the cool indigo water, the clouds just above it holding the last of the light. Warm pink and copper washed the entire sky, sifting itself into layers and meeting the dark water at the horizon. Sara flipped the top off her bottle of beer and leaned back in the worn Adirondack chair.

"Here's to not knowing what the hell I'm doing," she said, lifting the bottle and watching a ski boat cut through the water in the distance, heading straight for the setting sun.

Chapter Two

H ave you lost your fucking *mind*?"

Sara didn't even get the phone to her ear before her sister's screeching reached full volume, and she held the phone at arm's length while she searched for the zipper to the sleeping bag she'd thrown onto the bed in the loft the previous night.

"Do you have any idea how worried Mother and I have been about you?" Jennifer was clearly in full-on panic mode.

"Apparently not," Sara said, stifling a yawn.

"You can't just up and move across the country without telling someone!" Jennifer said. "What's the matter with you?"

Cue the over-dramatic sigh and Jennifer slowly rubbing her temples with her eyes closed. Sara didn't need to be in the same room to know exactly what her sister was like in this state.

"You do realize I'm a fully grown adult, right?" She tried not to let the irritation creep into her voice, but remembering that her coffee and French press were still outside in her truck made that difficult.

"Really, Sara," Jennifer said, her voice dropping to a whisper, "I'm starting to worry about your state of mind."

Jennifer had appointed herself the boss of Sara sometime in childhood, and it seemed to get worse with every passing year, despite being the younger sibling at twenty-nine. The fact that Sara had over three years on her never seemed to faze her.

"Mother says if she ever sees you again she's having you committed. Why would you leave Savannah for the fucking Northwest? You know they all wear flannel year round there, right?"

Jennifer had been married to her high school boyfriend for seven years, now an orthopedist, and spent a lot of time at the country club pool. She was too thin, and she always pulled her blond but still highlighted hair back into a tight bun or French twist. Sara didn't know why that bothered her, but it did.

"What's really wrong, Jennifer?" Sara said, pressing the heel of her hand to her forehead. "You can't really be this upset over me moving to Idaho. You love this town. It's where we went to camp, remember? Payette Lake?"

"Why didn't you tell me?" Her voice was suddenly quiet, and the first pang of guilt twisted in Sara's chest.

"Honestly, Jen," she said, "I thought about it but I knew you would just try to talk me out of it."

Jennifer started to answer, then paused. "You're probably right," she said. "I was just planning on coming to visit you in the next couple of weeks, that's all."

"Are you okay?"

"I'm fine, I just…" She covered the phone and spoke to someone before coming back to the conversation. "Look, let's talk about this later, okay? And don't move to Nepal or something before we get a chance."

Sara smiled, her irritation replaced by genuine affection for the sister who had driven her crazy the second she learned to talk, yet somehow had remained her best friend.

"I promise to stay put for the time being."

"Good enough," Jennifer said, "And until I get the real story I'll just tell Mom you joined a commune and are committed to a life of making goat cheese and never shaving your legs."

Sara shook her head and let that image sink in. "Where do you get this stuff?" It was the first time Sara had felt happy in a while, but by the time she'd replied, Jennifer was already gone.

She spent the morning cleaning the main room of the cabin and rubbing restoration wax into the brown leather couch that was in surprisingly good shape. All of the furniture was salvageable with some elbow grease, and most of it had its own charm, but she'd discovered that the bathroom was her favorite part of the cabin. Beams of sunlight that streamed through the picture window warmed wide plank oak floors, and an antique cast iron tub with claw feet sat just to the left of the window frame. It was white, with copper faucets, softened by a few worn places and chips in the enamel. A large mirror set into an old portrait frame occupied the opposite wall, and the same copper faucets sat above a white pedestal sink. There was no shower, but the idea of having to relax in a bath whether she liked it or not had started to grow on her. In Savannah, she was always either coming from or going to work in a rush; lounging around in a bathtub had been the last thing on her mind.

Later that day, Sara took her truck into town and loaded it up with cleaning products, lawn tools, and kitchen supplies. She'd managed to fit her chef's knives into her truck when she left Savannah, a custom Wüsthof collection wrapped in black leather, but she'd given away everything else except basic cutlery. Now, looking back, Sara wondered what she'd been thinking. Even if she wasn't cooking for a living, she genuinely enjoyed it, and maybe now she'd have some time to experiment with some different ingredients. The Savannah food scene was all about seafood, which she enjoyed, but she'd been missing classic Southern food, and getting to explore that again was an exciting thought.

After she had most of what she needed, she looked around for somewhere to have lunch, but the options were limited. Nonexistent, actually. McCall had a decent population for a mountain town, plus a boost in numbers once the camp season started, and it seemed likely a diner or luncheonette would do well here. But apparently not; there wasn't even a single fast food restaurant for a quick bite.

Odd, Sara thought. *Where do people eat?*

She didn't have a chance to look further before something at the community docks caught her attention as she drove by. A ski boat glimmered in the late afternoon sun, and a For Sale sign was taped to the front windshield. Sara parked and walked down the hill that separated the town from the water. The boat looked to be in good shape; it was white with a glittery blue stripe down the side that said *Ski Nautique.*

"You in the market for a new boat?" An older man wearing a faded Hawaiian shirt and ball cap walked up the dock from a boat slip halfway down the dock.

"No, sir," Sara said, with a glance at the white leather interior.

"I have no idea how to drive a boat, so I figure the residents of McCall might be safer if I stick to driving."

The man chuckled and pulled a pack of cigarettes from his shirt pocket. "Well," he said, lighting the tip with a brass zippo lighter, "you may be surprised to hear this, but most people don't know how to drive a boat until they decide to learn."

Sara smiled, declining the cigarette he offered her from the pack. "How long have you been driving one of these things?"

He looked out over the water and seemed to consider that for a moment, then turned back to Sara.

"Truth is, I bought my first boat when they banned smoking in restaurants, so not all that long ago in the big scheme of things." He grinned, flicking ash over the edge of the dock. "My wife had already outlawed cigarettes at the house, so I'd been smoking at McCall's diner until they had to ban them there too. Eventually I figured the only place I'd get some peace is the middle of the lake."

Sara watched the fading sunlight glint off the sparkly trim down the side of the boat. How hard could driving a boat be? It' wasn't like there was anything to crash into in the middle of a lake.

"Here," he said, handing her a sheet of paper from a storage box under the seats. "This has all the stats on it, so take your time and look it up online. I think you'll find it's listed well below current value."

He closed the storage box and held out his hand. "I'm Bart Riley, and you can usually find me at the docks. If you're interested, just let me know. I'll be happy to take you out for a spin."

"Sara Brighton," she said, as she shook his hand. "And I just may take you up on that."

Bart headed back down the dock with a tip of his cap, and Sara took a last look at the boat, gleaming in the setting sun. Her restaurant had been located on coveted downtown Savannah property, and between selling that land and the insurance settlement, she could afford the boat easily, even if she decided to buy real estate later.

This would literally give my sister a heart attack, she thought, giving it a last look before she walked back up the docks to her truck. *And I need all the entertainment I can get.*

By noon the next day, Sara held the title and keys to her new boat, and Mr. Riley had taken her for a spin around the lake and explained the basics of how to drive and pull the boat safely up to the docks. He also showed her where to gas up at the marina, which turned out to be exactly like filling up a car, so she was confident she could do that, if nothing else.

They pulled back up to the community docks in the early afternoon, and Bart offered Sara the wheel. She took his place in the driver's seat and patted the floor with her foot.

"Wait…where are the brakes?" Sara said, shading her eyes with her hand and peering down past the control panel. Mr. Riley didn't try to hide his amusement.

"Are you sure you don't want to take a stab at driving while you have me with you?"

Sara had opted just to watch as he gave her the basics earlier. There was one wheel, and a single throttle that, when pushed forward, propelled the boat in that direction and, when eased back, moved the boat smoothly into reverse. It wasn't exactly complicated. If she could find the brakes.

"There are no brakes on a boat, which is what makes parking it somewhat tricky," he said. He switched places with her, turned the engine off, and put his hand on the throttle to demonstrate.

"You just have to ease it in real gentle and create some current in the opposite direction by shifting into reverse to slow down or stop." Sara nodded, and he reached for his cigarettes as he stepped back onto the dock. He lit one, shielding it from the breeze with his hand, and took a long draw before nodding in the direction of her cabin.

"You have a boat slip at the Parker cabin or are you pulling in dockside?"

Sara had no idea. The closest she'd gotten to the dock was to sit on the back deck with a beer last night and watch the sun sink into the water behind it.

"Dockside."

"Good," he said. "That's easier to start with until you get the feel of things." He started to hand the keys back to her, then hesitated. "Want me to pull her out of the slip and get you going in the right direction?"

Sara nodded. That seemed like a good idea; better to get into the middle of the lake before she tried anything too complicated.

Like reversing out of a dock slip six inches from someone else's pristine boat.

Bart pulled them out of the slip in one smooth motion, spinning the nose out to face the open water. He shook Sara's hand and jumped from the back seat of the boat back onto the dock.

"It was nice to meet you, Miss Sara," he said, tipping his fishing hat in her direction. "You let me know if you have any problems with her."

Sara waved goodbye and leaned into the throttle, accelerating smoothly into the open water in the direction of the sun.

Sara drove the perimeter of the lake for hours, feeling somewhat like a fifties movie starlet with a new convertible and a long white scarf blowing in the breeze behind her. She wasn't, of course, but the J.Crew navy shorts and white polo shirt she wore were more her style anyway. This time, she stood behind the wheel as she drove so she could get a better look at the lakeshore. The water was a still, deep blue, and a perfect frame for the million-dollar lake homes just beyond it. She hadn't realized it until she was able to see it from the lake, but there was a marked difference between the north side of the lake, the side her cabin was on, and the shoreline in every other direction.

She'd done some research on the area when she'd finally slipped into her sleeping bag the night before. When she was a kid at Camp Yorktown Bay on the east edge, the lake had seemed vast, endless, a world of its own. It turned out that wasn't far from the truth. According to Google, Payette Lake was a 5,330-acre expanse of clean, glacial water at an elevation of about 5,000 feet in the forests of Idaho. When Sara looked at the map, she realized Ponderosa State Park, which was listed as a thousand acres of natural wilderness and mountain terrain, bordered the north side of the lake. It had to be privately owned up to the edges of the park, but there was at least a 150-acre stretch of buildable lakefront property there that was undisturbed. Now, as Sara glided by in the boat, she saw one house, a beautiful three-story log cabin with a single dock that looked out over the lake, that probably belonged to whoever owned that stretch of land. It was rustic, different from the rest of the north shore lake houses, each with hydraulic boatlifts on the dock to hoist the ski boats up and out of the water. This cabin was expansive but simple, built of honey-colored logs above sandy beaches and a private cove where the clear water lapped gently against the sand. She made a mental note to get an appraiser out to her cabin to see what kind of value it had; if Mary had been serious about wanting to sell, she was open to buying it, especially after she'd seen how close it was to the state park acreage.

Sara was starting to get hungry and knew from the angle of the sun it was time to start heading back. It had to be after four o'clock, and she still needed to park her boat at the cabin dock and walk the mile back into town to get her truck. She turned the boat back toward town and waved to the wakeboarders that passed her on the left, heading in the opposite direction. The loud country music that followed them as their boat sped away reminded Sara she might have a radio as well, and she bent down to check out the control panel for a dial. Her boat suddenly tipped to the right, and then violently back, throwing Sara headfirst into the controls, then shoulder first onto the floor as she landed under the wheel.

Her head flashed with pain and she slowly turned to lie on her back under the steering wheel, trying to determine if she'd broken any bones. There was blood coming from what had to be a gash in her forehead, and she found she could move her shoulder without the telltale sharp pain that would have indicated a more serious injury, so she tried to stand and find something to stop the bleeding. The boat continued to rock from side to side but with lessening force, although the motion had started to make her feel sick. She felt the wound gingerly with her fingertips. She must have cut her forehead on the control panel when the boat tipped her into it, but fortunately, that seemed to be the worst of it. Her shoulder was sore, and when she looked under the sleeve there was a nasty purple bruise starting to form, but there didn't seem to be any injuries beyond that. She stood, holding the side of the boat to keep her balance, half expecting to see another vessel sinking quickly beside hers, with an enormous hole in the side she'd put there with the nose of her boat.

But there was nothing. Just a vast expanse of sunlit, shimmering water and the ski boat she'd just seen disappearing in the distance. Blood dripped down her forehead and onto her shirt as Sara looked around for a first aid kit, making herself dizzier in the process. The flow seemed to be lessening as she checked out the wound in the rearview mirror; the actual cut was surprisingly small compared to the amount of blood it was putting out. Either there was no first aid kit or Sara couldn't find it, but either way, she decided at that point that it made more sense to just head back to the cabin and bandage it there.

She turned the key and pushed the throttle forward slowly, but as soon as the boat started, it sputtered and died. Waves lapped quietly at the sides of the boat as Sara turned the key over again, to no avail. She remembered suddenly when she reached for her cell phone that she'd left it in her truck to avoid getting it wet. She looked around her at the empty lake. How could she have wrecked her boat and injured herself with absolutely nothing else around her?

That takes a special talent, Brighton, she thought, as she sank back into the captain's chair.

The sun was sparkling onto the ripples of the water, which seemed to be deserted except for her boat, drifting aimlessly in the middle of the lake. Blood was still dripping down her temple; clearly she needed to get a better look at the cut, whether she felt like it or not. Sara raked her blond hair back into a bun with the elastic she kept on her wrist and tilted the rearview mirror closer to her. She looked at her cut carefully. She knew enough from a decade of working with knives that the cut wasn't going to close enough to stop the bleeding unless she applied some pressure, so she stripped her T-shirt off and held it against her head.

Sara was petite, with a feminine but athletic body, and rarely wore a bra; she'd never seen the need under a chef's coat and had gotten out of the habit over the years. There was no one here to see her anyway, and frankly, at that point, she wouldn't have cared if there was. She walked back to the white leather bench seat in the back of the boat and lay down, holding her shirt to her head, and closed her eyes against the pounding rays of the sun.

Chapter Three

Sam Draper walked into the police department and wordlessly handed a cup of coffee to the older woman at the front desk, before she walked through the double doors and down the hall to her office. When she'd first joined the force in McCall, almost twenty years ago, the same woman had taken an instant dislike to her. Sam was very fit, taller than she was by a good four inches, and wore her dark hair in a stylish but masculine cut. It was the mid-nineties in a small mountain town, and it didn't take a genius to figure out that Beth Thompson didn't like her. She was civil, and did her job well, but she never looked Sam in the eyes or made small talk like she did with the other officers. Technically, she was a receptionist, but in reality, everyone knew that the person at the front desk was the eyes and ears of the force, and Beth took her job seriously.

About a year after she'd started, Sam knocked on the door of the chief of police and asked if he had a moment.

"Absolutely," he said, clearing a stack of papers off his desk by dropping them in a pile on the floor behind it. "What can I do for you?"

She shut the door behind her and sat across from him in one of the two leather chairs. "Sir, I know Beth at the front desk isn't my biggest fan, but I've never given her a reason to dislike me. You've known her for years, and I was wondering if you had any advice on turning that around."

The captain looked at his desk and tapped a pencil on the calendar that covered it. "Why do you think she has a problem with you?"

Sam wondered if she was supposed to answer that frankly or if he was just asking if she'd ever had a run-in with her. He sat quietly behind the desk, waiting for her answer, and she decided to say what she really thought.

"I think it's because I look a little too much like you," Sam said.

Chief Draper pointed the pencil at her with a chuckle. "Well said."

"Unfortunately," Sam said, "I'm fresh out of dresses, so I've got to find some other way to make her see past this." She ran her hand through her hair, turning it into a ruffled mess without realizing it.

They sat there in silence for a minute or two after that, turning the issue over in their minds, until Chief Draper said, "You've been on the force now for a year, right?"

Sam nodded.

"So what's Beth's biggest pet peeve?"

Sam thought about the last time she'd seen her really annoyed. It'd been in the break room, and Beth had come through on her break, coffee mug in hand, only to find the pot empty. She'd muttered something under her breath about being the only one who actually worked, then turned on her heel and disappeared down the hall, a trail of resentment following her.

"She hates it when there's no coffee," Sam replied, wondering where he was going with all this. The chief looked out his window and nodded in the direction of Main Street.

"Don't you pass Moxie Java every morning on your way into work?"

It didn't take long for that to sink in, and Sam shot her father a smile on the way out the door.

Since that day, Sam had brought Beth a coffee every day on the way into the station and handed it to her as she passed. Even when she transferred to the Lake Patrol division, housed in a different wing of the station, she still brought one if she knew she'd be going by the front desk, by now out of habit more than anything else. Beth thawed toward Sam after a few months, and years later, one of her colleagues told her that when a visiting officer in the break room referred to her as *that dyke*, Beth had gotten up from her chair, calmly poured the rest of her coffee into his lap, and returned to her desk.

But now there was a new chief of police; Sam's father had passed away a year earlier. Sam had considered leaving the force but stayed to head the Lake Patrol division as captain, although she made a point to walk past her father's old office as little as possible. When she finally reached her office, she gathered the paperwork she needed to complete her rounds for the day and headed out toward the docks where the patrol boats were located. She always drove the same boat, and getting out on the open water was the best part of every day. In most places, crime happened on the streets, but in a small town dominated by a massive body of water, the majority of the excitement happened out on the water.

Sam patrolled the edge of the shoreline, looking for anything out of place, but the lake was quiet for a Thursday; not even the usual speeding water-skiers were present. She headed toward the north shore, unwrapping a ham sandwich from her backpack with one hand as she steered toward the Ponderosa National Forest. Camp Montauk came into view as she rounded the corner of the cove. Montauk was the largest youth camp in McCall; it was well known in the Northwest and a multimillion-dollar property, including a two-story waterslide built on the side of the dock. Sam kept her eyes straight ahead.

As she increased her speed toward the northwest quadrant of the lake, a flash of blue to the right caught her attention. About three hundred yards from the far north shore, an older model Ski Nautique was drifting. Sam knew from the water patterns that the engine was not engaged, and there didn't seem to be anyone in the boat. She accelerated toward it, then cut her engine. She utilized the currents of her wake to drift closer, picking up the radio to call back to the station when she saw what was onboard.

There was a blond female lying face up on the back seat with a bloody rag under her head. She was naked to the waist, and one arm was up to shield her face from the glare of the sun. She either didn't hear Sam approaching or she was unconscious, but her eyes snapped open when Sam tethered her boat to the side of hers and stepped in.

"Who the hell are you?" Sara scrambled to her feet, one hand pressed to her forehead, the other grabbing the bloody shirt to hold to her chest.

Sam motioned her back toward the seat. "I'm Sam Draper with McCall PD Lake Patrol, and I need you to remain seated until you tell me what happened."

Sara sat back down, holding her shirt against her body and looking through the glaring sun at the officer. She wore navy cargo pants and a crisp white uniform shirt, her gun clearly visible on her belt. Draper's voice was professional, but Sara saw her glance at the bloody shirt before she stepped back over into the patrol boat. She took a navy jacket with *MPD* embroidered on the back from the captain's chair and handed it to Sara, then discreetly looked away until she heard Sara zip the jacket up.

"Okay, ma'am," Sam said. "I can see that you're injured. Did you see who attacked you?"

Sara looked down without saying anything, and Sam took the opportunity to look around at the interior of the boat. Most of the blood was under the steering wheel, which indicated she was there when she was attacked.

"Did someone on the boat with you do this?" Sam said. "Or was it someone else you don't know?"

Sara just shook her head, and when she looked up, Sam saw she was trying not to cry. She softened her voice and knelt down to her level. "Whatever happened, I'm here to help you, okay? Just tell me who did this to you."

Sara wiped a tear off her cheek with the heel of her hand. "My stupid boat attacked me."

Sam took that in for a second. "So you were the only person on the boat when this happened?"

Sara nodded, then pointed to the control panel. "A big ski boat passed me and they had music blaring, so I leaned down for a second to find the radio."

She had a definite Southern accent, as if her words were covered in honey and clung together as she said them. Sam was willing to bet she was some rich girl from the South here on vacation, and even if she wasn't, she had no business driving a boat.

"So a boat had just driven by and then you leaned down?"

"Yes."

"Did you feel like something knocked you off balance right after that?"

Sara looked up, surprised. "Yes! How did you know that?"

Sam shook her head and tried not to smile. She was almost cute wrapped up in her jacket and insisting that her own boat attacked her. Almost.

"It was like a car crash," Sara continued. "But when I finally got up to see what I hit, nothing was there." Sara paused and touched the wound on her head. "Wait," she said. "What if I *did* hit another boat and it sank before I stood up?"

The color drained from her face and Sam thought it was probably best to take a guess at what happened before she passed out from shock, which looked to be about three seconds away.

"Ma'am," she said, leaning back on her heels and pointing at another boat in the distance, "if I had to guess, I'd say it was just bad timing."

Sara shook her head, trying to understand how timing had anything to do with crashing her boat into another and possibly killing everyone on board. "What are you talking about? I probably just murdered someone!"

Sam had to look away to keep her composure. "You didn't murder anyone," she said, turning back to Sara. "It was bad timing in that when you leaned down to look at the controls, the wake from the other boat no doubt hit the side of yours at the same moment. And because you were bending down at the time, your center of gravity was off and you went headfirst into the panel."

"Oh." Sara squinted up at Sam, clearly not sure she believed her. "So you're positive there was no other boat?"

"I'm positive."

Sam stepped away to radio the station and Sara heard her ask dispatch to send an officer out to drive her boat back to town.

"I think I'm going to need more than that," Sara said. "Like a towboat or whatever you call a tow truck for boats. On top of everything else, I somehow managed to break the engine."

Sam turned to look at the controls and stepped behind the wheel. "What made you think it's…broken?" Sam Draper was always professional, if even a little detached at times, but she was finding it hard to keep a straight face.

"Well, after it happened, I turned it on and it sputtered for a few seconds and then it died." Sara pulled Sam's jacket tighter around her shoulders. The sun was fading into golden afternoon light that hovered just above the water, and the wind was picking up.

Sam leaned down to look under the wheel. She flipped a tiny chrome switch, then turned the key and the engine roared to life.

"When you fell, you must have hit the lever that switches the engine from one gas tank to the other," Sam said. "It looks like the main tank is almost full, but the reserve was empty."

"Oh," Sara said slowly, "which explains why it died right away." She looked down at her hands and rubbed at the dried blood, then dipped them over the side of the boat to clean them.

"Do you think you're steady enough to step over to my boat and let me take a look at that cut on your head?" Sam said. "I can get the EMS boat out here, but I think that might just need some butterfly stitches, and I have that in my medical supplies on board."

"No, I'm okay," Sara said. "It's just a scratch. I think I'm just going to head home before I have to try to find my dock in the dark."

Sam shook her head. "I can't let you drive with a head injury, so driving home is not an option."

Sara stepped onto the side of the boat and almost lost her balance before Sam grabbed her waist and steadied her.

"Stay right there," she said, her voice low and controlled. "If you think I'm going to let you jump from here to the patrol boat, you're wrong."

Sam held her eyes until Sara stepped down and allowed Sam help to her get safely into the patrol boat. Sam motioned for her to sit, then rummaged through the storage compartments until she found the medical kit.

Sara watched her as she prepped a cotton pad and touched it gently to her forehead.

"Has anyone ever told you you're scary?" Sara winced as Sam carefully cleaned the area around the cut with disinfectant.

Sam smiled. "I've heard it once or twice."

Water lapped against the side of the boat, and Sara watched the blinking lights on the control panel long enough to make herself dizzy.

"Do you think it needs stitches?"

"If it was me," Sam said, "I wouldn't bother with stitches, but you may feel differently if you're worried about scarring."

"It's fine," Sara said, lifting her chin slightly. "I'm not as fragile as I look."

"Tough girl, huh?" Sam tried not to smile as she said it. "You're going to get a chance to prove that when I start cleaning the actual cut. I haven't touched it yet. Ready?"

Sara nodded, and put a hand on Sam's knee to brace herself. To her credit, she breathed deeply and stayed still while Sam worked, even through applying the butterfly strips, which Sam knew from experience wasn't easy.

The second patrol boat pulled up soon after, and another officer in the same navy jacket stepped in, a younger man with broad shoulders and a military haircut.

"You want me to drive this rig back to the station, Captain Draper?"

"Thanks, Randy," Sam said. "I'm going to drive her boat back to where she's staying, and I'll give you a call with the location so you can send someone to pick me up."

Sam and Sara stepped back into Sara's boat as Randy started up the patrol boat. "Where are you staying?"

"I'm renting a house on the north side…" Sara realized suddenly she hadn't memorized the address yet. Sam waited, noticing the blood that was starting to seep through the surface of the bandage.

"Do you remember the name of the person you're renting from?"

"Mary Parker?" Sara was almost sure that was right. "She owns the drugstore in town."

"You're at the Parker cabin?"

Sara nodded, closing her eyes and leaning her head back against the seat.

Sam was surprised; she'd expected to be driving her back to one of the five-star resorts across the lake. The Parker cabin was tiny, as Sam remembered it, anyway, and she'd be surprised if Mary had made it into a short-term rental. The last conversation she'd had with her, Mary was hoping to sell it and retire in Portland, to be closer to her daughters, and this girl didn't really look like the type to be roughing it in a fishing cabin.

The two patrol boats took off just then, and Sara lost her balance slightly when the wake hit the boat. Sam sat her down and wrapped a blanket she'd brought from the patrol boat around her shoulders.

"Keep that around you," Sam said. "The air is a lot colder now than when you started out."

Sam started Sara's boat and pulled smoothly out into the water. The sun was starting to set now, and the last of the sunlight lingered on the water like fairy lights as the boat carved a path through it.

Chapter Four

Sara woke the next morning to a stiff neck and a pounding headache, and instinctively touched her forehead before she lifted her head from the pillow. Sunlight warmed the bed from the loft window and Sara slowly stretched her sore muscles, which felt more as if she'd been in a fight than an accident. An appraiser was scheduled to be there in an hour to give her an idea what the cabin and land were worth. Apparently, in McCall, there was one appraiser and one home inspector, and it was the same guy in one truck, which Sara found amusing. Despite yesterday's disaster, McCall was growing on her; either that or she wasn't ready to go back to Savannah. She wasn't positive which one it was yet.

By the time he'd arrived, Advil, coffee, and a hot bath had made yesterday seem like a dream, and as she walked the perimeter of the property with him, she realized she was more relaxed than she had been in years. Northwest oaks turned the sunlight into dappled patterns on her arms as they marked the edges of the property, and even when she was too far into the woods to see the edge of the lake, she heard the water lap against the dock in a pattern that already seemed more familiar than not. It wasn't until she'd gotten out of the restaurant that she realized she'd been running on empty for at least the last few years. Fine dining was a challenge for any chef, but in Savannah's emerging food scene, competition was fierce. It felt good to finally wake without an alarm and listen to the cicadas on the deck while she watched the sun set over the water. The thought of being in such a competitive environment again was starting to feel foreign. Maybe she'd confused passion for the restaurant with the habit of working herself into exhaustion.

"Well, Miss Brighton," the appraiser said as he handed her the completed report early that afternoon, "there's good news and bad news."

"Well," said Sara, "there's a beer in my fridge that has your name on it if you can upgrade that to good news and better news."

"Deal," he said, "It's never too early for good beer."

She got them both her favorite Danish beer, and he took a long swig and looked at the bottle with real affection before he went on.

"Let's start with the good news. The cabin is solid, no termite damage, no indication of roof issues, and the plumbing is in better shape than my house, which is saying something."

"Any issues at all?"

"The roof over the porch is just plywood and shingles; it'll need to be replaced within five years if it's going to hold the winter snow load here, but that's a weekend project and fairly inexpensive." He took another swig of his beer. "And you'll have to have the chimney guy from the hardware store come out and take a look at that fireplace. This cabin's been empty for a couple of years, and you never know what's made a home up there in the meantime."

"I was hoping everything would check out well," Sara said, glancing at the report. "I knew I loved this place about five minutes after I'd walked in, so that's great news."

"The better news is that I spoke to Mrs. Parker about this place before I came out and she knows what she needs to get out of it as far as price. She's a pretty no nonsense gal, so I'd be surprised if she'd accept anything but that number."

"Great," Sara said, winding her hair into a quick bun at the back of her head. "That makes it easy."

"Well," Gerald said, "I'll let you decide what you want to do about this, but she wants $125,000 for the house and property. The plot of land is not big; the survey indicates it's just under three acres and the cabin is only 750 square feet, but because of where it is, it's valued at $340,000."

"The value doesn't surprise me," Sara said. "I've done a bit of research on similar properties on the north side, but what she wants for it is way too low."

"I know," Gerald said. "I'm not sure I've ever encountered

this problem before." He grinned and set his bottle down on the table as he took the check from Sara for the appraisal. "But she's a smart lady, so I'd bet the farm she has a reason. You two will figure it out."

Sara thanked him and watched him walk to his truck, until she remembered suddenly the last thing she wanted to ask him.

"Hey!" she called after him. "So what was the bad news?"

He smiled and tipped his hat as he got into the car and fired up the old diesel engine. "Take a look over your front door."

Sara watched his truck pull out of her drive and rumble up the road, preoccupied by the question of what to do about Mrs. Parker.

Sam leaned back in her office chair and swiveled around to face the window that perfectly framed the marina outside. The ropes and pulley from the flagpole were clanging in the wind, and the heat from the afternoon sun warmed her face, even through the glass. Routine paperwork was driving her up a wall suddenly. She hated it even on a good day, but when it seemed to be a self-replenishing pile, it reminded her how much she preferred being on the water. And not just because it was impossible to do paperwork in an open boat at sixty miles an hour. That was just a bonus.

A knock on her door made her turn her chair around. "Do you have a moment?"

Lily, the twenty-three-year-old temp sent from headquarters in Boise, stepped in and closed the door.

She was slender, startlingly pretty in a hipster way, with a dark angled bob and light blue eyes. The regular receptionist, Marnie, was on maternity leave for a few more months, and everyone but Sam was counting the days until she returned.

Sam got up from her chair slowly, walked to the door, and locked it behind Lily, her fingers brushing the small of her back. She pressed her slowly against the door with her body, one arm on either side of her head, then worked her fingers into Lily's hair and pulled her head gently to the side. She didn't quite touch Lily's skin with her mouth, just let the heat of her breath travel down to her shoulder, where she slid her finger under the strap of her sundress and dropped it down her shoulder.

Sam stepped back. Her voice was soft, but rough around the edges. "Take it off."

Lily wordlessly unzipped her dress as Sam walked back to her desk and leaned against it, watching as the dress dropped to the floor. "All of it."

Sam knew the sounds of her breath from across the room. It was fast, like her heartbeat; she'd memorized it over the last few weeks, her palm pressed between Lily's naked breasts, holding her body still while her tongue slid across her clit. Sam looked up and held her eyes.

Lily crossed the room and stood in front of Sam, who slid a thumb under her sheer panties, scraping them lightly down her thighs, then dropping them onto the desk behind her.

She lifted Lily into her arms, wrapping her legs easily around her waist, then turned and laid her down on the desk. Sam ran her hands down the insides of Lily's thighs, then lowered her mouth to Lily's clit, the slick heat of her body enveloping her fingers and dripping slowly almost down her wrist as she entered her.

"Do you want this?"

Sam waited. She asked her every time, and made her look her in the eyes and answer before she'd go.

"Yes," Lily said, arching her back, "Please."

"Please what?"

"Sam," she said, more breath than words, "Please fuck me."

❖

Where was that stupid business card the lake cop had given her? Sara rummaged around in the shorts she was wearing yesterday but came up with nothing, and a quick search of her boat yielded a bottle of out-of-date sunscreen and little else. *I remember her handing it to me*, Sara thought.

Sam had parked her boat in the slip, then handed Sara her card as she'd tied off Sara's boat and stepped into the patrol boat she'd called to pick her up. Sara wondered suddenly if it was in the pocket of the jacket when she gave it back to Sam, then remembered in a rush that she couldn't have given the jacket back when Sam dropped her off at the cabin; she'd been naked under it. *Great, at least returning her jacket won't be awkward.*

It was late in the afternoon when Sara made it into town and stopped by the drugstore, hoping to catch Mary, but no luck. She went on to the grocery store and picked up a few ingredients for dinner, then walked to Lake Patrol at the McCall police station.

"How can I help you?" The Lake Patrol receptionist raised one eyebrow, her eyes dropping to the jacket in Sara's hand.

"I just need to return this to Sam."

"Do you mean Captain Draper?"

Sara nodded and the door to her right buzzed open.

"Go down the hall, it's the last door on the left."

Sara was hoping she could just leave the jacket with someone and avoid Sam altogether, but that clearly wasn't an option. She went through the door and down the hall to her office, knocking lightly, half hoping she was out.

"Come in."

Sam was writing but paused to look up when Sara laid the jacket on one of the chairs in front of her desk. "It's you," she said, leaning back in her chair and spinning the pen slowly through her fingers. "Sara, right?"

"I just came to return your jacket."

Sam smiled. "Found a shirt, huh?"

Sara wanted to pitch the jacket at her. Was she so arrogant that it wouldn't occur to her that being found half-naked might be embarrassing? She picked the jacket back up. "Well, just for that, I'm keeping it."

Sam flashed her a smile. "How's your head?"

"It's okay." Sara rubbed the back of her neck with her hand. "My neck actually hurts worse than my head."

"You took quite a hit, judging from that cut, so that's not surprising." Sam got up from her chair and looked closer at the bandage. "Have you changed that dressing?"

"No. I went to the drugstore just now for those butterfly things, but it was closed. I must have just missed Mary."

Sam looked at her watch. "No, it's just time for *Days of Our Lives*. She closes for an hour every afternoon to watch it; she'll be open again around four p.m."

"You're kidding me," Sara said. "And everyone in town just knows that?"

"Well, I guess so since I just told you." Sam smiled. "Aren't you our newest local?"

"How did you know that?"

"There's not much going on that I don't know about," Sam said, leaning back on her desk. "But Bart Riley came in yesterday to register the title transfer on his boat and mentioned you'd be in eventually to get a boating license."

Sara looked at her, trying to determine if she was serious.

"You do know you need a boating license to be on the water, right?"

"Well," Sara said, resisting the urge to roll her eyes, "I do now." The lake cops clearly took water safety seriously. "Where do I buy one of those?"

"You get it here," Sam said. "But you may want to do a bit of practicing before you take the test if yesterday is any indication of your current boating skills, and a licensed driver needs to be with you in the boat at all times."

"There's a *test*?"

"Yes, ma'am." Sam shuffled the papers on her desk and held up a typed sheet with what looked like a hundred names on it. "Lake Patrol has to administer the test and pass you, and we're going into camp season, so all of their waterfront staff is already in line ahead of you."

"So," Sara said, "let me get this straight. I have to practice for this test, but I'm not allowed to get out on the water to do that unless I've already passed it." Sara paused, trying to keep the irritation out of her voice. "Then even if I somehow manage to get that done, all those people are in line to take the test ahead of me?"

Sam reached into her desk and handed Sara a book. "Everything you need to know is in there. Let me know when you're ready and I'll put you on the list. It's late May now," she said, running her finger down the list. "I'd say you should be close to the top by October."

It took everything Sara had not to slam the door on the way out.

❖

The next few weeks flew by, and unless it was to get supplies or shop for groceries, Sara rarely went into town. She'd closed on the cabin fairly quickly by real estate standards, which was exactly what she wanted. After the appraisal, Sara had stopped into the drugstore to discuss the price of the cabin, but Mary shook her head and shut her down mid-sentence.

"I'm not taking a penny less than $125,000."

Sara thought for a second then nodded. "I understand," she said. "It's a deal."

They shook on it and Mary persuaded her to stay and watch *Days of Our Lives*. Since then, every time she popped into the drugstore, Mary gave her a synopsis of what was happening in the storylines, and not that she'd admit it, but Sara had started to look forward to the updates.

She had the only real estate attorney in town write up the terms of the cabin sale for Mary to review, and just as Sara had hoped, she'd signed the papers without looking at them carefully and handed them back to Sara. Mary didn't realize until the closing that Sara had given her the appraisal value of the cabin, nearly three times the $125,000 she'd asked for.

"I agreed I wouldn't give you a penny less than the price you wanted," Sara said, "But I never said I wouldn't give you more."

Mary hugged her, and Sara was surprised to see she had tears in her eyes.

"It's what the property is worth," Sara said. "I wouldn't have felt right about it any other way."

"I won't forget this," Mary said, squeezing her hand. "Thank you."

Then she turned and punched the attorney in the arm for tricking her. Just in case anyone was thinking she'd gone soft.

❖

The cabin was starting to look like home. Sara had a restoration company refinish the floors and the interior surface of the log walls to the same golden honey color, finished with a satin gloss. She painted the ceiling beams white and replaced the loft ladder with a spiral iron staircase. New white linen curtains and a small farm table completed the main room, and soft ivory carpet warmed the loft. The worn leather sofa stayed, of course, as well as the turquoise fifties refrigerator with the dented door that Sara had grown to love.

A few weeks after she'd closed on the cabin, Sara stopped into the drugstore and pointed across the street at the abandoned diner she noticed every time she passed it on the street. It was small—the seating area looked to be only about 1,200 square feet—but there were floor to ceiling windows in the front. Sara stopped and looked at it frequently, and from what she could see with her face pressed up against the glass, there was an old-fashioned Formica bar at the back near the kitchen.

"How long has that been closed?"

"Well," Mary said, pouring Sara a mug of coffee from the pot she kept under the counter and sliding it over to her, "good morning to you, too."

"Sorry," Sara said, "I've always wanted to ask you about that place and just remembered."

"That was Gus's place, and it's been closed about two years now." She squinted out the window toward the diner. "It's a shame too. He was a stand-up guy and he made a kick-ass cheeseburger."

"Where the hell do people go for lunch around here? I've wondered that since the first day."

"Well, the tourists go to that fancy sandwich stop as you come into town that has fifty-seven varieties of lettuce and organic beer or whatever the hell they advertise, but the locals always went to the diner. I guess when he passed on we just stopped going anywhere."

"It sounds like everyone loved him."

"We did," Mary said, bending down and fiddling with the coffee to hide the emotion Sara had already seen. "He was the police chief here for twenty-five years, then after that he owned that diner for almost twenty. He used to spend most of the day at that counter, talking about God knows what with a group of old men who'd just sit there and drink coffee all day. They've all just kind of scattered since the place closed down."

"I'd love to get a look at the inside of that place," Sara said, looking out the window at the tattered awning above the diner's front door. "Do you know who has it listed?"

"Not a clue," Mary said, pulling a set of keys out of the cash register. "But if you want to see it, I've got the key."

Mary stopped as she rounded the corner of the counter and peered down the aisles. "Moira, I'm stepping across the street," she called out to the older woman at the back of the store, who was holding a bottle of vitamin E two inches from her bifocals. "Come get me when you're ready to check out."

Mary put a card on the door that said she'd be back in five minutes and they walked across to the diner. The light scattered across the tile floor as they went in, and Sara could smell the musty scent of an old building. Cobwebs sagged under layers of dust in every corner, and a broken sign hung from one end of a string on the inside of the door. Retro booths with black vinyl seats lined the far edges of the room, and matching chrome and vinyl chairs sat around the tables scattered between. It was small as restaurants go, just enough room for about twelve tables and the booths against the walls.

But the bar drew Sara. She ran her hand over the gold-flecked pale blue surface, following the curved chrome rim with her finger. She glanced back at Mary, who was leaning against the door with a smile that looked like a secret. There was a newspaper still lying by the cash register and scattered sugar packets behind the counter as if someone had left in a hurry. Sara pushed open the swinging double doors and stepped into the kitchen. It was all stainless steel appliances and work surfaces, customary for a commercial kitchen, but handwritten recipes and photos of the staff covered the walls. It wasn't hard to spot Gus, a portly man with a white beard to the center of his chest, his arm around someone in every shot.

"Look at this one," Mary said as she came through the doors, leading Sara into the tiny office. "It's my favorite."

Hanging over the desk was a newspaper cutting of a younger Gus, at what looked like a swearing-in ceremony. He held a Bible for that infuriating lake cop, who had one hand on it and the other on Gus's shoulder.

McCall Police Chief Gus Draper swears in daughter Samantha Draper as Captain of the McCall Lake Patrol Division for the McCall Police Department.

"Oh wow," Sara said. "Gus was her father?"

Mary nodded. "He and his wife Marcy adopted Sam when she was about six, and then Marcy died when Sam was fifteen. Gus loved that woman more than life, but Sam was his heart; they were always close." Mary leaned in closer to the picture. "I was worried about her when he passed last year. She just seemed to shut down and get hard around the edges."

"So Sam was adopted?"

"That's right," Mary said, nodding. "Her birth mother left her at the damn county fair with a note pinned to her shirt. They found her in the early morning, but they think she'd been there since the night before. I don't remember what the note said, but that woman was long gone."

Sara stared at the picture. "I can't believe anyone would do that to a child."

"She stayed with Gus and Marcy for the first few days, but of course Child Protective Services came from Boise and placed her with a foster family here in McCall after a while. But that girl ran away every chance she got and curled up on the Drapers' porch swing every time. They kept trying to take her back, but she kept running away, and eventually Gus and Marcy petitioned to adopt her."

"Wow." Sara stared at the picture just above the newspaper cutting of Sam and Gus in a boat, leaning back in identical chairs, fishing. "That's big love."

Mary looked at Sara and touched the edge of the picture. "Yep," she said. "That's exactly what it was."

❖

It didn't take long for Sara to find the diner listed online. The pictures were blurry, but she'd seen the place already with Mary so that didn't matter, and the price was reasonable. The listing said it had been on the market for nine months, so Sara prepared herself for the possibility someone had already put it under contract and the website hadn't been updated. From what she'd learned about the pace of business in McCall, that seemed like a distinct possibility. She decided to take a chance and call the agent.

"Hello, this is Stephanie Barton with Lakeside Realty." The woman who answered the phone sounded rushed. "How can I help you?"

"Hi, this is Sara Brighton." Sara tried to keep the eagerness from showing in her voice. "I'm interested in the diner for sale on Main Street. Do you know if it's still available?"

"It is," Stephanie said, and Sara detected the voices of children in the background, more than one of them talking to her with a touch of childish desperation. "I've had several people interested, but it's not yet under contract. Would you like to see it?"

Sara thought it best not to mention she'd already been inside, so she replied that she'd love to set up a viewing for that afternoon, if possible.

"I think I can do that," Stephanie replied, somewhat hesitantly.

"Bring your kids, if it's easier." Sara took a guess childcare might be an issue. "Not a problem at all."

"Really?" Stephanie said, relief in her voice. "That may make it easier."

"No worries. I'm looking forward to seeing it. I can meet you there in an hour…say around two this afternoon?"

"Perfect," Stephanie said. "I'll be there."

Sara arrived early and picked up a few doughnuts from Moxie Java on her way in. When Stephanie arrived in a minivan about five minutes later, she was waiting at the door.

"I love this place," Stephanie said as she unlocked the door. "I used to eat here all the time when I was in high school."

The door opened and Stephanie's three boys burst into the diner, heading straight for the old jukebox in the corner.

Sara stepped in and handed Stephanie the box of six chocolate-covered donuts.

"I brought doughnuts from Moxie just in case a snack was in order for the little guys."

"Oh, thank God," Stephanie said, looking at Sara with genuine surprise. "You're a lifesaver."

As the boys devoured the goodies, Stephanie walked the diner with Sara, pointing out the features, but also the areas that needed some cosmetic work, which was refreshingly different from the real estate agents Sara had dealt with in the past. Stephanie dug through her bag and brought out a stack of papers, which she handed over.

"The owner had a full inspection and appraisal done about six months ago," she said, "but you're welcome to go through the process again if you're interested in the property."

Sara recognized the name on the papers. "No," she said, "I'll look them over but the appraiser and I have already worked together on the purchase of my house, so I trust him."

"Great," said Stephanie. "Feel free to take those home, and I look forward to hearing from you. What are you planning to do with the space, if you don't mind my asking?"

"I'm thinking of putting in a gastropub," said Sara, looking around. "Something with an international beer selection and tapas or small plates. Something a little more upscale."

Stephanie nodded. "Well, let me know what you think," she said, "I know the seller is motivated, but she's stubborn, so we won't have much room for negotiation."

"Will do," Sara said. "And thank you for showing me around. I know you must be busy."

"I am, but this job is the least of it. I have three kids, well, four counting my husband, and I usually feel like I'm barely keeping my head above water."

Sara was about to reply when she felt a tug on her sleeve. A sweet blond boy who looked to be about four was looking up at her with an earnest look.

"Miss," he said, with a pronounced lisp, "Thank you for the sugar."

Sara laughed and squatted down to give him a high five. He looked very pleased with himself.

"I'm always threatening to limit their sugar," Stephanie explained, "So you may have a new best friend there."

Later that afternoon, Sara called the appraiser and chatted with him about the property, and he advised her to make an offer now if she wanted it. Sam had told him not long ago she was thinking about taking it off the market.

"It's a sound building," he said. "You'll see in the report there that the only issues were some drywall repair near the bar that you could put off indefinitely if you wanted, it's only cosmetic, and the back patio needs sealant." He paused. "It's a great property, and personally, I think it would do the town good to see it with some life in it again."

Sara thanked him and called Stephanie back immediately to tell her she wanted to make an offer. She wanted to offer about twenty thousand less than the asking price, approximately the amount she'd need to extend the back patio and put an open roof over it. The only issue she saw with the place being able to turn a profit was the lack of seating, so the extended outside area would almost double the usable square footage. Other than that, the inside needed an update, maybe some fresh paint and a few retro touches, but it was basically ready to go.

❖

The next few weeks were tedious, with Stephanie as the go-between in the negotiations. Sam refused to consider the price drop, and Sara wasn't going to give her the asking price out of principle. The principle being that Draper was an arrogant jerk and Sara refused to give her what she wanted. In the end, Stephanie suggested a compromise in that Sara pay the full listing price but retain all the kitchen supplies, serving ware, and pots and pans. Sara took a long second look at the pieces and agreed. She would have bought more modern plates and cutlery given the choice, but the white porcelain plates and bowls did have a classic look to them, and Sara had started to suspect Sam was tired of the negotiations and might pull out. Sara's only stipulation was she be given access to the building before closing, which Sam evidently thought was fine. Stephanie reported she'd agreed right away and signed the formal offer. The closing date was set for the following week—Sara was a cash buyer and all the paperwork like title searches and inspections had already been done, so what was normally a long, drawn-out process looked like it might be quick and easy.

In the meantime, Sara drove the two hours down the mountain to Boise to spend the weekend looking at colors and décor for the updates she wanted to put in place as soon as possible. She chose the same powder blue as the Formica countertop, with splashes of bright white and black for contrast. She wanted to keep the retro feel of the diner, but her plan was to elevate the cuisine to an upscale gastropub menu. She'd applied for a liquor license, which would take time, but Sara knew from experience that the less people ate, the more they drank. The profit margin on alcohol was twice what it was for food, with fewer staff and no kitchen time required, so she wanted to maximize that angle. She put in orders for the décor and a few updated serving ware pieces she needed to be delivered to McCall, and spoke to a graphic designer about the sign she wanted to put across the front windows. Sara wanted a simple design, so once they settled on the details, he assured her he would send a team to install the sign on Tuesday of the following week. Technically, the closing wasn't until Thursday but Sam had given her access to the property, so she couldn't really object.

Sara's legal first name was Elizabeth, but she'd never liked it and everyone just called her by her middle name, so the fact that it was her buying the property wouldn't be obvious to Sam just from the paperwork. Just in case, though, she'd asked Stephanie not to give Sam any details she didn't have to provide before closing. Something told her she might be enough of a jerk to shut the whole deal down if she knew she was selling to the woman she'd clearly decided was a pain in her ass. It still pissed Sara off that Sam had assumed she was an entitled resort tourist right away, as if she wasn't "cool" enough to actually live in town. If she didn't have to buy from Sam, she'd be happy never to speak to her again; it was just bad luck that she happened to own the only property in town worth developing into a restaurant.

The sign was screened onto the diner's picture window by late Wednesday; the colors weren't quite right when they were actually on the surface, so there was a delay because of the change. But when she stopped by the next morning to see at it in the morning light, it was perfect. She took one last look, then hurried to Lakeside Realty.

The closing was in ten minutes and she wanted to get it done and over with as soon as possible.

"Good morning!" Stephanie was waiting at the front desk when Sara arrived. "I have us all set up in the conference room."

Sam showed up about two minutes later, and stopped abruptly in the doorway.

"Sam," Stephanie said, gesturing toward Sara, "this is Sara Brighton, the buyer for your property, she—"

"Yeah," Sam interrupted, taking a seat opposite Sara, "We've met."

"Nice to see you again, Captain Draper." Sara gave her sweetest smile and officially started counting the minutes until the meeting was over.

"Well, that explains the cheesy sign that I saw on the way in here on the front of the diner," Sam said, rubbing her temples as if she had an instant headache. "Alchemy Gastropub? Are you seriously going with that? No one around here even knows what a gastropub is."

Sara looked at Stephanie, who quickly put her hands up and started for the door.

"I'm not getting involved here, ladies. You two figure it out and we'll start signing," she said. "I'm going to see if there are any muffins left in the break room."

The door shut and Sam held Sara's eyes, neither one of them speaking.

"Look," Sam said, breaking the silence, "I'm not trying to be an asshole here." She ran her hand through her hair and leaned back in her chair. "But this is not the easiest thing for me."

Sara thought of the picture of Sam and Gus in the restaurant office. "I know."

"What are you planning to put in there anyway?" Sam asked. "What the hell is a gastropub?"

Sara took a deep breath. "It's like a mix of a bar and restaurant with imported beers, tapas, and small plates." Sara paused for a moment while she pictured launching the stack of papers in front of her at Sam's head. "It's upscale, but still approachable."

Sam rubbed the back of her neck with her hand. "Approachable?"

Sara didn't answer, just raised an eyebrow, and eventually Sam just shook her head and pulled the paperwork over in front of them.

"I guess it doesn't matter anyway. Let's get this over with."

Sara went to get Stephanie and the papers were signed in record time. Sam stood to leave while Stephanie filed everything away and held out her hand to Sara. "Take good care of it."

Just for a second, Sara thought she saw tears in Sam's eyes. "I will," she said. "I promise."

That woman is infuriating, Sam thought, walking out of the realty office and back down to the station. *What is she thinking putting a pretentious gastropub with "small plates" and "international beers" in downtown McCall?*

Of course, Sam had heard of a gastropub, but just the name alone sounded like a medical procedure. Opening one on Main Street was the definition of a bad idea. Sure, Sara might pull in a few tourists in the summer, but what really kept a business going in this town year-round was the locals, and Sam knew for a fact that the locals didn't give a damn where the beer was from, they just wanted it fast and cold.

On the bright side, she thought, *it will be entertaining to watch her crash and burn.*

Chapter Five

The renovations on the diner were almost completed within just a few weeks. The painters gave everything a fresh coat of pale blue paint with the glossy black and white trim colors Sara had chosen. She'd installed lights underneath the Formica bar ledge and bought shiny black barstools, and the plates and saucers that had initially looked so plain now fit with the surroundings perfectly. The décor had a slight retro vibe, with the ancient jukebox in the corner and new chrome napkin holders, but Sara hoped overall it would offer a modern, hipster feel. The menu was coming along as well too, although it was hard to make decisions about what made it onto the final draft of the menu when she didn't have staff yet to taste it and offer opinions. But she had a good working menu ready to the stage of ironing out the kinks, so the end was in sight.

After working since dawn one day a few weeks after the sale was complete, Sara locked up and headed home in the mid-afternoon. The heat hung heavy in the air, and as she rolled the windows down in her truck and pulled out of town toward the cabin, she wished for the hundredth time she could drive her boat. What good was it to have it if she couldn't drive it? That lake cop told her she had to have a licensed driver in the boat with her at all times before she passed the test, but how exactly was she supposed to do that? Locals all had family or friends to teach them, and of course, the waterfront staff at the camps had on-site instructors. What was she supposed to do? Just walk up to random locals and ask them to teach her to drive her own boat?

The sunlight filtered gold patterns through the leaves and onto the roof of the cabin as she drove in. The lake was crystal blue on the other side of the cabin, and a breeze ran its fingers through her hair as she searched for her keys at the door. Then she saw it. The dead mouse just to the left of the door. Its fur was a brownish black and it was curled up in a ball on the wooden planks of the deck. Sara leaned down to see if it was still alive, but it was hard to tell. It was possible it could be alive, or maybe hurt; the only way to find out was to get a closer look. Sara quietly dropped her bag on the other side of the door and reached down to it. As she gently slid it onto her open hand, she noticed it couldn't be a mouse; it had brown wings that were motionless at its sides, the same color as its fur, and the tiniest little ears.

The bat was tiny, a baby no bigger than Sara's thumb, but it was already cold and it was too late to save it. Sara covered it gently in her palm with her other hand and tried to figure out what to do next. She didn't feel right just throwing its body into the woods, but the only other option was to bury it, and that seemed melodramatic. She stood for a moment, the dead bat ensconced in her hands, thinking. She lifted her hand up to look again and found that the bat was still motionless, but now was looking back at her. Tiny dark eyes blinked up at Sara, and its little ears wiggled in an odd combination of creepy and adorable. Its body felt warmer now, so it was definitely alive, but this presented a new problem. Where had it come from and what the hell was she going to do with it now?

Just then, Sara remembered that the appraiser had told her as he drove away to be sure to look above her door. She'd been too preoccupied at the time, but now when she slowly raised her head to look over her front door, thirteen small brown bats were staring down at her, hanging underneath the small boards that sheltered the door from the rain.

"Great," Sara whispered to them. "This totally doesn't look like the opening scene to a horror movie."

Eventually, she decided the only thing to do was try to put the baby bat back on the little ledge over the doorframe where the rest of the family was hanging. Sara knew enough about bats to know that they rarely bit humans, but slowly raising her hand directly into a group of them was not the most fun she'd ever had; the last thing she wanted was to scare them and have them all fly suddenly toward her face. She felt it stirring in her hand as she lifted it, and when she got it level with the ledge, the bats on either side unfurled their wings and enveloped the baby, pulling her from Sara's palm back onto the ledge. Sara stood there for a moment, amazed at what they'd done. If it was possible to feel gratitude from bats, she felt it from the ones she now shared a porch with. Sara watched them for a moment, then found her keys and shut the door quietly as she went into the cabin.

After she'd showered and popped the top off a Heineken, she stood looking out the window at her dock. Specifically at the boat she hadn't driven in two months. Sam said it was illegal to drive without a boat license, but what was she going to do, put her in lake cop jail? She grabbed her keys off the counter and walked down to the dock. When she reached the slip, Sara pulled the cover off the boat and started the motor, inexplicably pleased at the steady hum, until she remembered she had to back it out of the slip with barely six inches to spare between the sides of her boat and the dock. What possible reason could there be for making these things so small? It was like trying to park a car on the edge of a cliff.

Eventually she cut the engine and just pulled the boat back by hand using the tie rings on the dock.

One big push at the end cleared the dock, so Sara turned the key again and edged the throttle forward, picking up speed. What she really wanted to do was explore the little islands and coves dotted all around the perimeter of the lake. Captain Draper seemed to be the only other lesbian in McCall, so the thought of having a girlfriend to take there for a romantic picnic someday was out of the question, but still, the idea of having islands to explore was exciting.

She cruised past the point of the shoreline and back into the cove that curved around in a half-moon shape to almost touch the tiny island just beyond it. Sara cut the engine and let the boat drift toward the inside edge of the cove, wondering how she was going to anchor it if she got out to explore. She searched the control panel for an anchor button, although she had no idea if that even existed; unsurprisingly, there was no such thing. Eventually, she decided to just leave the boat drifting and swim to shore. She made a mental note to store a spare bikini on the boat in the future as she pulled off her shorts and dove into the water.

It was a short swim to shore, and Sara sat on the beach when she got there, stretching her toes into the sand. A few weeks ago, she'd noticed that the sand almost sparkled in direct sunlight. Mary told her the next time she stopped into the drugstore that the sand in McCall had naturally occurring pyrite in it, which explained why it glinted like powdered gold in sunlight. She lay back on the sand, the water lapping around her ankles, and soaked up the warmth. Without sunscreen, Sara knew she had only about fifteen minutes in direct sunlight before she started to burn, so she stood up and looked out on the water to make sure her boat was still there. It was there, but unfortunately, so was a Lake Patrol boat. The patrol boat started to make its way closer to the inside of the cove, and Sara saw it was Sam at the wheel. Of course. Obviously, she'd seen Sara now, so the only thing she could do was sit back down and wait.

Sam shifted the boat into idle as she stopped short of the shoreline. This whole situation was starting to strike Sara as funny, but Sam did not look amused.

"Are you kidding me with this?"

From the shore, Sam looked even taller behind the wheel of her boat. Tall and pissed off.

"I could ask you the same question," Sara said. "How did you even see me out here?"

"Believe it or not, we tend to notice empty ski boats drifting across the lake with no occupants." Sam picked up her radio and spoke into it, keeping her eyes locked on Sara.

Sara waited, the warm glow of the sun reminding her of how happy she'd been before Sam had shown up. There had to be thirty search and rescue officers in countless boats; Sara saw them every day from her kitchen window as they sped by. Why did Sam have to be the one to see her in the cove?

"I'm going to assume you don't have your boating license yet?" Sam raised her eyebrows, not trying to hide the sarcasm in her voice.

"No, Captain Draper," Sara said, matching her tone, "I do not."

"Did you drive the boat here?"

Sara felt her patience start to thin. "No," she said, "I walked."

Sara heard the radio crackle again and Sam spoke into it for a few seconds before she turned back to Sara.

"I'm going to need you to get into my boat and I'll have another officer pick up yours. You do realize I can arrest you and impound it, right?"

Sara ignored her and walked out until she was chest deep, then swam the few strokes it took to reach Sam's boat. She climbed up the ladder on the side and stepped in, suddenly very aware she was wearing a black lace bra and panties under a wet white tank top, water streaming down her body.

"You're seriously going to arrest me?"

Sam smiled, averting her eyes a second later than she should have.

"I should arrest you. I happen to know you've been warned about driving without a license," she said, sliding on a pair of sunglasses. "But I'm going to write you a ticket this time."

Sara squeezed the water from her tank top and focused on staying calm. She knew she was past the point of frustration. "Why do you have it in for me?"

"Sara," Sam said, the muscles in her arms flexing as she gripped the steering wheel harder than necessary and turned the patrol boat around toward Sara's cabin. "Do you realize there are kids in the water out here?" She looked over at Sara. "Wakeboarders, skiers, or just people swimming back and forth from the mainland to the islands?"

Sara looked out over the water. Actually, she hadn't thought about that.

"And if you lose control of your boat because you don't know what the hell you're doing and kill one of them, it's going to be a way bigger deal than just a ticket."

Sara didn't say anything else as they sped over the water back to her dock. It was easier to be angry than admit to herself that Sam was right, but she didn't really have a choice.

When they pulled up to Sara's cabin, Sam loosely tied her boat to one of the anchor rings on the outer edge of Sara's dock. She pulled what looked like a notebook in a steel binder out of a slot on the side of the control panel and wrote what Sara could only assume was a ticket. She took it without comment when Sam handed it to her.

"Will you be okay getting back up to the house?"

"I'll be fine," Sara said, stepping up on the side of the boat.

Just as she remembered she wasn't supposed to do that, her foot slipped on the wet fiberglass and she felt herself falling backward. Sam caught her, scooping her up in her arms and setting her back onto the stairs. If Draper wasn't so arrogant, the way she'd handled her might have almost turned Sara on. Almost.

"Thanks," she said, not quite meeting her eyes.

Sam nodded and had started to turn the boat around when Sara thought of something else and grabbed the side. Sam looked over at her fingers wrapped around the edge of her boat and had to laugh.

"You're a tenacious little thing, aren't you?"

"Sorry," Sara said, letting go. "It's just that I need one more thing."

"What is it?"

"It's just…" Sara looked over at the boat slip on the opposite side of the dock. "Do you think you could have the officer that returns my boat park it inside the slip, not just on the side of the dock?"

Sam looked over and instantly knew why she was asking the question, but feigned confusion anyway.

"Why is that?"

Sara paused, wondering if it was wise to actually tell her. "Because I don't know how to park it yet."

Sam smiled. "Yes, ma'am." She pulled away from the dock and accelerated, disappearing around the point.

❖

The next Saturday, Sara woke to find she was out of coffee, which seemed like a good enough excuse to go into town for a Moxie Java mocha. Everything was busier now that the *summer people*, as the locals referred to the tourists, were out in force. It gave the town a bright new energy that Sara loved, although it continued to bother her that outside of a handful of breakfast places or the few restaurants that offered upscale evening dining on the water, there was no everyday lunch spot like a pub or diner.

She threw on some white denim capris and a blue sleeveless T-shirt and walked into town, twisting her wavy blond hair into a messy bun as she walked. By June, Savannah was always intensely hot and humid, although Sara had grown more used to it over the years. McCall was nestled high in the mountains, with a similar elevation to Denver, so even in the summer sun, the air still felt cool and light.

Moxie Java was packed, but Sara picked up an iced mocha for herself and a black coffee for Mary. Even for a summer Saturday, town was unusually busy. There wasn't a parking spot in sight, the main street going down to the docks was blocked off, and there was even a white news van parked by the police station, setting up cameras. Sara pushed open the door to the drugstore with her shoulder and handed Mary her coffee.

"What the hell is going on out there?"

Mary tore the tops off five pink packets of Sweet'n Low at one time and emptied them into her cup.

"It's the Island Scramble." Mary tossed the packs at the trash behind her, where every one of them landed on the floor.

"What's that?"

"It's a swimming competition between McCall High School juniors and Boise High's junior class. Each team swims out to the island opposite the docks, and the first team to get all their swimmers there and back wins the race. It's more than a mile each way, so it's a crapshoot every year who's going to pull out the win."

"Well, it may just be high school kids," Sara said, looking through the crowds of families parked at the docks with chairs and coolers, "but it looks like they're serious about it."

"They've been doing it since the sixties, and it's hands down the biggest event of the summer," Mary said, blowing on the surface of her coffee. "The kids get sponsors to pledge a certain amount of money if they win, then collect that money and use it to fund their senior trip."

"I saw a news crew at the station when I walked by," Sara said. "Does it really make the Boise news?"

Mary leaned her elbows on the counter and looked through the glass door. "Every summer."

She pointed to the group of younger teens hanging out on the sidewalk behind the docks. "That's the sophomore class. The McCall Lake Patrol provides a catered pancake breakfast after the race every year, and the sophomores help serve and clean up. That's really what brings in most of the money for the kids. The sponsors are more to build excitement, but the catered breakfast people pay for afterward is where the bulk of the money comes from."

Mary narrowed her eyes as she stared out the window. "Last year, the sophomores thought it'd be real funny to all crowd in here together and see how much of my candy they could shove in their little filthy pockets." She dug out a rifle from under the counter and leaned it against the door. "This year I'm prepared. I'll shoot the little asshats before they know what hit them."

"Mary!" Sara stared at her, stunned. Until she saw the jar of paint pellets by the cash register.

"I'm going to shoot every single one of them with fluorescent paint so they'll be easier to round up when I call the police."

"So it's not real?" Sara picked up the "rifle" and looked closer.

"Of course not," Mary said, grabbing it back and putting it back within arm's reach. "But they don't know that."

Sara had to laugh at the look of blissful anticipation on Mary's face. She was clearly counting the minutes until she could whip out her gun and wave it around over the Snickers bars.

❖

"What do you *mean* you're not coming?" Sam Draper was pacing the docks, cell phone pressed tightly to her ear, voice low and hard. "You've catered this breakfast every year for six years."

She tried to listen but eventually gave up and kicked a buoy lying against the boathouse.

"No," she said, "I did not get an email that said you were double-booked. If I had, I wouldn't be calling you now."

She snapped her phone closed and shoved it into her navy uniform pants, rubbing her forehead with her hands. What the *hell* was she going to do? Countless parents were here, students were depending on the revenue from the breakfast for their senior trip, and to cancel at the last minute would be a PR disaster for McCall. The media was already swarming around, interviewing everyone.

Sam headed through the crowd toward the drugstore. The last thing she needed right now was a migraine, and she could feel one starting right above her left temple. The bell attached to the door clanged hard against the glass when Sam walked in. Sara and Mary looked up from their coffees, startled.

"Do you carry Excedrin Migraine?"

Mary pointed toward the last aisle on the right and raised her eyebrow at Sara, then they both turned together to watch what was happening.

Sam set the box on the counter and looked toward the door. "Mary, you know you can't have that gun in here, right?"

"I can have any damn thing I want in my own store, Samantha." Mary held her eyes until Sam looked away, but every muscle in Sam's jaw visibly tensed. "I live in the apartment upstairs, so technically I'm protecting my home."

"Sam," Sara said, "It's just for show. It's a paintball gun."

Mary looked like she was expecting a fight, but Sam just sighed and rubbed her temples.

"What's the matter with you?" Mary's voice was soft, which seemed like a bad sign.

"The caterers that always do the breakfast aren't coming."

Mary looked at Sara, then back at Sam. "Well," she said, "Who's coming?"

"No one," Sam said, "I just got off the phone with them. They claimed they notified us they'd been double booked, which they did not, and now I have to go out and cancel the fundraising breakfast."

Mary let out a slow, low whistle and the three women were silent.

"Sam," Sara said finally, with a glance at Mary, "when is the breakfast supposed to start?"

Sam opened the bottle of Excedrin and shook three into her hand. Mary handed over her coffee.

"It usually starts about an hour from now, maybe an hour and a half. The swimmers are supposed to take off in about fifteen minutes and it usually takes a little over an hour for them to start crossing the finish line."

"Have you told anyone what happened yet?"

Sam sighed. "No, not yet."

"Good," Sara said, turning toward her. "Because I have a proposition for you."

Sam looked over at her blankly.

"Now it's starting to get interesting!" Mary slapped her hand down on the counter and poked Sam. "Pay attention."

"I can solve your problem," Sara said, "Like it never even happened. But you have to do something for me."

"Jesus," Sam said, straining to look over the counter. "Mary, you don't have vodka behind there, do you?"

"Samantha," she said, motioning toward Sara, "shut up and listen."

"I swear to God, Mary, if you don't stop calling me that, I'll arrest you."

"Good," she said with a wink. "You let me know how that goes."

"You two need to stop fighting or I'm going to separate you." Sara leaned across the counter and grabbed a small pad of paper and a pen. "You're worse than children."

"Okay, she's listening," Mary said. "What are the terms?"

"First of all, I need Captain Draper here to teach me what I need to know to get my boating license. And then I need you to bump me to the top of the list to take the test."

Sam looked hard into Sara's eyes. "And if I do, you'll help me pull this off?"

"I'll more than pull it off," Sara said. "And all you'll have to do is pretend nothing ever went wrong."

Sam hesitated. "How do I know you can do this? If you crash and burn, it'll be worse than letting them down now."

Mary swatted Sam's arm. "Listen," she said, "I know you think you know everything about everyone,but trust me here, you don't. Take the deal."

Sam sighed but stuck out her hand to shake on it. "Okay. I accept."

"Great," Sara said, heading for the door. "Now introduce me to those sophomores."

Within five minutes, Sara had the sophomores in a circle around her and somehow managed to grab their full attention. Not a cell phone in sight.

"Okay," she called out, "my name is Sara Brighton, and I'm a chef."

Some of the boys were obviously checking her out, and everyone knew something was brewing.

"Captain Draper brought me in to make this the biggest breakfast fundraiser McCall High has ever seen."

Everyone erupted into cheers, and as it died down, Sara started scribbling on sheets of paper and tearing them off.

"Who has a car and a driver's license?"

Six students raised their hands.

"Great," Sara said, "I'm going to give each of you a list, and you need to get everything on that list and bring it back here as quickly as possible. Tell the cashiers that you're with the breakfast team and they will settle with us later, so go through the checkout like usual but don't worry about the money. Then get back here as fast as you can."

Sara leaned into Sam and whispered into her ear. "Can you call the grocery store and let them know we'll come by with a check for the bill after the race?"

"I'll do it now." Sam turned away, already dialing as Sara finished talking.

Sara handed each of the six students a list and they took off running toward their vehicles.

"Now," Sara called out to the remaining students, "how many of you have plates at home your mom might not miss for an hour or two?"

Every hand shot up.

"I'm not talking about fine china here, guys, just everyday dinner plates. Don't bring back anything expensive. They don't have to match, they don't even have to be pretty, just grab as many as you can and don't forget a fork and butter knife for each plate."

Every student took off at the same time, trying to outrun each other back up the hill to their houses.

"And a couple of pitchers and some mixing bowls," Sara called out after them, "And an apron!"

One of the boys turned around long enough to give her a thumbs-up, and then they were gone.

"Okay," Sara said, turning to Sam, "how many officers do you think you have in that station right now?"

She nodded toward Lake Patrol, which was somewhat hidden

by the two additional news trucks that had shown up and parked in front of the building.

"About fifteen, maybe seventeen."

"And how many of them have gas grills?"

"Probably most of them," Sam said. "Why?"

"I need every gas grill they can find, with a spatula for each, and I need you to show me where the caterers were supposed to set up."

Exactly seventeen minutes later, eleven gas grills strapped to a boat trailer pulled up to the site, a small grassy park just above the docks. Officer Murphy, Sam's newest patrol officer with the biggest mouth, jumped out.

"Captain," he said, popping a piece of Nicorette gum into his mouth and leaning against the truck, "you wanna tell me why I had to load everybody's gas grills up and drag 'em out here?"

"Murphy," Sam said, nodding at Sara, "this is Sara Brighton. She's your new boss. Unload those grills in five minutes or less and set them up anywhere she wants them."

The students who went to the grocery store and most of the kids who ran home to collect dishes were back by the time the grills were unloaded. Sara had Murphy set them up in a straight line in the center of the park. Sara had Sam line up the long folding conference tables she'd borrowed from the station, and told some of the boys to scatter some of the smaller square tables and chairs in little groups away from the catering station to encourage people to get their food and move away from the line.

"Okay," Sara said, once everything was in place. "Can I get everyone's attention?" The chatter died down quickly, and students looked expectantly at Sara.

"Captain Draper just told me the swimmers got a late start, so we still have a little over an hour from this point to pull this off."

A tall, lanky boy with red hair called out from the back. "So we're helping the caterers this year?"

"That's almost right," Sara said, "Except that we *are* the caterers."

The kids instantly loved that idea, and Sara had to whistle to get their attention again.

"Okay," she said, dropping her voice so low they had to lean in to hear her, "here's how it's going to go down."

❖

Almost an hour later, Sam pulled Sara aside and told her the swimmers were nearly back to the docks. "It looks like we have about fifteen minutes before people start lining up for the breakfast."

"Great," Sara said, smiling. "Don't look so nervous. We're ready."

Carefully laid pages from the *McCall Mountain Times* covered the gray plastic conference tables, with a brown craft paper runner down the center of each. The runners were dotted with blue mason jars filled with bright yellow daisies and lavender from Mary's garden, and more blue jars, lit up by sunlight and flowers, hung from an enormous oak tree at different lengths, scattered among the branches as if they'd grown there. Three of the cheerleaders were busy hanging the last of them, one of them running back and forth to the pharmacy for the rest of the flowers and jars Mary had loaded the counter with. At the far end of the tables, there was a charmingly mismatched stack of plates and a basket lined with a blue gingham apron for the silverware.

"How did you do all this in an hour?" Sam looked around at all the beautiful details and realized Sara had just put her no-show professional caterers to shame.

"I didn't really do much," Sara said, nodding in the direction of the kids, "But they did."

Sara had convinced ten of the Lake Patrol officers to man the grills, all topped with an interesting combination of frying and grill pans, and two of the students stood behind them with pitchers of batter.

"Okay, people," Sara turned and called out. "It looks like we're ten minutes out. Can we have the first pancakes on the grill, please?"

The sophomore girls holding the pitchers went down the row of grills one by one, pouring one even pool of batter on each, then held up a cell phone and looked at Sara.

"Great, that was perfectly done. Now make sure these guys flip them together when the timer goes off. We can't afford to have any that are over or underdone."

Murphy leaned out of the row to look at Sara. "You were serious about that?"

Sara rolled her eyes and looked over at the girls. "You're in charge," she said, "and I'd keep your eye on that one."

The girls started the timer and fell into fits of giggles.

"Chef Brighton?" Mara Rooney, a plump girl with deep green eyes, hurried over with a chalkboard in her hand. "You said you'd give me the menu for me to put on the board?"

"I did say that," Sara said, turning to look around her. "But I might have been lying because I have no idea where I put it."

Sam reached over, took the notebook out of Sara's back pants pocket, and handed it to Mara, just as the cell phone alarm beeped and all ten officers flipped their pancakes at one time.

Sam almost clapped.

❖

The breakfast was in full swing when the press arrived. Frank Sinatra played from one of the patrol cars, courtesy of the chief, and the serving table was piled high with summer berry pancakes drizzled with vanilla syrup, with a glass pitcher of golden maple syrup at hand for the traditionalists. The students topped up a platter of crispy bacon every few minutes, and there was even a big bowl of grilled potato wedges dusted in a mysterious spice combination Sara refused to divulge. The citrus lime spritzer, a simple mix of orange juice, sparkling water, and wedges of fresh lime, seemed to be one of the biggest hits with the crowd. It was guaranteed to look beautiful in the photos, which was the real reason Sara chose it.

Later, as the breakfast wound down and the kids started cleanup, Sam found Sara taking down the mason jars of flowers from the tree and reached above her head from behind to hand her a jar just out of her reach.

"I still don't know how you pulled it off, but every one of those kids thinks you're a superhero." Sam looked at Sara with something that almost looked like respect.

"I'm glad," Sara said, handing the jar off to one of the students to return to Mary. "I had a blast. They're great kids."

She shaded her eyes and looked up into the branches. "Can you reach that last jar up there on the right? I've been trying to hook it with a stick, but that plan's gone south a few times now."

Sam pulled herself smoothly up onto a lower branch and stood to reach the jar. She handed it back down to Sara and jumped to the ground.

"So," she said, "a deal's a deal. I'm at your service. When do you want me?"

You wish, Sara thought. *Although I guess watching her climb that tree wasn't the worst part of my day.*

"How about tomorrow around four p.m.?" Sara said. "You know where the cabin is."

"Great," Sam said, "I'll see you tomorrow."

As Sara turned back to the tree, Sam touched her hand. "Not very many people surprise me," she said. "Thanks for saving my ass."

CHAPTER SIX

The next evening, Sam pulled into the cabin driveway and grabbed the Lake Patrol life jackets she'd thrown into the back seat of her truck when she left work.

Sara stepped out of the cabin, the screen door slapping shut behind her. "You're not thinking I'm going to wear one of those, are you?"

"I *know* you're going to wear one," Sam said. "I haven't seen you really swim yet. How do I know you won't sink like a brick?"

Sara stood on the porch, hands on her hips. She was barefoot, in black chino shorts and a loose white linen shirt that was half tucked in, as wild as her hair.

"Why would I buy a boat if I couldn't swim?"

"I don't know, but I wouldn't put it past you." Sam smiled and held the vest out to her.

"Seriously?" Hands were still firmly on hips.

"Look," Sam said. "If you want to show me you're a strong enough swimmer once we get out there, I'll reconsider. Maybe."

Sara relented and they fell into step on the trail that led from the front porch down to the docks. The sun was glittering over the surface of the lake, and a great blue heron skimmed the surface of the water as they came around the corner of the cabin. The dark water lapped at the sides of the dock as they walked out to the boat slip, the boards creaking and shifting under their feet. Sam threw the boat cover off and left it on the dock with her shoes.

"Ready?" She offered Sara her hand. "And don't you dare step on the side of that boat."

"I'm so excited," Sara said, stretching out on the white leather lounge seat. "I've missed my boat, even if she did try to knock me out."

Sam laughed despite herself, then looked around her and noticed the boat looked brand new. The bloodstains were gone, and Sara had polished and cleaned every inch of it, including the chrome, and placed a tiny blue and white striped pillow in the captain's chair. Sam held it up by one corner and looked at Sara.

"You've *got* to be kidding me with this."

"Hey, I had to do something while you had me grounded, so I tidied up a bit." She was clearly pleased with herself as she slid her sunglasses from the top of her head onto her face. "You know you're jealous. You wish you had a pillow like that for the patrol boat."

Sam rolled her eyes, tossing the pillow at her and motioning for her to come to the front of the boat. "I'm not here to drive you around, Miss Brighton. You're going to back this thing out of the slip."

Sara looked at the six-inch space between the side of the boat and the dock on either side with concern. "I can't, I'll crash it."

"First of all," Sam said, "you're not going to crash anything with me here, and secondly, you've got to start sometime, and that's now."

Sara reluctantly traded places with Sam behind the wheel and turned the key.

"Okay," Sam said. "There are two kind of throttles in boats, foot throttles and hand throttles. Can you drive a stick?"

"Yep, my first car was a standard."

"Great, that will help you get the feel of the throttle faster, which is really the hardest part. If you can learn to handle that right, the rest will fall into place with practice."

Sara filled in Sam what she'd already learned from Bart Riley when she bought the boat, which wasn't much. Now she wished she'd paid better attention.

"Okay, let's try backing out," Sam said, sitting in the passenger's seat opposite where Sara stood behind the wheel. "You want to ease the throttle back slowly, giving it less gas than you think you should, and turn the wheel slowly when the nose clears the dock."

Sara tried to focus, getting a good look at the space she had on either side between the boat and the dock. When she felt like she had a grasp of it, she pulled back on the throttle. The back end of the boat jerked into the bumpers covering the inner corner of the dock with a sharp thunk, then bounced against the other side of the slip.

"Whoa," Sam said, jumping up and grabbing the edge of the dock to steady the boat. "You want to give it about half of that gas to ease it into reverse. Remember, you don't have brakes, so if you rocket out the back it'll be hard to correct."

Sam pushed them back into position by hand and told Sara to try it again, but obviously Sara and that throttle were not a good combination. The boat bounced like a ping-pong ball against the edges of the dock until Sam finally switched places with her and backed them easily out of the slip, turning the wheel smoothly as the nose passed the end of the dock, then easing the throttle forward and into the open water.

"It feels so graceful when you do it," Sara said, settling into the passenger's chair. "How old were you when you learned to drive a boat?"

"I was six," Sam said, her eyes on the horizon. "My dad taught me to swim and drive a ski boat in the same summer."

"How did you not know how to swim by the time you were six? The kids here seem to live in the water."

"You're right, they do," Sam said. "But I was adopted that year, so it was the first summer I'd had with my parents."

Sam accelerated around the end of an island point, then pulled them smoothly into the quiet cove Sam had busted her in last time. It was perfect conditions, though. There wasn't even a ripple on the water, and the sun had intensified into a deep gold, the light visibly hovering above the navy blue surface of the lake.

"Okay," Sam said, stepping back and turning the wheel over to Sara, "let's call a truce between you and that throttle."

"I know what the problem is." Sara started unbuckling the life jacket, tossing it onto the back seat before Sam had a chance to stop her. "This enormous vest is in the way."

"You'd better hope you have a swimsuit under those clothes," Sam said, "because you're wearing that vest until I know you can swim."

Sara unbuttoned her shorts and stepped out of them, then took off her shirt and dropped it on the seat. She wore a sleek white bikini top underneath, with white boy short bikini bottoms. She stepped onto the side of the boat before Sam could stop her and dove into the lake.

When she surfaced, Sam watched the water slip over her body, glossing the curve of her shoulders, then her hips, as she swam a perfect freestyle stroke fifty yards out and turned to come back.

"Fuck," she said to herself, killing the engine and pulling on her sunglasses. "She's gorgeous."

Sara reached the teak platform of the rear of the boat and pulled herself up to standing, twisting the water from the length of her hair.

"So," she said, "What do you think?"

The lines of her body were more feminine than Sam had expected. In clothes, she looked athletic and petite, but in a wet white bikini, shaking the water from her hair, she looked perfect.

"That'll do," Sam said, looking intently at one of the dials on the control panel. "Get dressed and we'll practice turning in reverse."

Sara slipped her white linen shirt back on. "Okay, I'm ready."

Sam looked down and shook her head before she caught herself. Sara was standing there in white bikini bottoms and an unbuttoned shirt. Sam was always professional, but this was going to be more challenging than she thought. She stepped out from behind the wheel.

"Okay, let's see you back up like you're coming out of the boat slip at home."

Sara slid past her and turned the key, letting the engine fall into an idle, then pulled back the throttle.

"That's better," Sam said, "But you're still hitting it too hard."

"I'm barely touching it!"

"I know it feels like that, but driving a boat is different from how it feels to handle a gearshift on a car. It takes a while to get used to. Try it again."

Sara took a couple more passes before Sam got up and traded places with her. "Okay," she said, "I think you're just trying too hard. Come closer."

Sara stood up and watched Sam slowly pull it into reverse.

"Do you see how my hand is barely touching the knob? You're wrapping your fingers around it more aggressively, which is getting in the way of learning the feel of it."

"What do you mean by the feel of it?"

"When you're driving a boat," Sam said, "you have to be aware of the water. You can make the motion and force of the water work for you, but you have to respect it as a partner and pay attention to how it moves."

"Okay," Sara said, "I think I understand."

Sam let Sara take her place behind the wheel but stopped her before she started.

"Put your hand on the throttle," she said, "But don't apply any pressure. Just stand there, think about how it feels in your hand, and what the water is doing underneath you."

Sara stood, listening to the water lapping at the side of the boat, and let her palm relax onto the throttle. She pulled back softly, with the pads of two fingers, and opened her eyes. The boat glided back effortlessly.

"That was beautiful." Sam smiled.

The sunlight was fading into soft violet evening, and eventually it got too dark to see, so they headed back to the dock. Sam drove, but Sara watched her hands, memorizing the way they moved over the controls. The wind blew Sara's hair around her face, and when Sam shifted down to cut the wake as they neared the dock, she looked across at Sara just as the last of the sunlight fell across her eyes. They were clear green, with amber flecks that looked like gold shimmering under water.

"Come here," Sam said. "Stand in front of me."

Sara hesitated, then stepped behind the wheel, aware of the warmth of Sam's body behind her. One of Sam's arms came around her on the left side and held the wheel, and the other held the throttle on the right.

"Okay," Sam said, "I'm going to pull her in, and I want you to put your hand under mine on the throttle and close your eyes. Don't think about what I'm doing, just pay attention to how it feels."

Sara felt her arms around her and slid her hand under Sam's. She closed her eyes and leaned back slightly into her chest, feeling it move with her breath. Sam's hand closed lightly over hers and eased the throttle forward, then back, turning the steering wheel with her other hand. They slid easily into the slip, and Sara felt Sam touch it into reverse with the pressure of one finger to gently stop the boat.

"You can open your eyes."

Sara stepped away from the wheel and looked at Sam, who'd turned to tie off the boat to the dock.

After the cover was secure, they walked up the dock in the semi-darkness, fireflies hovering around them like sparks from a fire.

Sara opened the back door and turned on the lights over the back deck. "Do you want a beer?"

"Next time," Sam said, her eyes holding Sara's for a second too long. "I've got somewhere I need to be."

Sam loaded the life jackets into the truck and pulled out of the drive, the headlights shining into the forest as she rounded the corner on the drive back into town. The window was down and she let the wind sift through her hair. Her mouth was set, tense, and she reached across to the glove box and pulled out a pack of cigarettes. She'd smoked through her twenties, until her dad said that it was the only thing about her that had ever disappointed him. She quit that day, but she'd always kept a pack in her glove box. She'd had the same box for the last three years. She shook one out of the box and lit it, drawing in the smoke and exhaling it against the wind.

The house was dark when she pulled in, but instead of knocking, she just walked around to the screened-in porch in the back. Sam knew she'd be there, and she was. Mismatched candles dripped wax on the table, Ani Difranco's staccato guitar played from the kitchen, and Lily was bent over a book, writing like there wasn't enough time to get the words on the page. Sam climbed the steps and knocked on the back screen door. Lily looked up, shocked to see her or shocked to see something existed besides her pen; Sam couldn't tell which.

"What are you doing here?"

Sam opened the door. "Can I come in?"

She nodded, picking up the pen. She raised one finger to let Sam know she'd just be a minute, so Sam sat on the hearth built into the porch and threw another log on the fire, pushing back the chill that had started to come through the screens with the dark.

Two months ago, when Lily had just started working at Lake

Patrol, Sam had been in the next booth at Moxie Java one morning and heard one of Lily's friends trying to talk her into coming back to Boise.

"Lils," she said, "don't be stupid. I've never even met anyone else with an opportunity for a book contract. They want to buy the last one and pay you to write two more. What the hell are you doing here? You should be writing."

She didn't hear what Lily said in return, or maybe she didn't say anything at all, but her friend had plenty to say for both of them.

"They want you, you idiot. They want to pay you to write. It's what you love more than anything in the world. What the hell is wrong with you?"

Sam was listening by then, and heard Lily tell her she felt suddenly trapped, as if she would be locked into a life that she wasn't sure she wanted.

"I want to write. I never said I wanted to publish. Those are two different things."

But now, here she was, writing in a quick stream across the page, almost bleeding onto the table before she remembered to go down to the next line. She paused, wrote one more sentence, then looked up at Sam and leaned back in her chair.

"What are you writing?"

She looked down, tapping the pen on her page. "Nothing."

"Lily," Sam said, "don't think for a second I believe that. I know you're a writer, a good one. You shouldn't be wasting your time at Lake Patrol."

Lily got up and walked into the kitchen, popping the top from a Corona and handing it to Sam, who put it on the windowsill behind her and guided Lily over to the sofa beside the fire. She sat and pulled Lily onto her lap, knees on either side of Sam's hips, facing her. Her hands followed her thighs up to her bare ass, and she wrapped it in her hands, pulling Lily's mouth down to hers. She kissed her, drawing her tighter against her body, the warmth between her thighs pressed into Sam's shirt. Lily pulled at Sam's belt, then unbuttoned the top button of her uniform pants. Sam looked at her and tightened her grip on Lily's ass.

"Did you ask permission to do that?"

She smiled and shook her head. Sam opened her shirt, one

button at a time, then slid her hands up her back until Lily arched and Sam pulled her nipple into her mouth. She circled it with her tongue, then scraped it lightly with her teeth until Lily groaned.

"God," Lily said, leaning back and smoothing the hair out of her face. "You always make me so wet."

Sam circled her nipple with her thumb. "Show me."

Lily touched herself, then put her slick fingertips in Sam's mouth. Sam stroked them with her tongue, holding Lily's eyes as her hands slid up her legs, then into the wetness that was dripping onto Sam's thighs. She held her still with one hand on her waist, running the thumb of her other hand over Lily's swollen clit.

"Are you sure you want this?"

"Goddammit, Draper," Lily said, breathless. "I'm going to die if you don't make me come."

Sam slid three fingers inside her. Lily leaned her head back and moved her hips against Sam's hand, her clit slick and hot under Sam's thumb. She gripped Sam's shoulders and circled her hips, her breath a hard whisper, begging her not to stop. Sam curved her fingers to slowly stroke the spot inside her that always sent her over the edge, and Lily's breath caught. A few seconds later, she bit down on Sam's shoulder as her orgasm shook her, a rush of warmth soaking through Sam's clothes to her skin.

Lily stayed where she was after, her thighs against Sam's, her bare breasts flushed and damp. Sam waited until Lily's breath slowed, until she relaxed against her and laid her head on Sam's shoulder, before she picked her up and laid her back down on the couch. She pulled a down throw from the couch to cover her and threw another log on the fire before she left, closing the screen door gently behind her.

CHAPTER SEVEN

A few days later, Sara changed into faded denim shorts and a white T-shirt and unloaded her bags from the car. She'd stopped by the farmer's market at the park after she'd left the diner and picked out some bright red and gold heirloom tomatoes, shallots, fresh celery, and a baguette. The tomatoes were perfectly in season, still warm from the sun, and she washed the celery and set it out to dry. She heard Sam's car come down the drive but waited until she knocked to go to the door.

"Ready?" Sam said when she opened the door.

She must have come from work; she was still in navy cargo shorts and a white polo embroidered with the Lake Patrol logo. Her light blue eyes looked even lighter against her tan, and even with her hands in her pockets, the muscles in her arms and broad shoulders were tight and defined.

"Ready for what?" Sara raised an eyebrow.

Sam silently reminded herself that Sara was straight. Clearly straight.

Sara smiled and opened the door. "I'm just teasing; I'm ready, let me just throw on a swimsuit."

Sam looked around. The last time she'd been here was on a fishing trip with Mary's husband, and there'd been bloody fish heads piled on the table and cases of beer stacked by the back door. She ran her hand across the back of the leather sofa just as Sara came back down the hall. She looked into the kitchen and paused.

"Would you mind if I chop those tomatoes before we go? I need to toss them in the marinade before it gets too late."

"Not at all, take your time."

She chopped the tomatoes and celery at what seemed to Sam like lightning speed, then dumped the pile into a glass bowl. She added balsamic and oil, and rubbed some fresh herbs between her hands before she added them to the mix.

"What did you just put in?" Sam walked over and peered into the bowl.

"It's just basil. I need it to be pretty strong to balance the tomatoes this late in the season, so I rub it to release the oils before I mix it in."

She washed her hands and they headed down to the dock, Sara pulling the door shut behind her. The sun warmed the back of Sam's neck, and the water shimmered in a broken reflection of the green spruce trees that lined the edges of the water. She took off her shoes as they walked down the dock.

"Okay," she said, settling into the passenger's seat. "Let's see what you remember."

Sara started the boat, the rumble of the engine vibrating under her bare feet, and put her hand on the throttle.

"Close your eyes," Sam said.

Sara was confused. Why was she telling her to close her eyes while she drove a boat?

"You can't rely on your eyes. Feel what the water's doing around you, then you can open them once you start moving."

Sara closed her eyes and touched the knob with her fingertips, pulling backward slightly with the current. Then she looked behind her and instantly overcorrected, sending the rear of the boat almost into the dock.

Sam grabbed the edge just in time. "That was great," she said, "It's a hell of a lot harder when you're not in open water."

Once she got safely out of the slip, Sara accelerated in the direction of the cove. When they got there, she tried to turn the wheel parallel to the shore like she'd seen Sam do yesterday, but ended up spinning the boat into a slow circle.

Sam leaned over Sara and cut the engine.

"Okay," she said, her hand still on the keys, "think of the wheel like it's your boyfriend's face. Don't touch it any harder than you would a person."

Sara tried not to smile.

"What?" Sam shaded her eyes with her hand and wondered where the hell she'd put her sunglasses.

"You're assuming I'm straight."

She finally spotted them behind Sara on the seat and leaned over her to grab them and slide them onto her face. "Well, you don't exactly look—"

Sara rolled her eyes. "I swear to God, if one more person tells me I don't look gay, I'm going to lose my mind."

"You don't look gay." Sam couldn't resist. It was too easy.

"Okay, Draper," she said, pulling her hair into a quick ponytail, "you're going in for that."

Sara's plan was to push her over the side of the boat into the water, but Sam easily grabbed her wrists and held them together at the small of her back. She waited a second, holding Sara's body against hers, then loosened her hold slowly. Sara looked up at her, then stood on tiptoe and slid her hands over Sam's shoulders, brushing her lips with her tongue, so lightly Sam wasn't sure she'd felt it. Then she kissed her, melting into the hard lines of Sam's body, until Sam let out a low growl and pulled her hips closer.

"You can't rely on your eyes," Sara whispered as she drew away, her breath warm against Sam's ear.

"Jesus Christ." Sam looked up to the sky. "Point taken."

❖

The sun was setting when they finally got back to the dock. Sam had insisted Sara stay on her side of the boat for the rest of the lesson, only half joking, until they pulled into the slip and she offered her hand to help Sara onto the dock. As they walked toward the cabin, Sara turned to Sam.

"Feel like grilling some bread for me?"

Sam stopped on the steps of the back deck and looked at Sara. Her blond hair was wild and tangled from the wind in the boat, and she was starting to get a little tan on the tops of her cheeks.

"I guess I owe you that much," Sam said, opening the door for her.

"Good," she said, "I'm going to take a quick shower and try to untangle this hair. The charcoal and lighter are on the deck."

"How do *you* not have a gas grill?"

"What can I say," Sara said over her shoulder, pulling her shirt over her head as she disappeared through the door, "I'm an old-school lesbian."

Sam shook her head and poured the charcoal into the grill. That little stunt was impressive; even she had to admit the girl had some game.

Sara was back just as the coals were ready, and she let the screen door slap shut behind her as she handed Sam a beer. She wore a simple white T-shirt dress, with only a touch of makeup and bare feet.

"Basic Sam Adams?" Sam said, holding up the bottle. "I half expected some kind of fruity craft beer with a pineapple slice hanging out of it."

Sara raised an eyebrow in her direction. "Well, if you need another lesson on faulty expectations, we can go right back down to the boat."

Inside, Sara cut thick slices of halloumi cheese and baguette, placing them on a large platter with onion wedges and deseeded serrano peppers. She drizzled everything with olive oil, then seasoned it with salt and pepper, and tucked a beer for herself under her arm so she had a hand free to open the door.

"What goes on first?" Sam said, looking at her with her spatula already raised.

"The bread, probably, then the onions and peppers. Cheese last."

"You're doing the cheese, Chef," Sam said. "Bread and vegetables I can handle, but I have no idea what that even is, much less how to cook it."

"Deal." Sara smiled, leaning back in her chair and propping her feet up on the porch rail. "Damn." She looked back toward the door. "I forgot a bottle opener."

She started to get up but Sam took the bottle, pried the top off with her hand, and handed it back to Sara.

"Why the shocked look?" Sam said with a wink. "I do have skills outside a boat, you know."

Sara's cheeks flushed, and she looked away. *That's not hard to imagine*, she thought.

❖

Later, as the sun set over the lake and the emerging bats wove an invisible pattern above their heads, they sat down to eat, listening to the wind move through the trees. Sara took a split clove of raw garlic and rubbed it across the rough surface of the grilled bread, then piled it high with the marinated tomatoes, basil, and raw mozzarella. Sara laughed when Sam ate the first slice in three bites.

"That's seriously good," Sam said, obviously surprised, as Sara handed her another slice. "What's in it?"

"Nothing fancy, just the tomatoes, balsamic, herbs, and olive oil," she said. "What do you usually eat at home?"

Sam thought, then slid the serving platter closer to her. "Nothing I don't have to unwrap."

"Hey," Sara said, sliding a slice of grilled halloumi onto her plate, "I was Camp Montauk for several summers as a kid. Did you ever go to camp there?"

Sam opened another beer for both of them. "I was a camper there for years, then worked there after graduation until I was twenty-one."

"That's how long ago?" Sara asked. "How old are you now?"

"Twenty years ago, I'm forty-one."

"Why did you quit?" Sara said, rubbing another slice of bread with garlic, then loading it up with the tomatoes and herbs. "Is that when you decided to join the police force?"

"I did join the force right after that," said Sam. "But I didn't want to leave Montauk. I was thinking about a career as a camp director. I loved it."

Sara paused and looked over at Sam. "They let you go? For some reason I have a hard time picturing that."

Sam paused. "I was fucking the director's daughter."

"Yep," Sara said, "that'll do it."

"Unfortunately," Sam said, "that was the year they installed a new security system with literally hundreds of cameras all over the grounds." Sam looked out over the trees, the tops swaying in the evening breeze coming off the lake. "We were the same age, it shouldn't have been a big deal, but it was. It was huge."

"What happened?" Sara pushed her plate away and sat back in her chair.

"The director called me into his office and started the video. No warning."

"Jesus."

"It was clearly me and Kiera, his daughter. We'd been putting life jackets away in the boathouse, and it started outside where the cameras were. Thankfully we still had most of our clothes on in the video, or at least we did at that point."

"What happened then?"

"Well," Sam said, "then I took her inside and unbuttoned her—"

Sara smacked her arm. "I meant what happened with the director, you perv."

"He fired me and told me he'd already sent a copy to my dad at the station. I hadn't even come out to him yet."

Sara shook her head, her eyes wide. "What did he say?"

"I didn't know how to talk to him about it." She peeled the label from her beer, then downed the rest of it and set it back down on the table. "We were eating dinner that night and I just told him I'd gotten fired that day. I remember being so scared that I couldn't eat. I was worried he'd be so angry he'd disown me, or just never want to see me again."

"What did he say?"

"He said he and Mom had always known I was gay, and he asked if he could have the rest of my ravioli."

"And that was it?"

"That was it. We talked about it again a few years ago and he said he was so angry with the camp director for invading my privacy that he never spoke to him again. They'd been friends since college."

"Wow," Sara said, looking out at the lake. "I wish I could have gotten your dad to talk to my mom when I came out." She flashed Sam a tense smile. "It wasn't that bad, though. I lived."

Sara gathered the plates and took them to the kitchen. She'd put everything away as she prepped dinner, so the kitchen was clean except for the dishes, and Sam stepped up to the sink and started the hot water.

"No way!" Sara said. "I can't let you do the dishes."

"Too late," Sam said, passing her the first plate to dry and put away. "Now tell me what happened when you came out."

"There's no story, really," Sara said. "I was twenty-one and had just finished culinary school. My sister, Jennifer, was still in high school, so I wanted to come out to my mom first."

Sam passed her the serving platter. "So how did you do it?"

"I didn't have a plan. I just walked into her room and said it. She didn't say anything, just slapped me across the face and refused to come out of her room for three days. Later, Jennifer said she'd told her she was ashamed to have me as a daughter."

"I can't imagine what that was like," Sam said, turning to face her.

"It's okay," Sara said. "I moved to Savannah after that and my parents bought me the building where I started my restaurant. I didn't understand until later that it was their way of paying me off to stay out of Memphis." She twisted the damp dishtowel around her hand. "I haven't been home since."

Sara put away the last dish and Sam pulled her into her arms. Sara felt fragile, more delicate than she expected. She didn't want to let her go, but if she didn't leave now she wouldn't leave.

"Same time tomorrow?"

Sara smiled. "Only if you're not carrying life jackets."

Chapter Eight

The next night Sam got called out on an emergency, so by the time she got to Sara's dock, they only had about an hour of daylight left. It was enough to work with, though, so Sam went through the technical names for the individual parts of the boat and the minor mechanical repairs she knew would be on the test. They pulled back into the slip with just enough daylight to be able to cover the boat and tie it off without a flashlight.

"Let's be real here," Sara said, starting up the dock. "I think I've already demonstrated my boating prowess when it comes to the mechanics the first time we met, so we both know if something goes wrong, I'm not exactly going to flip up the engine cover and start tinkering with the engine. I'm going to call you."

Sam laughed, picturing Sara's blond head leaning over the whirring engine parts, picking parts at random to remove and toss into the lake.

"Actually, maybe you should just call me," she said, "But the parts of the boat will be on the test, so as much as I'd like to be your beck-and-call butch, you may want to look over the diagram I drew for you before you take it."

Sara climbed the deck stairs and looked over at Sam. "Beck-and-call butch," she said, tilting her head and considering the words. "If I get you a shirt with that on it, will you wear it next time you have to come rescue me?"

"Not a chance!" Sam snapped her with a towel as she opened the back door to the cabin for Sara, then stopped short.

A woman sat at Sara's table with an almost empty glass of Chardonnay in front of her. Perfect makeup, matching cigarette pants and polo shirt, with her blond hair pulled into a bun. She looked like she'd walked right out of a magazine. She also looked like she needed a sandwich.

"Thank Christ you're here," she said, in a soft Southern drawl that exactly matched Sara's. "I was starting to think I was in someone else's house."

"Jennifer!" Sara rushed over and pulled her into a hug. "How the hell did you find me? I haven't even had a chance to give you my address yet!"

The two women hugged tight and long, then Sara stepped back.

"Wait," she said, holding Jennifer at arm's length by her shoulders, "why *are* you here?"

Jennifer looked past Sara to Sam and extended her hand. "Hi," she said, "I'm Jennifer, Sara's sister."

"I'm so sorry!" Sara said. "This is Sam Draper. She's teaching me to drive my boat."

"Wow," she said, with an appreciative scan of Sam's body. "You look like a taller version of Tom Cruise."

"Well, thank you," Sam said, checking her watch and trying not to laugh. "But it looks like I need to get back to the station."

Sam and Sara walked to the door, and Sam glanced back at Jennifer before she stepped out.

"Jennifer, it was a pleasure, I hope I see you again soon."

Sara whispered in Sam's ear and then closed the door behind her.

"Jesus," Jennifer said, taking the bottle of Chardonnay out of the fridge. "She's gorgeous. If you're not sleeping with her, you should be." She filled the glass almost to the rim and set the bottle back down on the table.

"Okay," Sara said, pulling out one of the mismatched chairs and taking a careful sip of Jennifer's wine. "Tell me what the hell is going on. And don't say nothing. I know when something's really wrong, and this is it."

Jennifer sat back in her chair. "I wish I could tell you what's wrong," she said, "but I really don't know."

"Okay, start at the beginning and just tell me what happened."

Jennifer took a long drink of the wine and set it back down between them. "Short version?"

Sara nodded. "To start with, yes."

"I came home from my spinning class early, day before yesterday, because I wasn't feeling well. I usually stay for back-to-back classes."

Sara looked at the sharp points of her sister's shoulders visible even under the fabric of her shirt.

"I walked in and just instantly felt like there was something wrong, you know?" She held the wineglass in her hand, watching the pale gold liquid like a crystal ball. "I went upstairs, and I wasn't even to the top before I heard them."

Sara had an idea what was coming.

"I walked into our bedroom and Trevor was in our bed, fucking some girl from his office."

"Who is she?" Sara said. "Do you know her?"

"I've seen her at the front desk, but I think she's new."

"Jen, I'm so sorry," Sara said, leaning forward and taking her hand. "Are you okay?"

"That's just it. I *am* okay. It felt like it was happening to someone else, like it was someone else's husband." She hesitated. "I just don't feel anything."

"He's always been an ass," Sara said. "So you left him?"

"I didn't get the chance," Jennifer said. "He packed a bag that night and I haven't seen him since."

"I'm glad you came here," Sara said. "Does Mom know?"

"Are you kidding? The first thing she'd do is ask what I did to drive him away."

The sisters sat silent, each sifting through her own thoughts.

"I'm just so exhausted." Jennifer's shoulders were rounded forward, her eyes down. "I'm always so tired."

"Are you eating?" Sara's voice was gentle, her words as soft as possible.

Jennifer shook her head, her body showing the truth despite what she'd said. "I'm eating."

Sara stood, holding her hand out to the other half of her heart. "Come on," she said, "Let's get you some pajamas."

❖

The next morning, Jennifer drove her rented Audi down the mountain to Boise to buy some clothes. She hadn't stopped to pack much when she left her house, and she didn't mention going back to Memphis. Sara went into town after she left to get some peppers at the farmer's market and buy some extra sheets for the makeshift bed on the couch. She wedged her truck in among the endless tourist cars parked in town and had managed to get everything except the peppers when she heard her text ping. It was Sam.

So now you've decided to stalk me until I give you a boat license?

Keep dreaming, Sara typed back. *Where are you?*

Her phone pinged again.

Over your right shoulder.

But before she could turn to look, she got another message.

That's exactly what a stalker would ask, by the way.

Sara spun around and saw Sam leaning out of a booth through the window of Moxie Java.

"This reverse stalking thing has got to stop," Sara said, sliding into the booth opposite Sam.

"You keep telling yourself that." Sam smiled, accepting the steaming mug the waitress brought to the table. She slid it over the table to Sara.

"What is this?"

"A skinny latte."

"Okay," Sara said, "How do you know that's what I order?"

"Let's just say I like to stay one step ahead of my stalkers."

Sara kicked her under the table and Sam asked the obvious question. "So what happened last night after I left?"

Sara added sugar to her latte and stole Sam's spoon to stir it. "I'll give you the abbreviated version."

"Hit me," Sam said.

"She finds her dickhead husband fucking some girl from the office in their bed. He leaves, she catches the next plane to Idaho, and here we are."

Sam leaned back in the booth. "Shit. That's rough. Are you two close?"

"We couldn't be more different," Sara said. "But yeah, it's always been the two of us against the world."

Sara stared into her coffee.

"What are you worried about?" Sam ducked her head to catch her eye.

"How do you know I'm worried?"

"Because you have that look you get when I make you back the boat up with your eyes closed."

Sara kept her eyes on her coffee. The last thing she needed was Sam to see the tears welling up in them for no reason. Or maybe it was a thousand reasons.

"Tell me?" Sam asked, her voice uncharacteristically gentle.

"She's so fragile, but she won't tell me what's happening in her head," Sara said, folding the sugar packet into tiny stacked triangles. "It's always been hard for her to talk. Mom is very controlling with Jen, and over the years, I think she just stopped telling anyone how she felt."

"And you're worried about her?"

"I am," Sara said, the words suddenly coming thick and fast. "When she was in college, she did two undergraduate degrees and a master's in four years at Dartmouth. She'll work herself to death if you let her."

Sam reached out and wiped a tear from Sara's cheek with her thumb, then sat back and held her eyes, listening.

"It's like she's fixated on being perfect. She thinks if she works hard enough or looks good enough, everything that's wrong won't matter anymore." She shook her head. "But she never gets to the point where it's enough, I guess."

"I understand," Sam said, nodding. "I think Tom Cruise feels that way about me." Her words were teasing but her eyes were kind.

Sara laughed and rolled her eyes at Sam before her face fell again. "I don't know what to do to help her. It's like the more I try to help, the more she disappears. And the worse she feels, the less she eats."

"Everyone thinks this isn't the case," Sam said, "but sometimes there's just nothing to say that makes it better."

Sam put her card down on the bill the waitress dropped off.

"It took me a long time, but I realized that after Dad died. Sometimes life is so shitty nothing makes it go away. All you can do is get through the moment you're in."

After a few more minutes, Sam had to get back to the station, so they gathered Sara's bags and Sam walked her to the truck.

"Hey," Sara said, unlocking her door and sliding onto the seat. "What are you doing for dinner?"

"Something involving Spam," Sam said. "Don't be jealous."

"I am jealous. But do you want to come over for dinner anyway? About six?"

"Are you sure Jennifer won't mind?"

"Are you kidding?" Sara said. "She'll be thrilled. Fewer chances for me to try to get her to eat or talk."

"Then I'm at your service." Sam shut the door to Sara's truck and hesitated. "Does she have a swimsuit?"

Sara shook her head. Jen couldn't have much in the tiny bag she brought.

"Get her one," Sam said, turning to walk back toward the station. "I'll see you tonight."

❖

Jennifer opened the door and took the bottle of wine Sam had tucked under her arm. "Tread lightly," she said, gesturing toward the kitchen. "She's in Chef Mode."

"Thanks for the tip," Sam said. "What's the best approach here?"

"Simple," Jen said. "Stay out of the kitchen, no matter what's happening, and the answer to every question is 'yes, ma'am.'"

Sam winked at Sara, who was holding a charred pepper aloft over the gas range, and accepted the beer that Jennifer brought her.

"How did you know to get me a beer?"

"Well," Jennifer said, "no offense, but you look a little more Sam Adams than Sauvignon Blanc."

"Well said." Sam laughed, clinking Jennifer's glass with her bottle.

After steak sandwiches dripping with caramelized onions, charred peppers, and British brown sauce, they took their drinks down to the dock to watch the sifting layers of evening light. Jet Skis crisscrossing the lake provided the background sounds of summer, and the water lapped under the dock in a relaxed rhythm. Jennifer barely ate two bites of her sandwich at dinner, which worried Sara, but she'd let it go—she'd learned the hard way criticism made everything worse. Jennifer watched an eagle glide over the lake and into the dark cover of the trees, then turned to Sam.

"So, what do you do for a living?" She dangled her foot in the water, then tucked it underneath her. "Besides teaching Southern belles to drive boats?"

"I'm with the McCall Police Department Lake Patrol."

"Like cops on boats?"

"Exactly," Sam said. "I'm primarily responsible for issuing tickets to blonds driving without a boating license." The memory of a topless Sara in her boat flashed across her mind. "What do you do?"

Jennifer looked at Sara. "Nothing, really."

"Jen," said Sara, pausing before she continued and dipping her toes just under the surface of the water, "if you could have any job in the world, what would it be?"

"I don't know," Jennifer said. "I'd love to teach high school, but Trevor would never go for that."

"Fuck Trevor," Sara said, rolling her eyes. "If you want to teach, you should do it."

"What would you teach?" Sam asked, downing the last of her beer.

"Math, probably."

"And by that," Sara said, giving her sister a look, "she means that she has a master's degree in Abstract Algebra and Numerical Theory."

"Holy shit," Sam said.

"Right?" Sara said, "I was doing well to graduate high school."

A Camp Montauk ski boat drove by and left a huge wake, which made Sara's dock feel more like a porch swing in downtown Savannah.

"I can see why you love it here," said Jen, looking out over the water to the mountains in the distance. "I know Trevor will make my life hell when I get home, but I'm starting not to care. I'd move here if there was a gym."

"Do you miss him?"

"I don't. I don't really feel anything." Jennifer paused, twisting her wedding ring around on her finger. "I haven't even cried."

They sat in silence for a while, listening to the sounds of evening falling into night.

"Do you see that island out to the far right from here?" Sam said, pointing into the setting sun. "That's Rock Island." She got to her feet and held a hand out to Jennifer. "We just have time to swim out there and back if we leave now."

"What?" Jennifer said. "Why?"

Sam turned to Sara. "What about you, up for a swim?"

"No way," Sara said. "This is my third glass of wine. I'm good." She nodded toward Jennifer. "But I bought you a swimsuit today in town. It's in a bag on my dresser."

Sam looked at her watch. "You've got three minutes."

To Sara's surprise, Jennifer started up the dock toward the cabin, and Sam sat back down on the dock. "Actually, that's a great idea," Sara said. "If she can just get out of her own head for a while, I think she'll start eating again."

Sam looked out at the island. "After Dad died, I spent most of last year in the water. I don't think I would have made it through if I hadn't."

"Wait," Sara said suddenly, looking her up and down. "Do you even have a swimsuit on?"

"Always," Sam said, standing up and waving Jennifer back down to the dock. Sam unbuttoned her shirt and left her jeans on the dock. She wore a black Speedo two-piece, and her muscles flexed slowly from shoulders to abs as she took off her clothes.

Jennifer stripped off the shirt she'd thrown over her swimsuit, dropped it on Sara's lap, then looked up at Sam, who had a good seven inches on her.

"Look, I don't want you to feel bad if you can't keep up," she said, reaching up and patting Sam's shoulder. "Just do the best you can."

She dove in and left Sam on the dock.

Sam smiled. "It's not hard to see that you two are related."

❖

The next day, Jennifer declared she had cabin fever and left for town after lunch. Sara had spent most of the previous night trying not to think about Sam's body. She wished she hadn't seen it. And she wished that she'd seen more of it. But she was certain she was losing her mind. A couple of days before, Sara had tried to bring up the progress she was making on the diner, but Sam shut her down, mumbling something about a gastropub being a bad idea not quite under her breath. Sara thought if they talked about it, or Sam saw the progress she was making with the space, she might come around. Apparently not.

They'd planned to have a lesson in the early evening, but Sam got pulled into a staff meeting, so they didn't have much daylight left by the time she arrived. They pulled out of the boat slip and Sam directed Sara toward the middle of the lake.

"Where are we going?" Sara looked back toward the cove they usually used for practice.

"I thought I'd teach you how to do something fun. People love it, but you need to do it carefully or it can be dangerous," Sam said, taking over the wheel. "Go sit in the back."

Sara hesitated. "Why?"

"Brighton," Sam said, slowly taking off her sunglasses, "if you don't take a seat in the back, I'll put you there myself." Sam stepped closer to Sara, looking down at her, holding the challenge between them.

"Fine," Sara said. "But remember, this boat has a tendency to attack me when you're not looking."

Sam took her uniform polo off and draped it over the back of the chair, leaving just her tank top and navy cargos.

Sara watched her from the back, then diverted her eyes to the shoreline. Checking out a hot butch with broad shoulders and a sexy smile was usually high on her to-do list, but this one would just be too complicated.

"Hold on to something," Sam called back.

Sara grabbed the handle on the side just as the rear of the boat swung suddenly into a full 180-degree sweep. A cold spray of lake water soaked Sara and the entire back seat as the boat skidded back into place and accelerated again toward the center of the lake.

Sara squealed, wiping the water from her eyes. "I *loved* that!" When the boat steadied, she ran to the front and nudged Sam out from behind the wheel.

"Will you teach me how to do it?"

Sara's white shirt was now completely transparent and clung to her soaked skin, although she was too excited to notice. The opposite was true for Sam, so she stepped behind Sara at the wheel out of self-preservation and put her hand on the throttle.

"Okay," she said. "It looks difficult, but it's really not. The trick is to pull the throttle back at exactly the right time."

She lifted her hand and Sara slid hers underneath. Sam's hand was tan, with long fingers and a broad palm that covered Sara's completely. She pushed the accelerator forward, bringing her other arm around Sara to hold the wheel.

"Here," Sam said. "Put your other hand under mine on the wheel. That way, when we go into the slide, you'll know how it feels to be able to recreate it later." She pushed the throttle forward, her voice close behind Sara's ear. "Don't move it. I'll move you."

Sara leaned back into Sam, thankful for the shelter from the wind. The water was surprisingly warm this late in the summer, but wet clothes and high-speed wind in the back of the boat changed that pretty quickly.

Fuck, Sam thought as she felt the warmth of Sara's body lean slowly back into hers. *Is she trying to make this as difficult as possible?*

Sara practiced power slides until it was too dark to see anything but the stars. The lake was quiet, water-skiers long since headed to the docks, and the only sound was the boat gliding through the water. A pale silver path of moonlight fell from the night sky to the lake.

Sam cut the engine.

"Ordinarily we'd do this in the daytime," she said, "But there's a section of the test called Wrap and Retrieve that deals with ski ropes and knots in the water, so we can get it out of the way if you have time."

"If you don't mind me doing it in a bra and underwear," Sara said, unbuttoning her shirt. "I mean, I could try to act modest here, but I think we both remember how we met."

"Yeah." Sam smiled, raising an eyebrow at Sara. "I don't think that mental picture will be leaving my head anytime soon."

Sam pulled a ski rope out of the storage and started to unknot it. "If you want to go ahead and get in the water, I'll show you what you'll need to do."

Sara climbed over the back seat to the platform made of teak slats at the rear of the boat, dropping her clothes behind her on the seat. She wore a sheer blue bra and underwear, and both, Sam noted, were still wet. This was definitely a bad idea.

She dove into the water and swam out, and Sam tossed the loose rope to her. "Do you know how to tie a carrick bend knot?"

"Sam," Sara called out, "you do remember I'm a chef, right?"

"How about a bowline hitch?"

"And that I'm treading water?"

Sam stripped to her bikini and dove into the water. She reached Sara and pulled the rope toward her, demonstrating how to wrap and knot it, then use the ends to create a second safety knot.

"Good God," Sara said. "No wonder the list to take the test is so long. Everyone has to retake it."

"It is a bit tricky." Sam smiled, running her hand through her hair. "Are you getting tired?"

She looked at Sam over the dark water. "If I say yes, will you rescue me?"

Sam tossed the rope bundle into the boat. Her voice was low and soft. "I'll do anything you want me to do."

Sara ducked under the water for a second, then reemerged. "Let's see if you mean it." She paused. "How about tossing this into the boat for me?"

Sam tossed Sara's bra and underwear in the boat, then wrapped her arm around Sara's waist and pulled her closer.

"What do you want?" she whispered into the space between them.

Sara hesitated. "I don't know," she said, eyes tracing the strong lines of her face in the moonlight. "But I need you to give it to me."

Sam pulled herself up onto the teak platform, then lifted Sara out of the water. She lay down in the back of the boat and pulled Sara on top of her.

"Sara," she whispered, her hands sliding up the back of Sara's wet thighs, "if I start this, I won't stop."

Sara kissed down the side of her neck, sliding her warm tongue over Sam's ear. "I don't want you to stop."

Sam flipped Sara underneath her body and slowly pulled her nipple into her mouth, circling it with her tongue, until Sara arched her back and pulled her closer. Sam paused to pull off her own bikini top and then lowered herself back down onto Sara's naked body. She ran her tongue down her body, then slowly across the inside of her thigh. She stopped just as Sara felt the heat of Sam's breath on her clit.

"Fuck," Sam said, sitting back in the back seat of the boat and dropping her face into her hands.

Sara sat up and slipped her shirt on. "What's wrong?"

Sam looked up, brushing a stray wave of damp hair off Sara's face. "I can't do this. Not yet."

"Sam, it's okay," Sara said, looking up at her in the moonlight. "I'm perfectly happy to go back to you stalking me from a distance."

Sam held her face with both hands and kissed her. Softly this time, as if she was trying to memorize her face.

Once they were back at the dock, Sam walked Sara up to the back door of the cabin. The lights were on in the kitchen, so Sara opened the door, calling to Jennifer that they were home.

Sam could see Jennifer through the window, sitting at the kitchen table. She didn't answer, just stared down into her plate.

"Are you okay?" Sara said, stepping in and shutting the door behind them.

"I'm fine," Jennifer said.

The plate of food Sara had left for her was on the table in front of her, but Jen had divided it up into multiple identical sections, placed around the perimeter of her plate. Jennifer finally looked up and leaned back in her chair.

"Really," she said, "I'm fine. I'm just tired."

She looked drawn and pale, and Sara noticed that her eyebrows crinkled together like they had since she was a kid, when she was nervous or worried.

"When did you get home?" Sara said, looking at the clock. Jennifer had texted her that she was almost home right before she went down to the boat with Sam, which was nearly three hours ago.

"Do you want me to warm that up?" Sara said, opening the refrigerator door and staring inside. "Or make you something else?"

Jennifer ran her hand through her hair and dropped her head into her hands. "Jesus, Sara," she said, frustration starting to creep into her voice. "I'm just not hungry, okay?"

Sam walked over to the table and picked up Jennifer's plate. She handed it to Sara, nodding toward the counter. Sara put it in the sink.

"How much have you had to drink tonight?" Sam said, her eyes locked onto Jennifer's.

"Not that it's any of your business, but I haven't had anything since yesterday."

Sam held out her hand to her. "Get up, Jen," she said, her voice more gentle than her words. "We're going for a swim."

Jennifer let Sam pull her up, and she walked wordlessly down the hall to change.

"What the hell is she doing?" Sara said, tears of frustration welling up in her eyes. "Why won't she just eat? If she'd just eat, all this would just go away."

Sam pulled Sara into her arms. "It's not about the food," she said, holding her closer. "And it's not about you. You're not doing anything wrong."

"I have to be doing something wrong," Sara whispered. "I love her so much, and all I seem to do is make it worse."

"You're not making anything worse, Sara…she's here. When she was really in trouble, she came to you," Sam said. "Jennifer has to get her head around it herself. You can't fix this for her."

Sara nodded.

"Let's just get her in the water, okay?"

"Okay," she said, wiping the tears from her cheek with the heel of her hand. "I'll send her down to the dock."

Sam stripped off her clothes as Jennifer walked down the

dock, wearing her swimsuit with a fleece jacket over the top and the sleeves pulled tight in her fists. She sat on the end of the dock with her feet in the water, but left her fleece zipped up.

"So," Jennifer said looking over at Sam, "it's just us here now. Why are you doing this?"

Sam lowered herself into the water to her shoulders and stood on the little aluminum stairs that hung off the end. The water was warmer than the sharp night air.

Jennifer shook her head, her blond hair almost translucent in the moonlight. "I mean, I know you and Sara are doing…" Jennifer searched for the right words. "Whatever it is you're doing, but it has to be more than that." She tapped her toe on the surface of the black water, sending ripples out in perfect circles around it.

"Do you really want to know?"

"Yeah," Jennifer said, "I do."

Sam looked down into the water, until Jennifer wondered if she was going to answer at all. "I know something about how it feels to not be able to fix what's wrong."

Jen paused, then shook her head, looking out over the water. "I appreciate what you're trying to do here, Sam," she said, "But you can't understand. Even Sara doesn't get it."

An owl swooped down suddenly over the surface of the water, then came to rest on the windscreen of Sara's boat about ten yards away. She turned her head toward them slowly, as if she was listening.

"Wow," Jennifer whispered, "I've never seen an owl in real life."

"Actually, they rarely hang out over the water." Sam pointed in the direction of the woods. "They're usually at the tops of Sara's trees over there. She must like you."

Jennifer took the hair band out of her hair and pulled it tighter into a bun at the nape of her neck, her jaw tense. "Why did you say that about not being able to fix something?"

Sam skimmed the surface of the water with her hand. "About a year ago, someone I loved died. I felt powerless, and I didn't deal with it well."

Jennifer nodded, and looked back toward the cabin. "Sara's always been the powerful one."

The water lapped at the dock and Sam climbed the ladder to sit on the dock, wrapping her shirt around her and listening.

"I mean," Jennifer said, "Sara's just a badass, isn't she? She doesn't take shit from anyone."

"Yeah," Sam said, smiling, "I've noticed."

Jennifer stared up at the stars. "I'm just so tired of everyone having an opinion about how I look. I wish I was Sara, so I could tell them to fuck off."

"Who's everyone?"

"My mom. Trevor. My friends." A tear slipped down her cheek and dripped slowly off her chin. "It's all they notice about me, so it's always made me feel like it's the only thing I have to offer." She shook her head, wiping the tear from her face with her fist. "And that makes staying skinny feel pretty fucking important."

Sam nodded. "I can understand that."

Jen looked at Sam and rolled her eyes. "No offense, but you're not exactly unattractive. I have a hard time believing you're insecure about your looks."

"Are you kidding?" Sam said, rolling her eyes and looking over at Jennifer. "I know how it feels to be stared at every day, and not in a good way."

"What do you mean?"

"Well," Sam said, "the fact that I'm a woman, but also very masculine, throws everyone off. I guess they don't know how to label me, and it can piss people off pretty quickly. It's like I have to fit the standard mold or they don't know what to think about me."

"I never thought about that." Jennifer thought for a moment. "Being judged every day about how you look must get old."

"Yep," said Sam. "So I get how shitty that must be for you too."

Jen looked up at her. "Thanks."

She unclenched the fist she didn't realize she'd made and stared at the little red marks where her nails had dug into her skin.

"I don't know why, but that actually makes me feel a little better."

"Okay," Sam said, "it's hard not to care what people think, but let's knock Trevor right off the list of people you give a shit about. Clearly he's an asshat."

Jennifer laughed. "I'll give you that one."

"And correct me if I'm wrong, but it sounds like from what Sara's said that your mom might be so critical of how you look because she thinks it reflects on her."

Jennifer nodded. "Always."

"Look," Sam said, running her fingers through her hair. "I'm not going to say this food thing is easy. It's not." She looked into Jennifer's eyes. "But before you let it ruin your life, think about how *you* actually want to look. Fuck them."

Jennifer thought for a few seconds and trailed her fingers back and forth in the water. "I can't believe I'm saying this, but I think you may actually have a point there."

"And I think we both know what the real problem is."

Jennifer looked up.

"You want to look like a tall version of Tom Cruise. It's understandable." Sam looked over at Jennifer with an angelic smile. "And I know it's hard, but you just have to accept that's not going to happen for you."

Jennifer stood and unzipped her fleece, dropping it on Sam's head. "Thanks for the head start, Tom."

She dove into the inky water, making an effort to splash as much water as possible in Sam's direction.

Chapter Nine

A few days later, Sam headed into the station earlier than usual and got a start on her paperwork. If drama was going to happen on the water, it was usually on a Friday, so she always liked to get a head start on patrol before anything kicked off. She unwrapped a cinnamon muffin she'd grabbed at Moxie Java on the way in and leafed through the duty logs.

"Hey, boss," Murphy said as he rounded the corner of her office door. "You wanted to see me?"

"Murphy." Sam leaned back in her chair. "Where are you from?"

"Jasper, Arkansas, ma'am."

"Did a little old lady flag you down from the dock on the east side last weekend?"

Murphy looked up, surprised. "She did. I thought she might need help, but I think she may have just wanted a little company."

"Well," Sam said, handing him a card with a rose on the front, "I just got a thank you card from her for the little boat tour you took her on to see the 'fancy houses' on the north side of the lake. She said she couldn't remember your name, but you were the perfect Southern gentleman, so I figured that was you."

"Yeah, that was me," he said, glancing down. "I probably should have been making better use of my time, but she was just so excited to see all those big lake houses."

"I looked at the logs from that day. Callouts were slow, so you had plenty of time to show her around. That's not what I called you in about."

Sam smiled, popping the last bite of the muffin into her mouth.

"It says in that note that you reminded her of her late husband. Even used the same brand of chewing tobacco that he did."

"Oh."

"Now, I'm just going to assume you weren't using that and spitting off the side of the boat while you were driving her around."

"Well, actually…"

Sam raised her hand. "Nope, just that mental picture is plenty, thanks."

Murphy nodded and started to leave, but Sam stopped him and took a sip of her coffee.

"Does the name Shawn Keough ring a bell?"

"No, ma'am."

"He's an Idaho state senator. And the woman you picked up is his mother-in-law. She called me personally to tell me about it, and I put two and two together. Keough has a lake house on the east side."

"No way!" Murphy said, scanning the card in his hand. "Come to think of it, I did think it was strange that she wanted to see all the fancy houses but I'd picked her up from the biggest house on the lake."

"I think you were right," Sam said. "She just wanted a little company. I appreciate you taking good care of her."

"My pleasure, Captain."

As Murphy left and closed the door behind him, Sam picked up her phone and texted Sara.

Lesson tonight after work? Around seven?

She went back to her paperwork until her phone pinged a few minutes later.

Depends on what you're teaching me, Captain Draper.

Sam laughed, leaning back in her chair and looking out over the water. She'd never wanted anyone like she wanted Sara that night in the lake. It took everything she had not to take her on the back seat of her boat, and she'd gone to bed every night since thinking about Sara's naked legs wrapped around her waist.

I guess you'll just have to find out, Sam texted. *I'll bring dinner.*

If it's spam, I'm calling the police and having you arrested.

Good luck with that, Sam typed. *See you tonight.*

❖

Sara smiled as she put her phone away and pushed open the door to the drugstore.

"Thank God you're here." Mary pulled a pan of cinnamon rolls from underneath her counter. "I would have eaten every one of these."

"Now you're keeping pastries down there with your coffee pot and gun?"

"Well, I always have a little something to eat up here, but it just kind of became self-preservation after McCall's closed." She looked across the street at the diner. "Samantha used to bring me leftover pie at the end of the day, and I walked over every day for lunch. It wasn't until Gus passed that I realized I missed the company more than anything."

They both stared at the abandoned diner. It was hard to imagine it full of locals and great food.

"Hey," Mary said suddenly, "I think I met your sister the other day. She mentioned she's staying with you for a while. She looks just like you, except she's too damn skinny." Mary ripped the top off yet another Sweet'N Low and dumped it into the black abyss of her mug. "That girl needs to hang out in here with us. I'll turn that around right quick."

"Yeah, I'm working on that," Sara said, looking down into her cup. "I can't get her to eat. I always say the wrong thing. It's gotten to the point that I'm worried she'll go too far and I'll lose her someday."

"I'm sorry," Mary said. "Me and my big mouth. I had no idea."

"You know what's weird, though?" Sara said, almost to herself. "Sam seems to be getting through to her somehow."

"So, Samantha's hanging out at the cabin lately?" Mary smiled, her eyebrow raised.

Mary got called away to help a hapless customer find Band-Aids, and Sara thought about the last night Sam had been at the cabin. To be honest, it still surprised her that she'd stopped them before they had sex. It definitely wasn't her idea. Just thinking about Sam on top of her, pulling her nipple into the warmth of her mouth… it made her wet every time she thought about it. Unfortunately.

"Actually," Mary said as she stepped behind the counter again, "it kind of makes sense that Sam might be able to get through to your sister. What's her name?"

"Jennifer."

"Jennifer," she said, clinking her spoon down on the counter. "After Gus died, it was a good few months before that girl got her balance back. Everyone was worried about her. She wasn't taking care of herself and worked to all damn hours of the night. The chief finally made her take a month of paid leave, which finally seemed to do the trick, thank God."

"She must have been so sad," Sara said, thinking of the picture of Sam and Gus in the diner.

"The Lake Patrol officers told me later that they took turns going by her dock every evening to check on her," Mary said. "She was easy to find, she just swam back and forth to that Rock Island for a few weeks straight, or that's what it looked like to them, anyway."

"Wait," Sara said, "Rock Island? That's across from my cabin."

"Yeah." Mary tilted her head, puzzled. "She's your neighbor, didn't you know that?"

"You're kidding me," Sara said.

"Nope, that great big log cabin is hers." Mary warmed up Sara's coffee and put the pot back under the counter. "Gus had an eye for business. All that time he was police chief, he was quietly making investments, though in what I have no idea. He never talked about it. He just said he wanted to make sure Sam was taken care of."

"Wait," Sara said. "So that's who has *all* that land between my cabin and Ponderosa National Park?"

"Yep," Mary said, plucking the rest of Sara's cinnamon roll off her napkin and popping it in her mouth. "Somewhere around 170 acres."

Sara was speechless. She didn't know what she was expecting, but that was not it.

❖

Sam pulled up a few minutes late that evening and knocked with her elbow, her arms full of brown paper bags. She was wearing faded Levi's low on her hips with a leather belt and a black T-shirt that highlighted the definition in her arms.

"Good Lord," Sara said, opening the door and taking a bag from her. "What did you bring?"

"I'm grilling steaks and doing garlic potatoes in the coals," Sam said, setting her bags down on the kitchen counter.

"Wait," Sara said, "I thought you couldn't cook."

"Any card-carrying butch can grill a steak."

"There's a card?" Sara said. "I'm gonna need to see that."

"Forget I said that," Sam said, dropping her voice to a whisper. "We're not supposed to tell anyone."

"I won't tell anybody." She paused, her breath warm against Sam's ear. "If you're lucky."

"I might be able to arrest you for it if you do," Sam said. "I'll have to check the butch handbook."

Sara laughed, heading for the kitchen with one of the bags. "Be sure and let me know the regulations on that."

An hour later, the coals were screaming hot and the potatoes Sam had stuffed with whole garlic cloves and obscene amounts of butter were almost ready. She'd wrapped them in foil and they'd been buried under the red-hot coals for the last forty-five minutes.

"Okay," Sam said, "I think I'm ready for the steaks."

Sara had just handed them to her, stacked and wrapped in brown butcher paper, when they heard a car pull into the drive. Thirty seconds later, Jennifer burst through the door, pushing a bike, a bright turquoise beach cruiser with a white leather seat.

"Sara," she yelled up to the loft, "look what I bought!" Sara and Sam opened the screen door from the deck.

"We're out here," Sara said, holding the door open for Jennifer.

Jennifer stopped in her tracks, leaning the bike against the wall. "Oh," she said, suddenly unsure, "I'm sorry. I didn't know you had company."

Sam leaned into sight, still at the grill. "What are you talking about?" She pointed at the coals with the spatula. "I brought steak for all three of us. I just need to know how you like it."

Sara watched Jennifer's face relax into a smile as she started chattering to Sam about her new bike. It was good to see her like this. She didn't know if it was the swimming or Sam that'd started to make the difference, but it didn't matter. Her sister looked almost happy, and until tonight, she hadn't realized how many years it'd been since she'd seen that.

A few minutes later, they were sitting around the table, and Jennifer looked over at Sara. "Hey," she said, "I talked to Trevor today."

"Whoa, what?" Sara said, her fork halfway to her mouth. "What did he say?"

Jennifer pushed a piece of potato around on her plate with her fork. "He said he'd made a mistake and that he wants me to come back home."

Sara and Sam looked at each other briefly, then Sam got up and busied herself with searching the fridge for another beer.

"And what do you want?" Sara said.

"To be honest, it felt like déjà vu," Jennifer said. "He cheated on me the day before Christmas last year, and he said the exact same thing after I found out."

"What?" Sara shook her head. "You never told me!"

"I was embarrassed," Jennifer said, lifting her bite of potato to her mouth, then putting it back on her plate. "I didn't want you to think less of me."

"Why the hell would I think less of you because your husband is a cheating…" Sara searched for the words.

"A cheating asshat," Sam said as she returned and sat, with a nod to Jennifer. "I think that title has already been established."

"True," Jennifer said. "Anyway, I went to see a lawyer in town today." She turned to Sam. "Is it true that there's only one lawyer in the whole town?"

"Yes," Sara and Sam answered together.

"Well, I went to see him and started divorce proceedings." She put a small bite of steak in her mouth. "I'm not going back to Memphis."

Sara dove for Jennifer and wrapped her in a tight hug. "Thank Christ," she said. "I was afraid I was going to have to shoot him."

When Sara let her go, Sam touched Jennifer's hand for just a second, looking her in the eyes. "Well done, girl."

Jennifer speared a piece of steak, but hesitated as she lifted it to her mouth.

"I swear, Jen," Sam said, leaning over and spearing three bites of her steak from her plate, "I'm going to eat your steak if you don't get a move on."

Jennifer smiled and put the fork back in her mouth, scooting her plate closer to her and out of Sam's reach. "Back off, Lake Cop," she said. "Eat your own dinner."

❖

Hours later, Sara walked Sam to her truck. "I'm sorry it got too late for us to go out on the water."

"I'll see you in the morning anyway," Sam said. "I'm coming over to swim to the island with her." She ran her hand up Sara's back, circling her neck with her fingertips. "But are you free after?" Sam stepped closer and bent to whisper in Sara's ear. "I can't stop thinking about you naked."

"I thought you might have forgotten that, Draper," Sara said with a teasing look.

"Trust me," Sam said, her thumb lightly stroking Sam's bottom lip. "That is impossible to forget."

After Sam left Sara's house, she went back to the station to grab some papers she'd wanted to work on at home. The station was unusually quiet—most of the officers were out on patrol and the support staff all went home at five, so Sam buzzed herself through from the front desk and stepped into her office, turning the lights on and digging through her inbox for the incomplete incident reports she came back to find.

"Hey," a voice said behind her, "I didn't see you come in."

Sam whipped around but it was just Lily, closing the door behind her and walking toward the desk. She had a white dress on that clashed perfectly with her Doc Marten boots Sam remembered from the nineties. Evidently, they were cool again.

Sam sat down on the edge of her desk. "What do you need?"

Lily edged herself between Sam's thighs. "Are you really asking me that?"

Sam's nipples hardened under her shirt and she tried not to look at the front of the dress that Lily was unbuttoning.

"Don't." Sam made a move to stand, but it just brought her body closer to the heat of Lily's skin.

"Don't what?" Lily leaned into Sam's neck and ran her tongue down to the collar of her shirt.

"Lily," Sam said. She was aching to crumple that dress around her waist and sink to her knees, mouth buried in the slick heat of her. "Just don't. I can't."

She didn't answer, just took Sam's fingers and pressed them into her wet heat between her thighs, then slowly brought them up and sucked them into her mouth.

"Goddamn, Lily," Sam said, closing her eyes and trying not to think about how wet Lily was, how obviously ready she was for Sam to fuck her.

"I can't," she said, pushing Lily gently away. "Not today."

Lily stepped back, unsettled, then buttoned her dress and walked out. Sam watched out the window as she left the building and walked to her Jeep.

"Fuck," she said, slumping down in her office chair. "Fuck."

❖

The next morning, Sam met Jennifer on the dock in the late morning and they swam to Rock Island, then on to Ocmulgee Island before heading back. Sam took a quick shower and changed, then found Sara leaning against the counter.

"Where's Jennifer?" Sam said. "She's more than welcome to join us."

"She's gone, actually. She was out of here in about two minutes, she said she had to go see a man about a boat."

"I'm not even going to guess what that means," Sam said, "But it sounds like she's up to something."

"You know what she did before she left?"

"What?"

"She made a peanut butter sandwich and actually ate it while she was getting ready. Whatever you said to her, it helped."

"It wasn't me," Sam said. "I think it's the water. There's just something about how it moves over you, or maybe it's the silence underneath the surface. It just smooths the edges of whatever's wrong after a while."

"I don't believe that's all it was for a second." Sara smiled. "But thank you."

"You're not doing terrible on the driving lessons, by the way," Sam said, "so I brought something new. Have you seen it yet?"

"What?" Sara followed her gaze out the window. A Lake Patrol boat was parked on the far side of Sara's dock. "Oh no, I have a bad feeling about this." She paused. "But it's technically illegal for me to get another citation if I'm actually in a Lake Patrol boat you're responsible for, right?"

"Technically. If you can drive one inboard ski boat," Sam said, "you can drive them all. Or you should be able to, at least."

Sam looked at Sara's rolled-up white chinos and cropped blue top that showed a slice of her tight abs when she moved, and wondered for a second if she was trying to distract her or if it just came naturally. "Are you ready to go?"

Sara nodded, but once they were at the dock, she refused to drive the patrol boat, so Sam got behind the wheel and headed for the open water. She cut through the lake toward the far north side. Just as they were getting close, the radio on the control panel beeped and Sam picked it up.

"This is Captain Draper, go ahead."

"Captain, this is Chief Davis, what is your location?"

"Heading north toward Ponderosa," Sam replied, her thumb on the radio handset button. "What's going on?"

"9-1-1 just got a call from the waterfront staff at Camp Montauk." There was a pause, then some static on the line. "They have a situation up there, but I can't get anyone to tell me exactly what's going on."

"Are there injuries?"

"That's not known at this time," Chief Davis said, his voice crackling through the radio, "but it's a possibility."

Sam slid the throttle to full speed, and Sara stood at the passenger's seat, holding on the rail and looking forward to the Montauk camp docks, just coming into view on the horizon.

Sam picked the radio back up, holding the button with her

thumb. "Are EMS and Lake Patrol en route?" she said into the handset, the wind whipping the words from her mouth.

"EMS has been dispatched," the chief replied, "but Lake Patrol was working the regatta on the south side, so their ETA is ten minutes, minimum."

"We're there in less than thirty seconds," Sam said. "I'm on it." Sam handed the handset to Sara. "I'm going to need to move quickly when I get there. You keep me posted on any radio communication right away," she said. "Can you do that?"

Sara nodded, her heart beating faster. As they neared the dock, she heard screaming and a crowd was forming on the docks, hovering behind the snapped boards and broken foam floats where it looked like the far end of the dock had snapped off and sunk toward the bottom of the lake. Sam headed straight for them, then slid the boat to a sudden stop with a sharp left turn, parallel to the dock, sending a spray of water ten feet into the air. The crowd had no choice but to back up off the ragged end of the broken dock. Sam shouted to the panicked staff that looked like they were frozen in place.

"Get those people off the docks now, it's sinking!"

Everyone was screaming at once; it was impossible to hear what they were saying, but as the boat idled closer, Sara looked down and saw it.

"Sam," she said, squeezing her arm and pointing down into the water a few yards ahead, "look."

Sam peered down into the water. "Jesus Christ," she said, pulling off her clothes and shoes and tossing them aside.

"I'm going in," she said. "I need you to stop the boat here. Don't let it come any closer. If the prop hits someone, it could kill them."

Sara nodded, and Sam dove into the water, disappearing toward the sunken vehicle several feet below the surface of the water. The screaming from the dock intensified, and Sara watched as it continued to splinter and sink.

"Move those people back!" she shouted, waving an emergency flag she'd pulled from the glove compartment. "The dock is sinking underneath you!"

That seemed to get through to them, and what seemed like

hundreds of staff and campers slowly started to back up. The broken end of the dock facing Sara started to rise.

"Keep going!" she called, gesturing with her hands for them to keep walking backward.

Just then, Sam broke the water's surface for air and dove back under, reemerging quickly with a dazed teenage girl. One of the waterfront staff dove into the water, took her from Sam's arms, and started swimming back to another staff member lying on the edge of the splintered dock, holding his arms out to take her. Sam loaded air into her lungs and dove again.

"How long have they been under?" Sara shouted toward the dock.

The staff member on the end who had pulled the girl onto the dock shouted back, "The dock broke off when they drove the car out on it, and it sank so fast. They tried to open the doors but they wouldn't open. It was a minute or so before..." He paused. "They didn't go under until right before you got here."

Sam emerged with another teenager, a boy, and passed him off to the staff member who'd been treading water and waiting.

"How many were in there?" Sara called out.

"I think just three," the staff member said, a question hovering in his voice. He shouted behind him again for everyone to back up and be quiet so he could hear.

"They were driving the car onto the dock as a prank. They were already out there before anyone knew to look."

Sara heard the Lake Patrol boats in the distance, but she could tell by the sound that it'd be several minutes before they arrived, even at full speed.

Sam suddenly surfaced again, forcing in breath and sinking under the water again. Sara saw her under the murky layers of water, dragging a body out of the front passenger's side, holding him under the arms and breaking the surface in a rush, pushing him into the arms of the waiting staff. He was barely conscious, choking and trying to breathe. Sam started to swim underwater toward the dock behind them, just as Sara caught sight of something out of the corner of her eye. Blond hair had floated up to the dark surface of the rear window like a ghost in a mirror. She started to shout to Sam but saw that she was underwater, looking toward the lake floor under the broken edge of the dock, searching for campers that might have fallen and gotten trapped when it split open.

Sara dropped her clothes and dove in. Her ears screamed with the pressure as she swam straight down to the car on the lake floor, about ten yards from the surface. The water was dark and the car partially covered by plant life. She saw nothing in the dark water until a hand suddenly floated by the side window. Sara opened her mouth to scream without thinking and almost choked on the water that forced its way into her mouth. She dove deeper to the door she'd seen Sam at, but it was barely open. She was running out of air. She had one chance, maybe ten more seconds before she'd be forced to surface, and by the time she returned, it would be too late.

She pushed the car door open with her foot as she reached in, but the force of the water allowed her to get it open only enough to put her head and shoulders in to search for the girl. It was pitch black inside, and Sara could see nothing, not even her own hands reaching frantically out in front of her. At the last second, she pulled her arms out and felt the faintest brush of hair cross her fingertips. She dove for more of it, wrapping what she found around her fist and pulling the girl toward the door with it. She pried it open against the force of the water with all the strength she had left in her legs and managed to pull the girl's head and shoulders out of the car before she realized she was close to passing out. She had just seconds left. Sara wrapped her arms under the girl's arms and pushed the door open with everything she had. If she couldn't break her loose from the steel frame this time, she knew she'd have to leave her. Then suddenly Sam was pulling on the other side of the door. She felt her own arms give way and her body start to sink as she blacked out.

Sara woke to a feeling as if she was vomiting in her sleep. She felt heavy pressure on her chest, as if something was still holding her underwater, and her limbs were too weak to move. She choked as a rush of water shot out of her throat, and she felt someone turn her to the side. Splintered wood from the dock scraped her cheek as she fought for breath, water still spurting out of her mouth and nose.

"Breathe, baby."

It was Sam's voice. Sara struggled to open her eyes as she fought for air.

"Don't move, Sara," Sam said. "Stay on your side until your airway clears, okay?"

Air rushed into her lungs, sharp as shattered glass, and Sara felt strength slowly returning to her arms and legs. She realized suddenly she was surrounded by EMTs speaking in soft voices, telling her to relax and breathe. She took a deep breath in and opened her eyes.

"Did she make it?" Her throat felt raw and ragged, and the words came out like molten steel, burning her nose and mouth.

Sam leaned over her, placing her hand between the splintered dock and Sara's face.

"We don't know yet," she said, looking over her shoulder at the emergency personnel behind her. "She hasn't come around, but they're still working on her."

"What about the others?" Sara turned over on her back and looked up at Sam's face.

"They're going to be fine," Sam said, smoothing the wet hair off Sara's forehead, "but they're already on the way to the hospital just to make sure."

A shout went up behind Sam, then screams and clapping that steadily increased in volume, which Sara finally recognized as relief.

"It looks like she's back," Sam said, turning to look back at Sara. "Thanks to you."

Sara looked past Sam's shoulder to see the blond hair that she'd wrapped around her fist lying limp on the dock, but she also saw the girl was moving, so that had to be a good sign. EMTs rushed her onto a stretcher and carried her off the dock into a waiting ambulance, squeezing what looked like a clear plastic football above a mask on her face. Then someone tried to lower a mask onto Sara's face as she watched the ambulance doors close.

"Get off me," Sara said, waving off the burly EMT hovering above her. "I'm fine."

He retreated, laughing, and squeezed Sam's shoulder. "You've got your hands full with that one, Captain. She should be fine, but watch her tonight, and bring her in if she's having any trouble."

"I will," Sam said. "Thanks, Peter."

The noise slowly died down as the last ambulance left and Sara tried to sit up. Sam wrapped her arms around her and pulled her gently to a sitting position.

"Captain!" someone shouted from the beach. "I'm sending your boat and the last rig out. Are you going to be okay on Carter's patrol boat?"

Sam nodded and waved him on. Sara realized then she was half-naked in a soaked T-shirt and underwear. Sam seemed to notice at the same time and waved one of the patrol guys over with a blanket. She wrapped it around Sara as she stood up, and guided her toward the boat waiting on the far end of the remaining dock. Two patrol officers tried to help her step into the boat, but Sara gave them a look and took a shaky step toward the edge. Sam swept her up in her arms in one quick motion and handed her off to the officer in the boat, who put her down and told her to stay seated. The boat took off when Sam was safely in the boat, and one of the officers handed Sara a life jacket.

Sara looked up at Sam. "Seriously?"

Sam smiled. "I've got her." She looked at the life jacket he was still holding out to Sara. "And just FYI, she may hit you with that unless you take it away."

The officer driving leaned over and caught Sam's eye. "Where to, Captain?"

"My house," said Sam, ignoring the looks that ricocheted like pinballs between her officers.

Sara half heard them discussing the details of what happened. Apparently, the kids intended it to be a practical joke in which they disconnected the far end of the dock after they drove the car onto it, setting it loose to float out into the lake.

The foaming water whizzed by the side of the boat and Sara suddenly felt dizzy. She closed her eyes until she felt Sam kneeling in front of her, hands on her shoulders.

"Are you okay?" she asked. "Do you feel like you're going to pass out?"

Sara shook her head, feeling the driver shift down and the boat slow underneath her. "I'm fine," she said, shaking her head. "I promise." She eventually felt the boat drift to a stop against a dock.

"Do you want one of us to help you get her up to the house,

Captain?" The officer still holding the life jacket looked up at Sam, concern on his face. "No," Sara interjected. "I can walk."

"How about you guys just hang out until you see us get in the door," Sam said to them as they got up to leave. They nodded, and Sam and Sara stepped up onto a polished wood dock that led to carved wood stairs set in a curved path up the hill.

"Wait," Sara said, looking back. "My bag. It has my phone in it, and I should call Jen."

Sam signaled the boat and one of the officers walked up and handed her Sara's bag. She guided her up the stairs to the deck of a three-story log cabin. Floor to ceiling windows overlooked the lake, and a polished wood deck spanned the entire backside of the cabin, with a cedar hot tub tucked into an alcove upstairs.

"Okay, we're good," Sam called toward the boat from the door, punching a code into a keypad.

The patrol boat took off and accelerated toward the center of the lake. Sam opened the door, noticing the wet blanket Sara was still clutching around her. Sara looked around her at a rustic living room that seemed straight out of a design magazine.

"I'm going to try to find some clothes that might have an off chance of fitting you," Sam said, guiding her toward the leather couch in the center of the room.

"Do you mind if I take a shower while you do that?"

"Of course." Sam pointed down the hall off the great room. "It's down that hall to the left. Just leave the door unlocked and I'll put some clothes on the counter for you. I'll knock, I promise."

"Okay," Sara said, trying to take in her surroundings as Sam went to find clothes.

The cabin was built in Aspen style, all three floors open to the endless floor to ceiling windows looking out onto the water. An antler chandelier hung in the middle of the great room, and a main sitting area centered around an enormous fireplace made her want to collapse on the cozy couch on the way to the shower.

Eventually, she found the bathroom and started to turn on the water but was suddenly too tired to move. She sat on the counter, thinking about the girl she'd tried to pull from the car, her blond hair splayed out on the dock while they worked on bringing her back to life. She wondered how she was, if there was any lasting damage or if she'd even continued to breathe. She shook the thoughts from her head, folding the patrol blanket wrapped around her neatly into a square on the counter. The shower itself was at the end of a curved corridor made of natural stone that led to a rainfall shower at the far end, forming its own separate room. There was no curtain or shower door, just a feeling she was under a quiet waterfall deep in the woods.

"I'm putting some clothes on the counter, Sara," Sam called, her voice muffled by the water. "Are you okay?"

"I'm good," Sara said, "I'll be out in a minute, but can you call Jen from my phone? Just leave her a message and let her know I'm okay."

Sara heard the door shut and she rinsed the shampoo from her hair, adding a bit of conditioner to the ends, then walked out into the bathroom and toweled off. Sam had set some sweatpants and a hoodie on the counter. Sara rolled the legs of the sweats up so she didn't trip on them and wandered back into the great room to see Sam in the kitchen.

She sank down into the couch and held up her arms, the sleeves of the hoodie Sam had given her dangling past her fingertips.

"How tall *are* you, anyway?"

"Taller than Tom Cruise, apparently," Sam said. "I'm five-ten."

"Thank you for the clothes; they're perfect."

"Are you hungry?"

"I can't imagine eating anything," Sara said. "My throat is still burning for some reason."

"That's probably a combination of water irritation and the forced air when we were trying to get you to start breathing again."

Sam brought some tea to the couch and wrapped Sara in a blanket from a basket beside it. She'd dimmed the chandelier, lamps spilled out gold light into the corners of the room, and a fire crackled in the stone hearth. Sam got up to get a bottle of scotch and two glasses from the kitchen just as Sara's phone rang. Sam picked it up and held it out to her.

"It's Jen."

"Will you talk to her?" Sara whispered, shaking her head. "My throat is killing me."

"Hey Jen," Sam said, holding the phone to her ear and walking toward the couch with the scotch. She then held the phone away from her ear as Sara heard the familiar sound of Jen running ten questions together at once.

"Give her to me," Sara said, holding her hand out for the phone. "She's not in the mood to miss out on the details, clearly."

Sam handed her the phone.

"Jen?"

"What the *fuck* happened?" Jen screeched. "Sam left me a message about an accident and said you were fine, but then someone at Moxie Java told me you almost died trying to save someone and they had to resuscitate you."

"I didn't almost die." Sara rolled her eyes. "I ran out of breath, but Sam got me out of the water. It was at Camp Montauk, and Sam got called out because her boat was the closest to it when it happened. Some teenage campers thought it would be funny to drive their counselor's car out the end of the dock, then unhook that section so it would float away."

She paused, pushing the sleeves of the hoodie back up her arms. "So the short version is, the dock broke, the car sank, and it was a tense few minutes before everyone was out." A long pause made Sara wonder if Jen was still there.

"Are you positive you're okay?" Jen said. "Do you want me to come get you? Where the hell does Sam even live?"

Sara smiled. "I'm good here. I'm just going to crawl into bed here if Sam will let me and deal with everything in the morning."

Sara listened to Jen for a minute or two after, then crinkled her eyebrows together and looked up at Sam, the phone still to her ear.

"Jennifer Brighton, what do you *mean* you bought a houseboat?"

Jen hung up quickly after that, and Sara put her phone down on the table.

"She bought a houseboat?" Sam asked.

"Don't even ask, I have no idea," Sara said. "Although she did say Trevor actually paid for it, not that I think he has any clue yet." Sara tilted her head, thinking. "Actually, that may have been a smart move."

"She's a smart girl," Sam said, pouring amber scotch over ice in her glass.

Just then, Sam's phone rang. Sara nodded for her to answer

it, and she clicked the answer button and put it to her ear. She gave one-word answers to whatever the person was saying, then put the phone down after thanking them for getting in touch.

"The girl you saved, Amy, made it through with no lasting damage. They're releasing her tomorrow."

"Wow," Sara said, sinking back into the leather couch, tucking her feet underneath her. "But you saved her. I think we both can agree that I ended up being just one more person to bring to the surface."

"Hey," Sam said, refilling their glasses, "I never would have gone back down to that car. It was pitch black in there and I had no idea there was even another person in it. The truth is that you're the only reason she didn't end up a body at the bottom of the lake."

Sara leaned against her shoulder, her eyes suddenly very heavy.

"I have a guest room," Sam said, running her hands through Sara's hair, "But I'd rather keep a closer eye on you. Do you mind sleeping in my bed?"

As sleep threatened to wash over her, Sara realized she wouldn't want to be anywhere else.

CHAPTER TEN

*W*ell, thought Sam as she headed out to her truck in the morning, her hair still wet from her cold shower, *that may have been the most sexually frustrating night I've ever had.*

And given Sam's penchant for straight girls after she came out during her twenties, that was saying something. Sam had tucked Sara into bed after they'd finished the scotch, and as soon as she'd brushed her teeth and slid under the covers beside her, a sleeping Sara rolled into her arms, slipping her hand under Sam's shirt. Her breathing was deep and even; it was obvious she was in a deep sleep, but as her hand traveled over Sam's abs, then down to her hips, Sam wished she wasn't. To make it even worse, she'd pulled off the sweatpants Sam had given her in her sleep, and since her underwear had been wet, she wasn't wearing anything underneath. So despite a gorgeous blonde lying in Sam's arms all night, soft, warm, and naked from the waist down, she'd somehow kept her hands to herself. Literally, in fact; Sam had to roll Sara off her body at some point and stroke herself to a quick orgasm just to fall asleep.

Sam headed into the station, stopping at Moxie Java to get Beth her latte, nodding to Lily at the front desk, who watched her walk through the double doors and halfway down the hall. Sam felt her eyes on her back, making a mental note to decide what the hell to do about her. They'd been having sex for two months, and since then, it was rare for a day to go by without her fucking Lily on the desk in her office after hours or bending her over the table at her cottage on the weekends. Lily was twenty-three, and technically worked for the Boise temp company that sent her to McCall, not Sam, so it wasn't wrong, but it wasn't technically right, either.

She got to her desk and stacked her paperwork into some semblance of order before there was a knock at the door.

"Come in."

Chief Davis stuck his head around the door. "I just wanted to come over and thank you for stepping in yesterday," he said, then hesitated. "If you hadn't been there, those kids would have died."

"I'm glad I was close enough to the camp to get there in time."

Chief Davis nodded. "The water pressure made the doors impossible to open, and the electrical system shorted out the window controls about the same time, so all those poor kids could do was watch the water rise around them." He looked down and shook his head. Sam knew he had teenagers about the same age at home.

"Anyway," he said, looking Sam in the eye, "I hear everyone's going to be just fine, so you got there just in the nick of time. Well done, Captain." He turned to leave, then paused. "You did Gus proud."

Sam listened to his heels click back down the hall and turned her chair around to look out over the lake.

❖

"Can I help you?"

The same pretty girl with ice blue eyes sat behind the receptionist's desk, one eyebrow raised, waiting for Sara to answer.

"I'm here to see Sam. Is she in?"

Lily reached for the buzzer to open the double doors, still looking at Sara. "You've really got to start calling her Captain Draper."

The doors buzzed, so Sara headed toward Sam's office and knocked lightly on the last door in the corridor.

"Come in."

Sam was looking out over the lake, her chair turned away slightly from the door.

"Hey," Sara said, "You were gone when I woke up; I didn't get to say thank you for last night."

Sam turned her chair around and smiled. "You're easy to take care of."

"Well," Sara said, "you're great at it."

"Except that begging me for sex in your sleep thing."

Sara rounded the corner of Sam's desk and punched her arm for effect. "I can't believe you just said that!" She smiled and ran a hand through her hair, twisting it up into a quick ponytail. "You were amazing at that camp, by the way." Sara paused. "It was actually pretty sexy."

"That was my plan the whole time," Sam said with a wink.

Sara took a step closer, between Sam's knees, and closed her eyes when she felt Sam's hands move slowly up the back of her thighs.

Just at that moment, Sam's phone rang, and Sara stepped back.

"I have to go anyway," she said, "But I'm doing a tasting at the diner later if you want to come by."

"I'll try," Sam said, not meeting her eyes as she picked up the phone.

❖

Sara spent the afternoon in town, leaning over the prep table in the kitchen, trying to get a list of dishes together for the tasting. She'd decided to do a free tasting of the dishes she'd chosen for her menu that afternoon, just small bites that people could just walk by and sample. She hoped to get a general idea of whether her ideas were good or if she needed to make any changes. She'd hired Mara, the sophomore who'd helped with the fundraising breakfast, just for the day.

Sara let herself into the diner and got to work pulling several of the tables outside on the sidewalk in front of the diner. They would place samples of each dish at each of the small tables, bistro style, along with a small sign explaining what the dish was and what was in it. Bottles of sparkling water were chilling in the walk-in, and she'd have small glasses ready at each table. Mara would run back and forth from the kitchen with additional samples if they ran low, and Sara would be there to answer questions.

She'd decided to serve the five dishes she was positive she'd end up putting on the menu, and some alternatives she was considering if time permitted. She prepped the food all morning, getting the actual cooking time and assembly down to the bare minimum so she'd be able to get the food out quickly and refill it when necessary. She'd decided to go with a spin on British roast beef pie, with a side of braised cabbage and wholegrain mustard, buckwheat noodles with prosciutto and truffle oil, micro greens with shaved cheeses and balsamic reduction, duck fat frites served with a lemon garlic aioli, and lavender mousse. Each sample was about half a regular serving, served in a kraft paper boat. Her menu would be more thematic and cohesive by the time she opened, but she hoped this would be a great gauge of what the locals thought of the food. Mara arrived right on time and helped Sara get the tables set and décorated, and put a chalkboard sign on an easel at each end of the sidewalk, telling them more about the menu and encouraging them to try each dish. She also provided notecards and pens for guests to leave comments.

As soon as the first tray of samples went out, people came out of the woodwork, and the turnout did seem to be primarily locals rather than tourists, which Sara couldn't decide was a good thing or not. Mary came over right away and took two of the roast beef plates back to the drugstore, "for research purposes," and once Sara explained that the frites were basically just fries cooked in duck fat, several people reluctantly tried them. They were generally wary of the aioli, however, and so many people asked where the ketchup was she actually considered just putting it out on the table.

A few hours later Sara looked around at the tables as the tasting wound down. No one tried the lavender mousse, which surprised her, although in hindsight it occurred to her she shouldn't have listed in the description that it contained an "unexpected kick of habanero pepper." Still, though, it was beautiful, and food-wise not that far off the beaten path, so the negative reaction was unexpected. Most of the plates people had sampled and left on the tables had only one or two bites gone, if that. It was as if they picked them up, tasted them, and put them right back down, which to a chef was the worst possible outcome. The one thing that did fly off the tables was the roast beef pie, wrapped in a layer of flaky crust, so it wasn't a total loss.

"Well," Sara said to herself as she started to gather everything to take back into the kitchen, "at least they liked one of them."

She and Mara had the kitchen clean and sidewalk back to

normal in record time, and Sara included an extra hour's pay in the envelope she'd handed Mara when she left.

The roast beef was a hit. Mara was great. Everything else was an undeniable disaster.

"Shit," Sara said under her breath as she pulled the door shut and locked up the diner. "What's wrong with these people?"

Sara took the comment cards home with her to go through with a glass of wine. Jennifer had all but moved into her houseboat that Sara hadn't even seen yet, so the house was quiet. Sara took a long sip of her Chardonnay and read the first card.

I liked the French fries, it said, *But not sure what the side of mayo was for.*

Sara looked into the golden depth of her glass and started to reconsider the wine. This was quickly turning into an evening that required scotch.

I wanted to try the dessert but was afraid the lavender stuff would taste like soap.

Liked the salad, but I'm not sure I'd be able to find something here that my husband or kids would eat.

I can tell the cook knows what he's doing, but I would have liked that bacon stuff on a regular burger. What's up with the noodles?

Even better. Now they were assuming Sara was a line cook. And a man.

Only one of the cards was wholly positive. *Beautiful food, would love to take a date here.*

Which, of course, was the complete opposite of what Sara set out to do. She wanted the gastropub to be a casual place for locals and visiting foodies, with elevated but familiar dishes, but clearly that wouldn't be popular, to say the least. What did they want? Deep-fried mac and cheese balls?

Sara sighed and pushed the cards away. She knew she was being petulant and unprofessional. The locals liked what they liked, and if Sara was going to run a successful business in McCall, maybe she needed to rethink the whole concept of the restaurant. But was that really the kind of food she wanted to put out? Dishes that any line cook worth his shift beer could put out in four minutes or less?

The doorbell startled Sara enough to knock over her wineglass. The Chardonnay quickly soaked into the comment cards and dripped off the table down to the wood plank floors with an audible splat.

"Well," Sara said, shaking the wine off her hands and going to get the door, "at least I don't have to reread them now."

It was Sam. Sara suddenly remembered they were supposed to go out on the boat. She motioned Sam in and closed the door.

"I may not be the best student tonight. I'm not sure I can take any more embarrassment today."

She grabbed the paper towels and Sam took them from her when she came back to the table, gently pushing her into a dry chair and refilling her glass.

"That good, huh?"

"Don't you dare make fun of me, Draper." Sara couldn't even look at her. "I already get it that you predicted this."

"Sara," Sam said, soaking up the rest of the wine with a paper towel, "I'm really sorry if it sounded like I was making fun of you. I honestly wasn't. And you and I both know I was just being a dick when we closed on the diner."

She held up the cards that weren't soaked through, blotting them with dry paper towels.

Sara shook her head. "You don't have to do that. I've already read them," she said. "And I have no desire to read them again."

Once everything was almost dry, Sam sat down at the table opposite Sara. "Is that your first glass, by any chance?"

"Second," Sara said. "I totally forgot about our lesson. I'm sorry."

"Actually," Sam said, looking over to the window, "It's supposed to dump rain on us in about twenty minutes, so it doesn't matter at all. I just came over to bring you this."

She pulled a paperback booklet, *Boating Safety and Regulations*, out of her pocket and leaned back in her chair to toss it onto the kitchen counter. "You're fairly close to being ready."

"Really?" Sara said, "How long is the wait before I can take it?"

"Usually only a couple of days," Sam said, trying not to smile.

"I totally made up the story about a long waiting list just to get under your skin that first day."

"You're fucking kidding me." Sara smacked Sam with the stack of wet cards.

"Afraid not, Miss Brighton."

"And did I really even need a licensed driver in the boat with me until I pass the test?"

"That part was true," Sam said. "But you have every right to punch me for the waiting list thing. I think I just wanted to see what you looked like pissed off."

Sara thought back, remembering how much she'd wanted to ball up that list and pitch it into her smug face. "Mission accomplished."

Sam grabbed a beer from the fridge and sat back down. "Are you in a time crunch with this restaurant thing, or could you be gone for a few days?"

Sara looked up. "Well, considering that I'm now back at square one, a few more days won't make any difference. Why?"

Sam smiled. "I've got way too many vacation days stacked up that the chief is always on me to use. What do you think about getting the hell out of town for a while?" She picked up the limp comment card next to her hand and balled it up in her fist. "I've got something I want to show you."

"Really?" Sara said, "What?" *Now this is getting interesting,* she thought.

"It's not one thing," Sam replied, hesitating. "It's more of an… experience."

"I bet you say that to all the girls."

"Maybe," Sam said, with a smirk Sara tried like hell not to find sexy. "But this is purely educational, I promise."

"Why should I trust you?" Sara asked, narrowing her eyes at Sam and trying not to smile.

"Because I think I may know how to help, but you're just going to have to—"

"Trust you?"

"Yeah," Sam said, smiling and clinking her bottle to Sara's wineglass. "Exactly."

Sam finished her beer and told Sara to pack a bag as she walked out to the patrol truck. "I'll pick you up here at eight in the morning."

"Wait," Sara said. "What do you drive? I've never seen you in anything but a Lake Patrol vehicle."

"I'll be in the truck that's sitting in your driveway at eight in the morning."

Sam pulled out of her driveway and turned onto the road toward her house, just to the other side of Sara's property line.

❖

The next morning, Sam pulled up and found Sara's bag already on the porch. She stepped out of the cabin just after, holding two travel mugs, and locked the door.

"You're ready right on time?" Sam asked, picking up her bag. "I'm impressed. Have you eaten?"

Sara shook her head, handed her a mug of coffee, and climbed in the passenger's seat of a late model green Land Rover.

Sara ran her hand over the leather seats. "I've got to say, I was planning to tease you about some beat-up old truck, but I actually like this."

"Hey," Sam said, pulling out of the drive and onto the road to town, "I don't drive this thing because it's pretty, I drive it because it's the least likely to leave me stranded in four feet of snow on the side of the mountain."

"Oh my Lord, you don't drive it because it's pretty?" Sara said, fanning herself with her hand, and doing her best Southern belle impression. "I'm simply faint with the shock."

They cruised out of town and onto the road that wound down the mountain toward Boise. There wasn't much in the way of other small towns that Sara remembered, although she hadn't ever really paid attention. Twenty miles down the road, Sam pulled left onto a small paved road through the trees, passing a sign on the right. *Mountain Harbor, population 865.*

"What's this?" Sara said, watching the tiny town unfold on either side of the car.

"This," said Sam, "is where McCall eats on the way down to Boise."

"I had no idea this was even here!" Sara said, leaning out her window to check out the old-fashioned town square, tiny by any standard, but certainly charming, and it seemed right out of a fifties television show.

They parked next to the courthouse and walked to the north side of the square. Sara smelled what could only be biscuits and frying bacon, then she spotted a plate glass window with a white posterboard sign taped to the inside: *Just Deb's.*

"They used to have a regular sign out front," Sam said, opening the door for Sara, a brass bell announcing their arrival. "It was called Mel and Deb's Mountain Cafe."

"What happened?"

"No one really knows, but one day Deb paid some teenagers to pull down the sign, trash it, and stuff it into the cab of Mel's truck. Ever since then, there's been that posterboard sign with the new name of the place on it. Just Deb's."

"Let me guess," said Sara. "One of her waitresses was suddenly fired as well."

"Good guess."

They slid into a booth by the window, with coffee cups already in place and paper placemats. "Interesting," Sara said, looking around. "Where's the menu?"

Sam turned her placemat over and pointed at the menu printed on the back in old typewriter font. There were three sections: breakfast, lunch, and supper.

"This is to the point." Sara said, scanning the short list of options.

"You have no idea," Sam said, turning over her coffee cup so the next waitress that passed could fill it.

Sam didn't need to look at the menu. In the breakfast section, there were three options listed: egg breakfast, pancakes, and biscuits and gravy. Six words total.

"Wait," Sara said, "is this it?" She turned over the placemat again.

"Let me give you a word of advice," Sam said as she noticed the waitress on her way over to the table. She dropped her voice to a whisper and leaned over closer to Sara. "Choose what you want and say it just like it's written. Don't get picky with it."

An older waitress in jeans and a Six Flags T-shirt dug a paper order pad out of her apron with one hand and filled Sam's coffee cup with the other. Sara caught on and turned hers over too.

"What can I get ya?"

Sam nodded at Sara to order first.

"I'll have this one, please." She pointed at the last line in the breakfast section.

She nodded once, then poised her pen over the pad and looked at Sam.

"I'll have the egg breakfast, over easy."

She jotted Sam's order down and headed toward the order window. Sara watched her put the order sheet in the window and ring the bell. A hand reached up to grab it and clipped it to the wheel with the others.

"Was that Deb?"

Sam looked around before she answered. "Probably. Deb's usually in the kitchen on the line. She and Dad were good friends back in the day."

"So that's how you grew to like the place?"

"I spent a fair amount of time here in the years after Mel took off. Deb was too proud to ask for help, but Dad would stop in once or twice a week and just ask what needed doing."

"Wow," Sara said. "That was really kind."

"They both grew up in McCall. Dad went to high school with her."

"So has the food here always been the same?"

"Nope," Sam said, pouring an alarming pile of creamer into her coffee from a glass holder with a steel spout. "When I was in sixth grade, she dropped the tuna melt from the lunch section."

"Seriously?" Sara couldn't tell if Sam was kidding or not. "That's been the only change in all those years?"

"That's all I know about, anyway."

A few minutes later, the food arrived, and the smell of the smoky peppered bacon alongside the biscuits was mesmerizing. It was cooked perfectly, crispy but tender, and had a hint of maple sweetness along the edges.

"This might be the best bacon I've ever had," Sara said, closing her eyes and leaning back in the booth with it in her hand.

"Want to know the secret?"

"God, yes."

"She takes a square block of bacon and brushes the edges with maple syrup before she slices it into strips."

The biscuits had been split open and lightly browned for a bit of texture, then smothered in sausage gravy with a light dusting of cracked pepper.

"I'm assuming you know how amazing these biscuits are?" Sara raised an eyebrow in Sam's direction.

"I do," Sam said, "but they're dangerous. When she runs out of them on a Sunday, which always happens at some point, people have been known to get a little testy."

They finished their breakfast and the waitress cleared the plates, topping off their coffee and laying a handwritten paper bill on the table. Sam stirred more creamer into her coffee and reached for the sugar.

"My dad died suddenly of a heart attack," she said, looking into her cup. "There was no warning, no chance to figure anything out. But by eight o'clock the next morning, Deb had driven to McCall and had Mary let her into the diner. They both stayed there all weekend and cleaned the place top to bottom. They donated all the leftover stock, cleaned out the walk-in refrigerator, then made sure all the books were wrapped up and the staff were paid."

"I can imagine all that would have felt impossible if they hadn't jumped in and just gotten it done," Sara said.

"I couldn't have done it," Sam said. "Not with everything else. It was just me and Dad by then, so there was no other family to help." Sam looked toward the kitchen. "Every Friday evening for three months after he died, Mary would text me and tell me not to forget to get the casserole."

"The casserole?"

"Mary calls everything casserole." Sam smiled, dropping her voice and leaning closer to Sara. "Deb would bring pot roast or a pan of lasagna up to McCall and drop it off with her every Friday and I'd pick it up on the way home from work. Neither one of them ever said a word about it. Mary just handed it to me over the counter, but I'd been eating Deb's cooking since I was a kid, and somehow just that made me feel like not everything was suddenly different."

After they'd finished, they walked out into the bright sunlight and Sara looked back at the front of the cafe. Faded plastic mistletoe still hung above the door from the previous Christmas, and the edges of the posterboard sign were yellowed and curling up toward the center. But somehow, now it looked a little less shabby.

Chapter Eleven

The drive down the mountain toward Boise was crisp and beautiful. Even when she was a kid on the way home from camp, Sara had always loved the sight of the river crashing and falling down the mountain. It followed the road, and every twist and turn brought beautiful white rapids that eventually settled into a gentle flow during the straighter parts of the drive. Sara rolled down her window and let the cool air slip under her hand, the wind smoothing the edges of her thoughts until no sharp remnants remained. Boise eventually surrounded them, then slipped into the rearview mirror as Sam turned into Lucky Peak State Park. Thick pines bordered the winding road that eventually led to the ranger station. Sam picked up a set of keys at the desk and they took the road that followed the edge of the lake, deep blue and shimmering in the sun.

"So where are you taking me, anyway?"

"One of my favorite places," Sam said, looking over at Sara. She'd rolled her window down and her blond hair whipped around her face. "I've always had a thing for log cabins, and I found this one when I was here for a canoeing trip when I was twenty-one."

"So is this where you take all the girls you're stalking, or am I special?"

Sam winked at her. "I refuse to answer that on the grounds that I may incriminate myself."

She turned down a wooded road that ended at the lake, with an old log cabin at the shoreline. It was small, just barely bigger than Sara's, but had an enormous wraparound porch with white Adirondack chairs lined up and facing the water. Sam parked and tossed Sara the keys to open up the cabin while she got the bags.

Sara let herself in and instantly saw why Sam loved the place. There was a loft bedroom with a handmade ladder, a kitchen to the left, and a gorgeous stone fireplace with a wide hearth and a stack of logs beside it. A heavenly looking sofa with a navy slipcover and white and cherry striped pillows begged Sara to stretch out on it. She didn't resist.

"Look," Sam said, pulling a cooler into the kitchen with the bags on her shoulder. "I appreciate the offer and all, but it's not even dark."

Sara tossed a pillow in her direction. "You wish, Draper!"

Sam caught it and leaned into Sara on the couch, holding her face in both hands, kissing her slowly, then deeper, catching her lower lip between her teeth for just an instant before she let her go. "Time to go." Her breath was warm on the delicate skin of Sara's neck.

Sara's hands slid over the hard lines of Sam's arms. There was a quiet power to Sam that made her instantly wet.

"What makes you think I'm just going to jump up and follow you, Draper?"

"Nothing. I know you better than that by now," Sam said, picking Sara up before she realized what was happening and setting her down at the door.

"But I'll do it for you."

Once they were back in the truck, Sam drove them back into Boise, searching side streets in the downtown area until she found what she was looking for: a food truck, painted with bright splashes of yellow and green, parked on the side of the square with dozens of people standing around waiting for food. Warm Mexican spices wafted toward them as they walked up, specifically mole sauce made with what smelled like charred chili and dark chocolate. The menu, written in chalk above the service window, was entirely in Spanish.

"Can you read that?" Sara asked.

"I'll order for us," Sam said, still looking at the menu. "Do you trust me?"

"Absolutely not."

"Smart girl." Sam smiled. "But I'm still ordering for you."

When they got to the window, Sam ordered in perfect Spanish, and nodded toward Sara more than once while she was talking.

"What did you say?" Sara said, as they stepped to the side to wait for their food.

"Nothing I'm telling you about, but you're getting something that's not on the menu. They have it if you ask, and it's amazing."

"What is it?"

"Pork mole and pineapple tamales with pork belly salad."

"Wow," Sara said, "I underestimated you. You don't strike me as the pork belly type."

"There are two types of foodies," Sam replied, taking their food from the pickup window and handing half of it to Sara. "People who like to talk about food, and the people who'd rather eat it."

The steam rising off the tamales was intoxicating, and Sara inhaled deeply, trying to determine what spice they'd used for the filling. Roughly chopped ripe avocado, crushed cilantro, and onion in a rumpled paper boat surrounded two plump musa wrapped tamales. They sat down in the grass and Sara kicked off her sandals.

"Looks like the county fair," Sam said, spearing her tamale with her fork. "Tastes like heaven."

The tamale melted in Sara's mouth as soon as she bit into it. The mole sauce was silky and intense, a nice balance for the spicy shredded pork and sweet grilled pineapple.

"Wow," Sara said, looking down at the tamale in her hand. "Just wow."

"Wait," Sam said, cupping her hand behind her ear. "Did I just hear you say that you don't know why you ever order for yourself when I'm so amazing at it?"

Sara smiled. "Just for that, I'll be ordering for you next time."

After Sara finished the tamales and made a swiftly interrupted play for the rest of Sam's, she started on the salad, which turned out to have an interesting presentation. It was served in a bag of tortilla chips that had been cut open along one side, then filled with crisp smoky pork belly, sliced jicama, fresh lettuce, and onion.

"Actually," Sara said, "This 'serve it in the bag' concept is genius. It's got to be cheaper and probably produces half the waste."

The salad was excellent, but Sara could only eat about half so she slid it over to Sam, who finished it in three bites.

They stayed in the square for about an hour, enjoying the late afternoon sunshine, then stopped by the ranger station at Lucky Peak on their way back and rented some bicycles. They spent the rest of the afternoon biking through the park, stopping to take pictures of the sailing competition on the east side of the lake. By the time they got back to the cabin, the sun was fading and the fireflies were sparkling in the last of the evening light.

Sam started some coals in the grill while Sara went in to take a shower. She returned to the deck in a few minutes, her hair damp and falling around her shoulders, wearing a white skirt and black tank top. She was holding her phone in her hand.

"Do you know someone named Murphy?"

The grill sizzled as Sam transferred food from a plate to the hot coals. "If Murphy is the last name, I have an officer on Lake Patrol named Brian Murphy. He's the one that helped you with the grill setup at the pancake breakfast."

"Well," Sara said, tapping her phone on her shoulder, "I just called my sister and she couldn't talk because she's at my house and he's coming over to swim to the island with her."

"Oh really?" Sam looked amused. Sara did not.

"Is he a good guy? The last thing she needs is another Trevor right now."

"Honestly," Sam said, "I can tell you I've learned that if we have a difficult time with someone on the water, Murphy's the one you want to deal with the situation. He's great with people, and," Sam paused, a smile flashing across her face, "smarter than he looks."

"Great," Sara said, looking less than convinced. "I hope you're right, because she said she's been spending a lot of time with him since she bought the boat. Evidently, he's helping her fix it up."

"Can your sister even drive a boat?"

"No," Sara said, beginning to find the humor in the situation, "I'm pretty sure she's never been in one. At camp, she refused to take water-skiing because she didn't want to get her hair wet."

Sara's phone pinged and she looked at the text, smiling. She walked over to the grill and held up her iPhone. "But look at her now."

Jennifer was standing on the deck of her houseboat, pulling up a rope and winding it around her forearm. Her hair was loose and wild, and she looked like she might have even gained some much-needed weight.

"Well," Sam said, "That explains how she met him. That's Murphy's houseboat. It didn't occur to me until just now that he was talking about selling it a few months back."

"Well," Sara said, "I like him already. Look how happy she looks, and she's been eating."

Sam saw the tears in her eyes and pulled her into a hug. "I'm going to assume those are happy tears?"

Sara nodded.

"Good," Sam said, letting her go and turning her attention back to the grill. "Then now's a good time to mention that he dips."

"He…what?"

"Dips," Sam said. "Like chewing tobacco."

"Ew. Well, I give that about a week with Miss Bossypants in charge." She looked at the grill; she'd been so distracted she hadn't noticed what Sam was cooking. "What are you making?"

"Grilled rueben sandwiches on rye and charred peaches in Chardonnay."

"I thought you said you couldn't cook." She raised an eyebrow, looking down at the perfectly golden sandwiches and lightly charred peaches.

"I can't cook," Sam said, sliding the sandwiches onto their plates. She dropped a grilled fresh peach into each wineglass and poured a buttery Chardonnay over it. "I can grill. Totally different."

They took the plates to the deck chairs and watched the sun set over the lake as they ate. Sam had changed into a snug white T-shirt and faded Levi's jeans, her tan skin a dark contrast. Her eyes mirrored the same blue as the water.

"I don't think I've ever seen you drink wine." Sara looked at Sam's glass.

"That's because I don't," Sam said. "I love beer but I've just never seen what all the fuss is about with wine. It's all made with grapes. Aside from white and red, how different can the bottles be?"

"Oh, good God," Sara said, pelting her with a napkin. "I can't believe you just said that to a chef."

After they'd eaten and cleaned up the kitchen, Sam went to

light a fire in the fireplace. She sat on the hearth, the light playing with the angles of her face, while Sara lay back on the couch, scotch in hand.

"I poured one for you," she said, nodding toward the old steamer trunk that served as a side table. "I didn't intend to bring it, but I found the flask in my bag that Jen gave me the last time Mom threatened to come to Savannah for a visit."

Sam picked it up and sat on the couch, pulling Sara's legs onto her lap.

"So, why did you stop that night on the boat?" Sara said, looking into her glass. "If you're not attracted to me, you can just tell me. I promise I won't throw myself off a balcony or anything."

"Are you kidding me?" Sam tangled her fingers into Sara's. "I wanted you more than I wanted to breathe."

A log in the fireplace crackled and split, flames spilling out onto the coals.

"Then why?" Sara said.

Sam stared into the fire, her voice low and soft. "Because I realized I wasn't willing to risk losing this."

Sara watched the shifting gold reflection of the fire in Sam's eyes. "That might be the most romantic thing anyone has ever said to me."

Sam looked at her for a moment, then took the fleece throw from the back of the couch and laid it in front of the fire. Sara watched her as she added two more logs, sending a spray of sparks up toward the chimney, then sat on the hearth.

"Come here."

Sara put down her glass and sank down on the blanket, fire warming the side of her face, as Sam lowered her body down on top of her.

"Take this off for me," Sam whispered, her hand sliding Sara's skirt up to her waist.

Sara pulled her skirt and tank off, then slid her hands up the back of Sam's shirt, following the strong lines of her back with her fingertips. Sam pulled it over her head and tossed it onto the couch, leaving her naked to the waist. She kissed down Sara's body, tracing the outside curve of her breast before she pulled her hard nipple into her mouth, working it with her tongue, her hands wrapped around the small of Sara's back.

Sam moved lower, resting Sara's thigh on her shoulder, and traced the edge of her sheer panties with her tongue. Sara felt the heat of her breath on her skin and tangled her fingers into Sam's dark hair.

"Sam," she said, breathless. "Please."

Sam slowly slid her panties down her legs. The firelight cast shifting layers of gold and copper light across Sara's skin as Sam sank down slowly between her thighs. She slid her hands up the outside of her hips as Sara's hand slipped again into Sam's hair, less gentle than before. Sam lowered her mouth and touched her clit with just the tip of her tongue. It felt like an electric jolt, and just for a moment, Sara thought she might come.

"Tell me what you want," Sam whispered.

"More." Sara's voice caught. "I want more."

Sam slid two fingers slowly inside her, achingly slowly, her eyes locked onto Sara's. She stroked her gently, giving her less than she wanted, only adding a third when she felt Sara's body beg her for it. Sam felt her G-spot start to throb under the pads of her fingers, and she slowed her pace, curling her fingers in to increase the pressure.

"Oh my God," Sara said, her eyes shut tight.

Sam felt her holding her breath and knew she was right on the edge. She reached up with her other hand and rested it on Sara's chest.

"Breathe, baby."

When she felt Sara relax, Sam slid her fingers out and lowered her mouth again to the warmth between her legs. This time she pulled Sara's clit gently into her mouth, slowly stroking the underside of it with her tongue. She felt Sara's thighs tremble and she stayed there until the last second she could without sending Sara over the edge.

Sara pressed a clenched fist to her forehead. "Jesus, Sam, are you trying to kill me?"

Sam crawled back up her body and kissed her deeply, wrapping Sara's legs around her waist. She rolled Sara's nipples between her fingers, pausing to draw them into the warmth of her mouth again and again before she moved back down between her thighs. She dragged her tongue back over Sara's stiff clit, feeling the tremors that moved through her body, then slid her fingers back inside, stroking her slowly, Sara's juices running into her palm. She was breathing hard now, her chest rising and falling with the flames beside her.

"Don't stop, Sam…please don't stop."

Her skin was flushed, her eyes heavy with desire. Sara opened up to Sam and she slid another finger inside, her tongue higher, stroking inside and her clit with the same strong rhythm. Sara trembled, then arched her back hard and cried out, slicking Sam's hand to the wrist when she came.

Sam waited until Sara's body settled, then moved up to lay beside her, pulling Sara into her arms and wrapping the rest of the blanket around them. The flames sparked and danced beside their bodies, and Sam kissed the top of Sara's head, memorizing her scent.

Sara woke the next morning in the loft bed, a white duvet soft against her face. She turned to look at Sam still sleeping beside her and it all came back in a rush. Sam's mouth on her clit, the way she'd handled Sara's body, bringing her to the edge over and over again, then to the most shattering orgasm of her life. That was all she remembered. She didn't remember falling asleep, or how she got up the stairs and into bed. She remembered the climax—it was so intense she'd wondered the second before if she could die from pleasure. She moved to settle closer into Sam's arms and realized her lower abs ached. She'd come so hard that her muscles were sore. *Fucking hell*, Sara thought. *She knows what she's doing.*

She fell back into a heavy sleep and woke to the sun streaming into the loft window, illuminating tiny dust particles in the air that danced in the wide beam of light. Sara heard Sam below the loft in the kitchen and smelled what had to be a combination of eggs and sharp cheddar. She pulled the sheet around her body and held it to her chest as she climbed down the ladder.

"Good morning." Sam smiled, pulling her in for a kiss, her

hand strong at the small of Sara's back. She'd already showered and was barefoot, in jeans and a blue plaid shirt, the sleeves rolled up to the elbows.

Sam handed her an adorably messy plate of scrambled eggs. They took the plates to the couch and Sara curled up with her feet tucked underneath her, knotting the sheet so it would stay up while she ate.

"Wait," she said, a forkful of eggs halfway to her mouth. "You're not a morning person, are you?"

"I've spent the last fifteen years getting to work before seven a.m.," Sam said, smiling at the look of disbelief on Sara's face. "I'm guessing that you're not?"

"Well," Sara said, reaching over for a bite of Sam's eggs before she'd finished her own, "even if I was a morning person, I'd lie about it if it got me these eggs every morning."

They finished breakfast and Sara showered, dressed, and packed her bag. Sam threw them in the back with the cooler and they started driving out of the park and back to Highway 80. They'd been on the road for a while before it occurred to her to ask where they were going.

"I'm taking you to lunch at Ruby's," Sam said, moving her hand to Sara's thigh and smiling as Sara covered it with her own. "It's a diner just south of Pocatello in Blackfoot."

"So, basically, you're taking me on a food tour of Idaho?"

"Something like that," Sam said.

"I love it," Sara said, closing her eyes and leaning her head back in the warm sun streaming through the window. She sat there for a moment before she turned her head again to look over at Sam.

"What the hell did you *do* to me last night?"

"I'll take that as a compliment," Sam said with a sexy smile in her direction.

"I've never been that turned on in my life," Sara said, closing her eyes again and leaning back with the sun on her face. "You were…" She paused, searching for the words but coming up with nothing. "Wow. That's all I can say."

Just then, Sara's phone rang, and she dug for it in her bag, grabbing it on the last ring.

"Sara?" It was Jen. "Do you never answer your phone anymore? I've been trying to reach you since last night. What the hell have you been doing?"

Sara looked over at Sam, where it was clear from the smile on her face she was hearing every word of it.

"Jen," Sara said, trying to ignore the dramatics. "I'm here. What's going on?"

"Nothing."

Clearly, it wasn't nothing. Sara just waited.

"Okay," Jen continued. "Remember when I told you about Brian?"

"Wait," Sara said, "what does he do for a living?"

"He's one of Sam's lake cops."

"I thought so," Sara said, nodding at Sam. "Go ahead."

"Well, he's been helping me fix up the houseboat and teaching me how to work it and everything. I really like him."

"So what's the problem?"

"We've been spending every evening together," Jen said, hesitating, "and last night he took me canoeing to one of the islands where he had a picnic set up. It was amazing. He even had candles he'd lit and set in the sand around us. I mean, I didn't even know men did stuff like that."

Sam smiled and raised her eyebrows, keeping her eyes on the road. "So you had a good time?"

"More than that, I'm totally falling for him. I mean, I never felt this way about Trevor, not even at the beginning."

"I'm still vague on what the problem is. He sounds like he's really into you."

Jen hesitated. "That's just it, I'm not sure he is. So, we were sitting by the fire on the island last night, and he wrapped us both up in a blanket. But when I turned my head, expecting him to kiss me, he *didn't*."

"Did you try to kiss him?"

"Yes," Jen said, "Which was stupid. He stopped me and said he wanted us to 'do this right.'"

"What? He wants to wait until the divorce is finalized?"

"Yes, which makes no sense. If he really liked me, he would

have kissed me," Jen said, her voice quavering. "Am I an idiot here? Did I just read this entirely wrong?"

Sara looked at Sam, who shook her head.

"Jen, I know it seems like that, but let's get the facts straight here. He's a great guy, and you like him, right?"

"Yes," Jen sniffed. "Not that it matters."

"And he's been spending a ton of time helping you with the boat, then went to a huge effort to impress you on your date, right?"

"Yes, where I made a complete fool of myself." Jen pouted. "If you're trying to make me feel better here, it's not helping."

"And instead of taking advantage of you while you're going through a hard time, he said he wanted to wait and do it right." Sara paused. "It sounds like to me that you're worried he isn't serious about you but it's actually the exact opposite."

Sam nodded, pointing at Sara to let her know she'd gotten it right.

"Oh. I think I'm getting what you're saying," Jen said slowly. "So this is actually a good thing?"

"Definitely," Sara said, "I think he's just a gentleman. It sounds like he actually sees something in the future for you two."

"Why the hell didn't you answer your phone last night and tell me this?" Jen was back to full volume, but Sara heard the relief in her voice.

"Because I have a life," Sara said, her tone teasing and reassuring at the same time. "Just wait. It will be worth it, I promise."

Sam reached for her hand and squeezed it. As they were saying goodbye, Sara asked Jen to check on the cabin, just to make sure everything was still locked up.

"Actually, I already did," Jen said, "I went over there to borrow one of your tools, but I couldn't find them so I went down to the boat and looked there."

"Did you find what you needed?"

"The wrench, no. But I did find your bra and underwear crumpled on the back seat."

Sara slid down in her seat, trying to hide the flush creeping up to her cheeks. She'd forgotten Sam had thrown them back into the boat that night in the lake.

"So how is she?" Jen said, not even trying to hide her curiosity.

"Sitting right here."

"Fine," said Jen, undeterred, "But when you get back I want details."

They spoke for another minute or so, then Sara hung up, promising to let her know the minute she was back.

"You were right about Murphy, by the way," Sam said, looking over at her. "He's got some integrity about him; I'm not surprised he's holding off." She paused. "But I am impressed."

When they got to Blackfoot, it was after two and they were starving. Ruby's diner turned out to be tucked into the corner of a large stone building built in 1930s style. The stools and chairs were mirror finish chrome, and a bright cherry red covered the booths that lined the windows. The white tiled floor and eighteen-foot ceilings instantly made the space seem expansive and clean. A glass pie case sat on the counter, and a waitress in a pale yellow uniform pulling out slices of chocolate pie told them to sit anywhere. Sam chose a booth by the window, and the waitress came by briefly to drop off menus and take their drink orders.

"What's a Monte Cristo sandwich?" Sara asked, looking up from her menu.

"You've never had one? Maybe it's not a Southern thing." Sam folded her menu and laid it on the table. "But if I was ordering my last meal, I'd probably start with one of those."

"Well, there are no descriptions, so I guess I'm going to have to trust you," Sara said.

When the waitress returned, Sara ordered a Monte Cristo and a salad; Sam got a cheeseburger and fries.

"Okay," Sara said, "what did I order, now that I can't change my mind?"

"It's a ham and Swiss sandwich on...what is that soft bread that's slightly sweet?" She paused, trying to remember the name of it.

"Brioche?"

"That's it. They coat it in an egg mixture with a touch of nutmeg, then deep-fry it and serve it with powdered sugar."

"Seriously?" Sara said. "I just ordered a deep-fried sandwich?"

"Yes," Sam said, "and it gets even better. There is raspberry jam inside with the ham and swiss."

Sara laughed and the older couple at the table beside them looked over and smiled. Sara dabbed at her eyes with a napkin and tried to get it together.

"So what did you study at culinary school?" Sam asked.

"Primarily traditional French cuisine," Sara said, "Although I just love food, so I guess I was really all over the place."

"Is that what you served at your restaurant?" Sam dumped sugar into her sweet tea.

"Not really, but it did have an influence. Savannah is low country, right on the coast, so we served elevated traditional Southern cuisine with a lot of seafood thrown in the mix."

"Did you like it?"

"The food or the concept?"

"Both," Sam said.

"When I started out, I had a vision of what I wanted it to be," Sara said, folding her napkin and tucking it under her plate. "But as the years passed, what I put on the menu became more and more dictated by trends and the food critics I knew would review it. It was successful, but by the end I didn't feel a real connection to the dishes."

The waitress set down their plates, and Sam piled the lettuce, purple onions, and pickles on the side of the plate precariously onto her burger.

Sara cut into her sandwich, which looked somewhat like a block of French toast dusted in powdered sugar. When she sliced through it, bright raspberry jam and melted Swiss cheese dripped from the center over the layers of ham and down onto her plate. She cut a bite from the corner with her knife, but Sam stopped her before her fork reached her mouth.

"You can't eat a Monte Cristo with a knife and fork," she said in a whisper, laughter sparkling in her eyes, "And certainly not at Ruby's. I've got my reputation to consider."

"How do you eat it?"

"Just pick it up. It'll get all over you, but it's the only way to do it."

Sara closed her eyes and bit into the sandwich. The tart bite of the jam balanced the mild creaminess of the cheese perfectly. The ham was the perfect contrast, salty and rich, and the crisp egg crust was divine.

"Amazing," Sara said with her eyes closed and her mouth full. "How am I thirty-three and just now tasting this?"

"I told you," Sam said, smiling and nudging her foot lightly under the table. "You should listen to me. I've eaten a fair bit of diner food."

"I bet you have," Sara said. "What's your favorite dish?"

"It depends on the place, but here it's the Monte Cristo."

Sara looked at her plate, then over at Sam's. "So why did you order a burger?"

"I wanted to have something to trade you if you hated it."

Sara looked over at Sam, pouring ketchup onto a pile of French fries. Sam was getting to her. A lot. Maybe it was her kindness, or the way she laughed, whatever that was that she did to her last night, but she needed to be careful. Sooner or later, they had to go back to McCall, where Sara would open a restaurant that Sam hated, in the diner she loved.

"So," Sara said, "what did Gus have on McCall's menu?"

It was a risk, bringing it up, but the words were out of her mouth before she could catch them.

"It was a lot like you'd expect," Sam said, pushing her fries around on her plate. "Classic diner food like patty melts, burgers, mac and cheese…" She paused. "And the best Monte Cristo."

Sara reached across and entwined her fingers with Sam's. "Will you teach me how to make it?"

Sam nodded, putting down the burger and looking out the window.

It was nearly evening when they left the restaurant. They stopped in town to pick up some supplies and refill the cooler with ice, but on the way out, Sara pointed to a little stone building on her side. The sign read *Parker's Wine and Fine Cheeses.*

"Can we stop there for just a minute?"

"Absolutely, as long as you're not planning to make me drink wine."

"What if I balance it out with cheese?" Sara said, with what she hoped was her most charming smile. "Serious cheese. Something butch, like a strong, herby chèvre?"

Sam laughed so hard she had a hard time putting the truck in park and had to wipe her eyes when she finally got it together enough to speak.

"I can assure you that the terms 'butch' and 'herby' should never be in the same sentence. But you tried hard so I'll give you a pass."

Sam wandered around the store for a few minutes while Sara sampled some cheeses. She bought brined olives, some wedges of cheese, three bottles of wine, and a baguette. Sam pretended to struggle with the weight of the bags as they left and headed back to the truck.

"Are you expecting us to be snowed in tonight?"

"No, smart-ass, but you'll be begging me for more of this before I get done with you tonight."

"Really?" Sam said, looking over at her as they slid into their seats. "Because I seem to remember exactly the reverse last night."

Sara leaned over and kissed her, instantly wet when Sam's hand wrapped around the back of her neck, pulling her closer. It took everything she had to remember they were in a busy parking lot and reluctantly pull away.

"Well then," Sara said, "I guess we'll just have to see, won't we?"

Sam brought Sara's hand to her mouth and kissed her palm, holding her eyes and running her tongue lightly over Sara's fingertips before she let her go.

"I think you'll find I usually come out on top, Miss Brighton."

Sam drove them almost out of town, then turned right down a winding dirt road. She drove what seemed like forever through the trees, then eventually slowed when she came to a small log cabin tucked right off the road.

"Hang on," she said, getting out of the truck, "I'll be right back."

Sara watched her climb the steps to the front porch and grab an envelope that someone had taped to the front door.

"What's that?" Sara asked as she got back in the truck.

"Just the key to where I'm hiding all that wine before you make me drink it."

"Hey!" Sara said, smiling and swatting her arm with the back of her hand. "Watch it, buster, you're going to be eating your words later."

Sam just smiled and put her hand on Sara's thigh as she drove down an increasingly narrow road, finally emerging in a small clearing with an enormous tree at the center. A spiral staircase built beside the trunk led up to an intricately detailed treehouse, built on two levels, with a wraparound deck on both connected by stairs. String lights, made of tiny mission style lanterns and strung around the porch railing, mirrored the golden glow of the setting sun behind the trees.

"This is amazing," Sara said, too busy staring at the treehouse to actually walk to the staircase. "I've never seen anything like this."

Sam held out her hand, both their bags slung over one shoulder. She led Sara to the base of the tree and up the spiral staircase, then unlocked the glass door to the treehouse. As they stepped inside, Sara instantly fell in love with it. There were two overstuffed white sofas with a coffee table in the center, and a rough-hewn antique table to the side with a collection of mismatched chairs that looked like they'd been taken directly from Sara's cabin. The bright kitchen, painted a sunny yellow, was to the right of the main room, with small fairy doors attached to random cupboards and floorboards.

"My buddy built this place for his daughter when she was young and built onto it over the years," Sam explained. "And when he tried to renovate it after she went off to college, she flatly refused to let him take down the little fairy doors, so he just left everything the way it was."

She took the bags up to the bedroom while Sara wandered out to the deck and looked at the copper fire sky as the sun dipped below the trees. Translucent clouds in pinks and oranges melded into each other against the last slice of azure sky, and it was that moment that Sara knew she had more chance of pulling the sun back up into the sky than not falling in love with Sam.

Chapter Twelve

J ust try it."

Sara swirled the ruby wine around the sides and held out the glass.

"What am I supposed to be tasting?" Sam took the glass but glanced longingly toward the cheese and torn baguette on the table.

"Nothing specific," Sara said. "Just hold it in your mouth for a few seconds and tell me what you taste. Or maybe the fruit it reminds you of, like black or red fruit."

"Seriously?"

"It could be worse," Sara said, leaning close and whispering in her ear. "I could make you do it while I'm sitting in your lap, then give you a test later."

"Wait," Sam said, "I'm almost sure I like that option better."

Sara scooted her chair closer and picked up her glass. "Take a small sip and hold it in your mouth. Then breathe in through your nose. Try to draw in the air over the wine in short breaths."

Sam sipped, then set her glass down. "Okay, I'd love to torture you about this, but I actually do get what you're saying. If I had to say what it reminds me of, it would be maybe...plums, or overripe blackberries?"

"You couldn't be more right." Sara looked very pleased with herself.

"So what do you like so much about wine?" Sam said, setting her glass down.

"Well," she said, swirling the wine in her glass, "I think most people assume that women tend to like fruity whites or sweet moscato, but for me that couldn't be further from the truth. I like tannic wine that parches my mouth. I love it gritty and dirty, like liquid asphalt."

"Somehow that doesn't surprise me at all," Sam said. "There's more to you than meets the eye."

Sara spread a slice of baguette with Humboldt Fog cheese and handed it over. "I'll take that as a compliment."

"What's this?" Sam looked at it suspiciously. "And why does it look like there's dirt in it?"

"It's a dense, velvety goat cheese," Sara said, choosing a slice of a different cheese for herself. "And the gray line through the center is actually ash; it's a great contrast to the creamy, earthy quality of the cheese itself."

"So why aren't you eating it?" Sam asked, as she popped the baguette slice into her mouth.

"Now that it's in your mouth, I'll tell you. I can't stand goat cheese. To say it's gamy is putting it politely." She set the knife down and gave a little shiver.

Sam closed her eyes. "Actually, I love this," she said. "I would eat this every day."

"I'm glad. I thought you'd like it." Sara looked around the table and over to the counter. "I swear I had three bottles of wine. What happened to the Sauvignon Blanc?"

Sam spread another piece of baguette with the goat cheese. "It's down at the end of the road."

"What?"

"With a sign on it that says 'Free.' "

Sara hit her lightly on the arm. "You'd better be kidding!"

"Of course I am," Sam said, popping the second half of the baguette slice into her mouth. "I taped a five dollar bill to the bottle to make sure it found a good home."

Sara stood, sliding her knee between Sam's and leaning over her, both hands on the chair behind her.

"I'm going to check the fridge for that bottle, Draper. It'd better be in there."

Sam sat back in her chair, amused. "And what are you going to do about it if it's not?"

She thought for a second. "Pout."

"Actually," Sam said, "I've seen you pout, and it's adorable. I'd go with that if I were you."

Sara stood, laughing, and pulled the white wine out of the fridge. She brought it back to the table and cut the foil, glancing over at Sam.

"When have you ever seen me pout?"

"Well," Sam said, "it started about five minutes after I met you when I wouldn't let you step on the side of my patrol boat. Then again in my office when I told you that you couldn't drive your boat without a license, and then yet again when I insisted you wear a life jacket." She leaned back in her chair. "Shall I go on?"

Sara opened the Sauvignon Blanc and poured them both a taste in new glasses.

"I think I see where you're going wrong," she said, meeting Sam's eyes and swirling the wine in her glass. "You're confusing pouting with just being right."

Sara thought she might laugh, but Sam slowly took the glass out of her hand and kissed her, possessive and tender at the same time, holding her face in her hands.

"You're putting me on dangerous ground here, Sara."

"Good. That's exactly where I like you."

After they'd put the cheese away, they sat out on the deck, gold light spilling from the lanterns, watching the squirrels chase each other across the railing then jump directly into the tree and scurry off.

"I'm not sure this is a phrase I've ever said before," Sara said, glancing over at Sam eating a green olive. "But the way you eat olives is sexy as hell."

Sam laughed, taking the pit out of her mouth and launching it over the railing. "In that case, I'll have another."

She looked tan and lean, and wore jeans with a blue fleece jacket zipped over the white tank top that was warm enough to wear earlier. Her dark hair clashed with the vivid pale blue of her eyes, and even with her sleeves just pushed to her elbow, the muscles in her forearms brought back a vivid image of Sam on top of her the night before.

"Are you seeing anyone right now?" Sam asked, putting her feet up on the railing and looking over at Sara.

Sara laughed, pelting her with an olive. "That's a loaded question." She leaned back in her chair and looked at Sam. "Are you?"

"Present company excluded," Sam said, "no one I can remember."

Sara sneezed suddenly, then sneezed again. "Sorry," she said, her mouth still covered. "That's the worst timing in the world."

Sam laughed, looking at her watch then up to the wind moving through the trees. "It's later than I realized. It's cold up here. Let's move you inside where it's warmer."

Sara went to take a hot shower and climbed into the loft afterward. She pulled on sheer black underwear that laced up the back with a velvet ribbon and one of Sam's white T-shirts she'd found on the bed. She towel-dried her hair and gathered it into a loose bun, then lay on the bed on her stomach with the book she'd been halfway through before they left. She heard Sam turning out the lights and locking up the house below, and then she finally climbed into the loft, stopping in her tracks when she saw Sara on the bed.

"Let me get this straight," Sam said, taking her in. "You're in bed waiting for me, wearing one of my T-shirts, and…" She glanced down. "Jesus, the hottest underwear I've ever seen, and you're reading a book?"

Sara held her gaze. "Looks like it."

Sam took the book out of her hands and laid it on the bedside table. She lifted the hem of the shirt and kissed the soft skin of Sara's waist, warming it with her breath, then moved up her body to cover it with her own.

"Come to bed," Sara said, then turned over and slid her hands under Sam's shirt to brush her nipples lightly, feeling them harden under her touch.

"I'll be back in just a minute. I just came up to grab some clothes for the shower."

Sara took her hand and slid it from her waist into the silky wetness between her thighs. "Are you sure?" she said, whispering the words into Sam's ear, then following them with her tongue.

Sam groaned, hesitating twice before she stepped away. "You make it very hard to resist you, Sara Brighton." Her words were soft, and she swept her eyes slowly over Sara's body again as she climbed down the stairs.

❖

Sara was almost asleep by the time Sam got back to the loft with damp hair and skin still hot from the shower. That lasted about three seconds. Sam pulled the covers back and Sara into her arms, then tossed Sara's shirt on the floor.

"If you want me naked, you're going to have to figure out how to get these off," Sara whispered.

She sat on the bed, facing away from Sam. The almost transparent black silk, laced together from both sides of her hips with a black velvet ribbon, accented the plush curves of her bottom. Sam loosened the laces and the material fell to both sides, barely staying on her hips.

Sam's voice was a low rumble behind her. "Fucking hell, Sara."

Sam edged the panties slowly down her thighs and off, then rose to her knees behind her, nudging her thighs apart. She leaned back to sit on her feet and pulled Sara with her, her ass warm against Sam's thighs. Sam slid her fingers slowly into Sara, facing down, stroking the spot she knew would make Sara's thighs start to tremble. When she felt her getting close, she slowed, just long enough to let her calm down before she started again. Sara closed her eyes and leaned back against Sam's chest the next time she felt the wave of her orgasm start to break.

"Not yet," Sam said, her voice a warm whisper at the back of her neck. "Hold on to it until I tell you to come."

Sam stayed inside her, working her, keeping her at the edge, then started to massage her swollen clit at the same time with her other hand. Sara's breath caught.

"Please, baby," Sara said, her voice raw, muscles tightening around Sam's fingers. "Please now."

Sam rose to her knees and pressed Sara's shoulders forward into the bed. She cried out in pleasure, pushing back against Sam's hand as she slid a third finger inside and stroked her to the hardest orgasm of her life.

Afterward, Sam pulled Sara into her arms again and covered them both with the duvet.

"No one has ever turned me on like you do," Sam said quietly. She ran her fingers through Sara's hair and then turned over onto her back and looked up at the ceiling. "And I've already been too damn distracted since I met you. If you could just be less hot, that would help quite a bit."

"I'll work on that." Sara smiled, trailing her fingertips from the center of Sam's chest to the waistband of her underwear. She leaned up on one elbow, facing Sam.

"Can I touch you?" she whispered.

Sam looked at her, tracing her bottom lip with her thumb. "I don't usually do that."

Sara held her eyes. "I know."

Sam pulled her into a kiss, then hooked her thumbs under her shorts and pulled them off, dropping them beside the bed. Sara slid her hand over Sam's nipples, watching them harden under her fingers until Sam wrapped her hand around the back of Sara's head and pulled her to her chest, her breath quickening as Sara scraped her nipples lightly with her teeth. She lowered her hand to smooth her palm over Sam's tight abs, pausing to look up before she slid her fingertips over her clit. She stayed there, not dipping lower, just circling it, feeling it harden under her touch.

Sam draped her forearm over her eyes. "Fuck," she said, the tension showing in her abs.

Then suddenly Sam covered Sara's hand with her own and pressed Sara's fingers against her clit, their hands moving together, harder than Sara would have been brave enough to try alone. A fine mist of sweat was gathering on her chest, and she moved her hips to meet Sara's touch. Sara leaned in and sucked Sam's nipple hard into her mouth and Sam groaned, continuing to move Sara's fingers over her clit. The muscles in her torso started to clench, and when Sara felt her arousal reaching a new peak, she drew her hand away and straddled her, sitting just above Sam's hips.

"So you think you can just stop like that, huh?" Sam's hands were on her thighs, her voice husky and teasing.

"I won't stop," Sara said, looking into her eyes, "unless you tell me to."

Sam ran both palms farther up Sara's thighs, slicking her thumb across Sara's clit. Sara reached behind her, palm down, the inside of her wrist pressed tightly against her back. She looked into Sam's eyes and started to ride her, her fingers curved down onto Sam's clit, setting the rhythm with her hips.

"Fuck, Sara." Sam's voice trailed off, the thrust of her hips starting to match Sara's.

She felt Sara's thighs tighten around her, felt her leaning back, her hand stroking Sam's clit with the same pressure she'd just shown her. Sara slid her hips back and forth, building the heat between their bodies. She watched Sam's body start to glisten, her breath ragged as Sara ground her center harder against Sam, arousal quickening her pace. Sam had been close since Sara started, and watching Sara ride her was taking her over the edge. She passed the point of no return and arched her back, her voice guttural and raw, her orgasm almost shaking her body with its intensity. Sara watched until Sam's body started to relax, still riding her with her hand slick and firm against Sam's clit, only closing her eyes when the waves of her own orgasm threatened to overtake her.

"Come for me, baby." Sam's words were dripping with sex.

She wrapped her hands around Sara's hips and started to move her, then slipped one hand between them just enough to enter her as Sara threw her head back and came hard and hot against her palm, her body flushed and slicked with sweat.

They slept late the next morning and woke to find the morning sun streaming through the treehouse window, painting intricate patterns of light and leaves on the walls. Sara's eyes closed again immediately and a little pouty face emerged as she tried to block out the sun with her forearm draped over her eyes. Sam looked at her, the sunlight dappling her skin, falling over the light pink of her nipples and skin still creased with sleep.

"Morning, blondie."

"Why is the sun up in the middle of the night?" Sara groaned and ducked her head under the covers until she sneezed several times in a row and had to emerge.

"You look flushed," Sam said, covering her cheek with her palm. "And you're a little too warm to be fine, which I know is going to be what you say next."

"Sam," Sara said, burrowing her head back under the covers. "I'm fine."

A stifled cough under the duvet underscored her point, or maybe Sam's, and Sam got up and pulled on some clothes and a fleece.

"I'm going to make coffee, sickie. Don't move out of that bed."

Sara kicked at her from under the covers, unaware she was already halfway down the stairs, and Sam had to stifle a laugh. She had quite a little attitude on her when she was sleepy. Sam started the coffee and sliced some bread to toast in the pan as she whipped some eggs together in a bowl with salt, pepper, and some chili flakes she found in the cupboard. The familiar scent of brewing coffee started to fill the room, and when the eggs got to a perfect soft scramble, Sam turned off the heat and dropped a pat of butter on them to melt while the bread finished toasting. She tried to imagine going back to McCall and carrying on as normal, but she knew it was pointless. The road trip was supposed to have been about the food, but everything was different now and she knew it. She poured a cup of coffee and snapped off the heat under the toast. It would be fine to sit there for a minute. Sam took her coffee out to the deck and leaned against the railing.

She knew everyone assumed she didn't remember how it felt to be left at that fair. Someone said to her once years later that it must have been so hard to spend the night there and wonder if her mom was coming back for her, and she'd nodded, but really, that hadn't even happened. She knew as she watched her mom walk away, holding the hand of the new tattooed boyfriend, that she wasn't coming back. Her heart had started to go numb that night as she curled up between some hay bales behind the tents, blocking out every memory of her life to that point. It was self-preservation in a way, although she hadn't realized at the time she was doing it.

For the first year she lived with Gus and Marcy, she woke every morning curled into a ball, her fists clenched. Then slowly, she started to forget, although for years she still sometimes got up and sat in the hall at the door of their bedroom in the middle of the night.

She could fall into a deep sleep there because they couldn't leave without her knowing. It was the only way to be sure she wouldn't wake up alone. If she was at the door, she knew she was safe enough to close her eyes.

Marcy died years later when she was in high school. Sam missed her terribly, but she still had Gus, and they just became a little family of their own. But the moment she knew he'd died, she suddenly felt the hard ground under her body and the damp stench of the hay bales around her in the dark. Then her heart returned to numb.

Sam remembered the eggs and ran back into the treehouse to find them cold, but it didn't really matter. She cracked new eggs into the bowl to start again. She needed a moment before she climbed the stairs anyway.

❖

"I'm not sick." Sara sat in the center of the bed with her legs crossed. "I have allergies."

"What you have," Sam said, taking the empty plate from her, "is a fever, which I think you'll find is totally different."

Sara peered up at her from under the covers. "What if I was the teensiest bit sick? Would that mean we have to go back today instead of tomorrow?"

"If I say no, will you let me get you some medicine in town and stay in bed while I do it?"

"Maybe."

"Damn, girl," Sam said, trying to suppress a smile, "You are the most stubborn—"

Sara hit her with a pillow before she finished her sentence, then reached up and pulled Sam down on top of her. Sam relaxed into the soft warmth of her body and leaned in to kiss her.

"No way!" Sara turned her head. "I'm not getting you sick."

Sam turned her chin back to her with two fingers and kissed her deep and slow before she spoke. "Not an option, Brighton."

Sara smiled and wrapped her arms around Sam. "Good, because I didn't really mean it anyway."

They finally got showered and packed up in the late afternoon and headed back into town to grab Sara some cold medicine and restock the cooler before they headed north.

"Where are you taking me anyway?" Sara said, propping her bare feet on the dash. Sam smiled over at her.

"Totally not telling you that."

"What? Is it against Stalker Code or something?"

"It's actually not far. We'll be there in thirty minutes," Sam said, "So it looks like you'll have to wait."

"What is it about making me wait do you love so much?"

"So many things," Sam teased her.

Sara took some phone calls on the drive up from the design company that she'd hired to put the finishing touches on gastropub's décor, another from the printer in Boise about the menu she'd put a hold on, and still another from a potential manager Sara had contacted for an interview. She scheduled the interview at the diner for the following afternoon, then finally switched her phone off.

"Sorry," she said, "I just feel like I'm running out of time to get everything done."

Sam nodded but didn't say anything, just kept her eyes on the road, and Sara sat back in her seat with a worried feeling in the pit of her stomach. Not just about Sam, although getting closer to her over the last few days had only made the diner problem potentially worse. Now she was wondering if she was on the right track at all. The more she went round and round in her head about the menu, the less it came together in the end. And she couldn't risk another disaster like the last tasting. She knew she could only do so many of those before she generated a bad reputation before her doors were even open.

Sam finally turned off the main road and onto a rocky side road that seemed to lead straight up the mountain. Sara rolled down her window and stuck her arm out as far as it would go.

"What are you doing, crazy girl?" Sam looked over at her and smiled.

"None of your business, Draper."

It felt like they were climbing the mountain forever before Sam turned off the dirt road into a small parking lot with a trail marker and a sign. *Wampas Pass.*

"Um," Sara said, coughing for effect, "please tell me you're not taking me hiking?"

"Well, I should since you're still insisting it's just allergies, but we're going to drive."

Sam continued past the parking lot to a small access road Sara hadn't noticed. There were several signs warning hikers it was a restricted area, but Sam drove past them.

"Why do I get the feeling you know everyone in law enforcement around here?"

"Because it's true," Sam said, smiling and pulling Sara's hand onto her thigh and covering it with her own.

They finally parked under a cluster of spruce trees, and Sam unloaded Sara's bag and another large duffel bag from the back of the Land Rover. Sam put the two bags over her shoulder and pulled out the handle to the rolling cooler. She handed Sara a flashlight.

"This is all I get to carry?"

"Yes," Sam said. "Luggage dispersion is covered on page 387 of that butch handbook I was telling you about."

"Ah," Sara said, "I see. I'm liking that thing more and more."

They walked about fifty yards farther and around a sharp bend, where endless blue summer sky and white clouds came into view above the edge of a cliff, as if the earth had just broken off underneath it. An eagle glided across the treetops and came to rest on the ragged edge, but then Sam guided them down a path to the right with stone steps leading down, then around, to reveal the huge mouth of a cave. About fifteen yards beyond was the cliff edge, and beyond that, an incredible view of the sky and outlying snowcapped mountains.

"We're facing west here, so the sunsets are pretty spectacular," Sam said, pulling Sara into her chest and kissing her neck.

"This is gorgeous," Sara said.

It was then that she saw it over her shoulder. A tent set up just inside the mouth of the cave. Fairy lights twinkled inside and in the semidarkness of the cave behind it. Tiki torches were set up at the entrance and the cliff's edge. A circle of stones formed a fire pit a safe distance from the tent, and a bottle of wine and two glasses sat beside it.

"How in the world did you do this?" Sara spun slowly, taking it all in, then turned and sneezed directly on Sam's shirt. "Oh no, I'm so sorry!" Sara covered her face with her hands.

Sam laughed until she had to stop and catch her breath. "No," Sam said finally, "That was actually perfect." She pulled Sara into her arms and kissed her, running her hands up her back and into her hair.

"Wait," Sara said, leaning back to look at her. "You never told me how you did all this."

"It's no big deal," Sam said, nodding toward the cave. "Someone owed me a favor."

Sara turned to look back out at the endless sky. "Well, to me it's a big deal," she said quietly. "No one has ever done anything like this for me."

She looked back at Sam, whose eyes reflected the same powder blue as the sky. And at that moment, suddenly everything in her life became a lot more complicated.

CHAPTER THIRTEEN

I can't believe this stuff won't light."

Sam shook the wet paper, as if that would make it less waterlogged. Whoever had set everything up in the cave had set the wood and fire-starting supplies directly under a spring water drip. It probably hadn't seemed damp when they were there, but by the time Sam and Sara had arrived, everything was waterlogged.

"Unfortunately," Sam said, "it looks like we may be fireless."

A short rain in the morning had left everything in the surrounding woods just damp enough to render it useless as well, which was why Sam had asked for paper and dry tinder when she'd finalized the plans by text when they were on the road.

"I don't care a bit," Sara said, looking around. "But if I had to guess, I'd say there's a good chance you have a knife somewhere?"

"I do," Sam said. "But don't get your hopes up about finding dry wood. Everything got soaked this morning with the rain."

Sara took the pocketknife from Sam and gathered the pile of kindling and sticks that were left for the fire. Sam watched as she sat cross-legged by the fire pit, chipping the bark off the sticks until they were bare, the wet, discarded bark in a pile to the side. The sun was starting to fade. They had more than an hour until sunset, but the hints of it were starting to pile up on the distant indigo horizon. Sara carefully carved, then bent, thin layers of wood along each stick, curling them out from the center like a pinecone. When she'd layered one to be as fine and airy as possible, she moved on to the next. After ten minutes or so, she had a small pile of sticks that now more closely resembled wooden feathers, the edges raw and thin.

She dug a lip gloss out of her pocket and ran it over the edges of each stick, then stacked them in a cone shape, with fine wood shavings at the center.

"What the hell are you doing?" Sam said, teasing her about the pale pink lip gloss she continued to dab on the edges of the wood and shavings.

"None of your business, Draper."

As the light started to fall into violet evening, Sara lit the first wood shavings, fine as dust, patiently adding coarser shavings as they caught and flamed under the pyramid she'd created. When the flames reached the base of the smallest logs that Sara had stripped of bark, Sam watched as it climbed, until the pyramid of fire was burning strong.

"It should be hot enough now to burn the moisture out of those logs if we add them one at a time," Sara said.

"Seriously," Sam said. "Lip gloss?"

"It doesn't always work," Sara said, "But most of them are petroleum based, so if the tinder is fine enough, it can help light it."

"So where did you learn all this?" Sam asked. "Do chefs spend a lot of time out in the wilderness armed with lip gloss and wet wood?"

"Yes," Sara said, "when we're not knocking ourselves out with our own boats."

She added another log to the fire, which spit and sputtered as the flames started to dry out the moisture. The fire was beautiful in the fading light; sparks and rising ash shimmered in the air as they rose. The air had started to cool and sharpen, and Sara reached in her bag for a jacket as she spoke.

"I went to camp in McCall for ten years as a kid," she said, "Everyone was always bigger and tougher than me. You pick up a few tricks along the way out of self-preservation."

"That's right," Sam said. "I keep forgetting you spent summers in McCall as a kid."

"That's actually why I decided to come to Idaho. After the restaurant burned, I didn't even know who I was anymore. I'd worked too hard to have a life, or a girlfriend. So I just tried to remember the last place I was really happy. And McCall was it."

"What about high school?" Sam said, turning the log over in

the fire. "You seem like you'd be a popular girl. You weren't happy then?"

"Honestly, high school was hell for me. My brother and sister were always so smart and it was a lot to live up to. I just never understood things like they did, I guess."

"Were your parents supportive?"

"Well, my dad just ignored me—there was nothing about me that he could brag about to his golf buddies about, and Mom was just waiting for me to get married, hence the dramatic interlude when I came out. But it wasn't a big deal." She looked out from the mouth of the cave to the sun starting to set over the mountain.

Sam knew it was a big deal, but Sara didn't want to talk about it, and she knew how that felt.

"Okay," she said, looking over at the tent. "Are you ready for the bad news?"

"Thank God," Sara said, "I'd love to hear the bad news."

Sam unzipped the tent and pulled out a cardboard box. "My buddy was supposed to leave us some stuff to make dinner, and it's in this box."

"Great," Sara said, reaching for it. "Let's see it."

"Brace yourself," Sam said, sliding the box out of her reach. "I've been to his house. This is guaranteed not to be pretty."

"I love this," Sara said, settling in and leaning over to the box. "Hit me, I can take it."

Sam opened the box and pulled out the first item. "Saltines."

Sara tilted her head, considering their potential. "It all depends on what he sent to go with them."

Sam brought out a can of Kraft spray cheese. Bacon flavor, apparently.

"Now we're talking," Sara said, surprisingly genuinely pleased. "Toss that over here."

She loaded up a saltine with the aerosol cheese and put the whole thing in her mouth, closing her eyes with a look of bliss.

"I've never thought that stuff was actually edible."

"You've never had spray cheese?" Sara said, loading up another cracker. "What the hell have you been doing with your life?"

Sam reached in for the next item and held it up. "Oreos."

"You've got to love Oreos," Sara said.

Next, there was a hunk of butter, some sliced ham, and a round loaf of bread.

"Believe it or not, my buddy actually makes this bread," Sam said, handing it to Sara. "No one really knows why, but he'll only eat bread he makes."

"This looks great," she said. "I can tell it's airy on the inside. He knows what he's doing."

Beyond the food, there was a single knife and some bottles of water, and Sam and Sara took everything near the edge of the cliff to eat while they watched the sun set.

Later that night, after glittering stars had swept across the black velvet sky, Sara was asleep in Sam's arms inside the tent, the entrance unzipped to the night sky and the dying fire. She still had a sore throat, so Sam insisted on going to bed early to keep warm. Sam stroked her hair, looking out past the cliff to the mountains, the white snow still barely visible in the darkness. This road trip had been centered around food, and sitting in the same diners she'd grown up in and talking about what it all meant to her had torn open the raw edges of losing Gus. She'd only stepped into the diner once after Gus died, and that was when Sara bought the place and she knew she had to go get all his pictures. In the end, she'd only taken her favorite, the one on his desk. Being there brought everything back. It still smelled exactly as it always had. Even the creaks in the floor were as familiar as breath. Before she left, she stood in the dining room, letting it wash over her. It was the one place she could still feel him.

And now the woman she'd fallen in love with was taking that away.

CHAPTER FOURTEEN

After Sam had dropped Sara off at her cabin on the way to work the next day, she'd climbed the ladder to the loft and burrowed under the covers, an arsenal of cold medicine scattered across her nightstand. She stayed there for the next two days, only sitting up once to eat the chicken soup Mary asked Sam to deliver for her, then pulling the covers back up over her head. On the third day, Sara finally felt well enough to take a shower and get dressed. She pulled on some yellow chino shorts, a white tank, and a jean jacket, then headed toward town, lucky enough to grab the last free parking spot in town.

The brass bell clanged against the glass door as she walked into the drugstore, and she waited at the counter while Mary finished with a customer in the back. When she saw Sara on her way back to the front, she pulled her into a hug, then handed her a mug and reached under the counter for the coffee pot.

"Spill it," she said, her eyes twinkling. She sat on the stool behind the counter, her cup poised.

"Spill what?" Sara said, reaching for the sugar.

"What? Hmm…let me think," Mary said. "The most eligible person in town whisks you away for a road trip and you come back with a ten-mile smile on your face. Let's start with that."

Sara laughed, stepping aside so Mary could ring up a customer. After he left, Mary sat back, clearly ready for some serious gossip.

"What did Sam tell you?" Sara said.

"Are you kidding?" Mary replied. "You can't pry a secret out of Samantha with a crowbar, never could."

"Okay," Sara said, "It was amazing. The tasting I did outside the diner the other day was a disaster, so she took me around to all the places she ate in as a kid and still loves. We even checked out a food truck in Boise that was the best food I've eaten since I got here."

"Uh-huh," Mary said. "And was it all about the food?"

"I think it was supposed to be, but we were definitely closer by the end."

"Well," Mary said, tapping her fingers on the counter, "if you want my two cents, she'd be lucky to have you. I just hope she doesn't let her pride get in the way with that diner over there."

"You heard, huh?"

"She didn't say much, just that she was having a harder time than she thought with it. I told her to get the hell over it." She cleared her throat and fidgeted with the register tape before she went on. "I know how it is. I miss my husband. It was hard to let his cabin go. But I just finally had to tell myself that he wasn't in it anymore."

Sara was quiet for moment, thinking about what she said.

"Mary, do you remember that one day I was in here and you had that amazing lasagna we had while we watched *Days of Our Lives*?"

"That was just regular old lasagna," Mary said.

"I think that may be exactly what I've been missing."

Sam wrapped up her weekly maintenance records for the patrol boats and sat back in her chair. It had been two days since she'd seen Sara, and it felt strange being without her. She reached for her phone.

Want to go to Wine and Fire with me tonight? It's at Moxie Java, 7 p.m.

Sam pressed send and waited. Her phone pinged in just a few seconds.

Sorry, I can't. I'm kind of seeing someone.

Sam read the text twice, her stomach sinking like an anchor. Then her phone pinged again.

And she hates wine. So, I'm on my way to her office now to let her know her phone's been stolen.

A minute later Sam heard a knock at her door and she opened it, pulling Sara inside and against the wall. She kissed her, then pressed her forehead against Sara's.

"So we're seeing each other now?" Her voice was teasing but the hand running up her back and pulling her closer said the opposite. "How do I know you're not just in it for the boating license?"

"Well, I guess you're just going to have to trust me, Captain Draper."

Sara's hands slid under Sam's shirt and she leaned into her body. Sam groaned and pulled Sara's hips to hers, wrapping her hands around her ass and biting her neck lightly.

"If you start this in here, Brighton, I'm going to finish it," Sam whispered, looking slightly over her shoulder. "Against that wall with your legs wrapped around my waist."

A loud knock at the door made Sara jump. Sam stepped away and sat behind her desk, coolly stacking papers into a neat pile.

"Come in."

Lily walked into the office and paused, looking first at Sara, then over to Sam. She started to say something but seemed to think better of it and left, pulling the door shut behind her.

Sara arched an eyebrow. "Do you think she knew something was going on?"

"Absolutely," Sam said, looking amused. "But it's none of her business."

"Well, I'm going to get out of here and hope not quite everyone has heard about it by the time I reach the door."

"Good luck with that," Sam said. "See you on the back deck of Moxie Java at seven?"

"There's a back deck?"

"Yes," Sam said, "And Sunday nights it's closed for locals, for Wine and Fire, invitation only."

"I'll be there."

Sara turned to leave, but Sam stopped her.

"I almost forgot," Sam said, "I have something for you." She reached into the top drawer of her desk and handed a small card to

Sara. "Don't get excited. I'll still arrest you if you continue to insist on sunbathing topless."

Sam gave her a teasing look, and Sara tucked her license proudly into her pocket and pulled the door shut behind her.

❖

Sam got to Moxie Java a little early and chose a spot in the risers. The back deck was built in two levels: there were chairs and tables on the upper level, then a staircase that led down to the ground level, where stone risers, built in a bowl shape into the earth below, surrounded a huge sunken fire pit. Even in the winter, the locals gathered every Sunday night to talk and share a bottle or two, watching the embers rise into the frosted air.

The incident with Lily had unsettled her a bit. She needed to have a conversation with her, but the office was not the place. She made a mental note to remember to stop by her cottage at some point and talk. Soon.

By the time Sara arrived, Sam had set up a space for them on the risers, a blanket folded beside her from the stack the coffee shop provided for night events. Sara was wearing navy blue linen pants that sat low on her hips, and a white strapless top. Her shoulders were toned and golden from the sun.

"Good God," Sam said, still taking her in. "You look amazing."

Sara was carrying a bottle of rosé, and set it down beside the bottle of red that Sam had already bought.

"Seriously," Sam said, her eyes reflecting the shifting light of the fire, "you brought pink wine?"

"It's not pink, it's rosé. Totally different."

Sam picked up the bottle of Syrah that was on the other side of the blankets. "I'm one step ahead of you, Miss Brighton."

"Damn," Sara said, teasing in her voice. "I was so looking forward to finding a delicate little glass and watching you squirm while you held it."

"So now that you have your boating license, you think you're in charge, huh?"

"No, ma'am."

"That's better," Sam said, her eyes sparkling, leaning in to whisper in Sara's ear, "Not that I wouldn't love to show you who is if you have any doubt."

Something about the way Sam handled her made Sara hot. What she really wanted to do was go home and make her back that up. She let her hand rest on Sam's hip while she leaned in to whisper an invitation for later into her ear.

"So, this is the girl."

Sam and Sara looked up to see Lily standing there, her eyes narrowed, with her hand on her hip. A worried-looking friend stood behind her with her hand on Lily's elbow.

"I thought it was her." She looked Sara up and down, before turning her attention back to Sam.

Sam sighed, leaning back against the risers. "Lily, this is not the place."

"Where is the place?" she replied, her voice barely above a whisper. Anger made the edges of her words razor sharp. "Maybe your office, right before you fuck me on the desk? Or does she not know you've been having sex with me for the last three months?"

Sam stood up and just as quietly told Lily she needed to leave.

"No," Sara said, gathering her things and avoiding Sam's eyes. "I'll leave. You two look like you need to talk."

The only way out of the row of risers was past Lily, and when she tried to step past her, Lily intentionally bumped her with her shoulder. Sara stopped, took a breath, and kept walking, disappearing into the crowd on the top deck.

"First of all," Sam said, her voice low and controlled, "don't ever touch my girlfriend again."

Lily sat down beside her, her head in her hands. "I know. I'm sorry. I totally lost it."

"What the hell, Lily? I would have been happy to talk about this anywhere else. You should have just asked me."

"I just," Lily looked up at Sam, tears threatening to spill over, "didn't want to be replaced."

Sam nodded, waiting for her to go on.

"I mean, I know this wasn't about love," she said, "for either of us. I just didn't want to be nothing to you suddenly."

"Lily," Sam said, opening the Syrah and handing Lily a glass. "You'd never be nothing to me. We shared time." She leaned down to catch Lily's eyes. "I haven't forgotten that, and I won't forget you."

Lily looked into her glass. "I'm so sorry. I'm sure she hates me now."

Sam shook her head. "She's actually pretty sweet. I'd bet right now she's thinking about how upset you are."

"Really?"

"And about how pissed off she is at me."

"Sorry."

"Don't be," Sam said, giving in and filling a wineglass for herself. "I had it coming. I should have talked to both of you about this way before now."

"Yeah," Lily said, clinking her glass to Sam's, "it's totally your fault. Let's go with that."

Sam laughed and looked around. "Where did your friend go?"

"She left. I think she thought I was going to get a little crazy."

"Smart girl," Sam said.

"Hey!" Lily said, hitting Sam's arm lightly with the back of her hand. "Don't go telling people that. It's a secret."

Sam elbowed her gently. "All writers are a little bit crazy, right?"

"About that," Lily said, then paused. "I need you to fire me."

"Why? This really wasn't that big a deal."

"No, I need you to fire me because this is the last week I have to sign a contract I need to sign for another job, and I can't seem to get it done."

"Lily, I know about the book contract," Sam said. "I was in Moxie Java that day when your friend was trying to get you to sign it."

"Oh." Lily handed Sam her empty wineglass and took her nearly full glass. "It's not that big a deal. But I think I'm going to take it."

"It's a huge deal, and hell yes, you're going to take it," Sam said, "Because as of now, you're fired. If I see you back in the office, I'll make a big damn scene kicking you out." Sam's eyes were kind, and she took Lily's hand. "I always read what you were writing when you left the room, and it's amazing. You deserve this," she said. "Take it."

"I had them fax it to me at the office again today. I'll sign it when I get home and get it in the mail tomorrow morning."

"And I'll be checking up on you to see that you did."

"Thanks, Captain." Lily looked up at her. "Wait, do I get to call you Sam now?"

"I guess you do," she said. "Calling me Captain Draper would sound a little dirty now."

"Shhh!" Lily looked around and put one finger to her lips. "No one needs to know that we slept together or that you couldn't quite keep up with me." She looked at Sam with no hint of a smile. "I know you've got your reputation to protect."

"Yeah," Sam said, smiling and thinking that she would definitely miss this girl. "Let's not tell anyone that."

Lily laughed, and an easy comfort settled between them as if it had always been there. Now Sam just had to explain it all to Sara, somehow.

❖

Lily's friend reappeared and Sam left Lily at Moxie Java soon after that. She texted Sara the second she got to her truck.

I know you're angry and you have every right to be. I didn't cheat on you; I would never do that. Please let me explain.

She pressed send and waited. No reply.

"Fuck," Sam said, leaning her head back on the headrest and closing her eyes. She still smelled Sara in her cab of her truck from the road trip. She was in love with her. Losing this was not an option.

She drove the mile to Sara's cabin and knocked on her door.

I'll leave if you want me to, she texted, still at the door. *But please let me tell you what really happened.*

There was no answer, so Sam turned and got in her truck, slamming her fist into the steering wheel as she started the engine.

The next morning, Sam wrote several texts to Sara, but deleted each before she sent them. At this point, she couldn't afford to screw up again. A cold, hard ball of fear had started to settle into her stomach, and she didn't want to think about the growing possibility that Sara would never speak to her again. Sam left work early that afternoon, stopping by Sara's cabin to slip a small white envelope under her door. Sara's truck was there but she left without texting. At this point, she was fairly certain she wouldn't want to read her reply.

❖

After the disaster that was their first official date, Sara decided to walk into town that morning to clear her head. She had a second interview later in the morning with the woman who applied for the management position, so if that went well she could open in just a few weeks, but this was not the best day to have to concentrate. The air was crisp, and the sun shone through the fir trees lining the road in golden squares. A doe munching on leaves to her left turned toward her and dashed back into the forest as she approached, and Sara pulled on her jacket, holding the sleeves in her fists. Not surprisingly, she couldn't think about anything but Sam fucking that receptionist. The young, very pretty, obviously infatuated receptionist.

She'd left Moxie Java furious the night before, not because Sam had cheated on her, but because she had to find out the way that she did. Until that afternoon, they hadn't said anything about being a couple, so maybe it wasn't even cheating, but regardless, it was humiliating, and then that girl had intentionally bumped her shoulder on the way out. Sara's cheeks burned at the memory. Obviously, she'd been kidding herself for the last few weeks—Sam hadn't even said anything to her in Sara's defense.

She stopped into Moxie Java first as she got into town, the scent of roasted freshly ground coffee and baking pastries washing over her as she waited in line. Sam or no Sam, she loved McCall. She wasn't going to let her brief lapse in judgment drive her out of the first place that had ever felt like home. She ordered a coconut latte and a blueberry muffin, the espresso machine whirring in its familiar high-pitched whine. There was something so comforting about the suddenly warm air and familiar sounds of a coffee shop, no matter where you were, as if nothing bad could ever happen inside. As she took her coffee and turned to leave, she saw Lily, sitting in a booth alone, her hand moving furiously across the page in a journal.

It was one of those moments where Sara had a choice: she could choose to be petty and walk past her, or she could sit down and try to talk through it because it was the right thing to do. Someone cleared their throat behind her. She suddenly realized she was blocking the path to the door and stepped aside, glad Lily was too busy writing to notice her. Lily was just young and made a mistake. As much as Sara didn't want to admit it, she had been in a similar situation at about Lily's age and remembered how desperate and awful she'd felt.

"Do you mind if I sit for a minute?"

Lily jumped at her words and visibly held her breath when she saw it was Sara. She nodded toward the seat and closed her book. The words came tumbling out of Lily's mouth the second Sara sat down.

"I owe you an apology."

Tears shimmered in her blue eyes, and despite the previous night, Sara found herself wanting to reach out and hug her.

"There's no excuse for what I did, and I don't blame you if you hate me."

"I don't hate you, Lily." She touched her hand to Lily's for emphasis. "Sam should have told you what was going on, and me too, for that matter."

Lily looked up, relief starting to smooth the worry on her face.

"Besides, I was once in an almost identical situation myself."

Lily perked up, her eyes wide. "No way! When?"

"When I was in culinary school. I was twenty-one, newly out, and had never had a girlfriend." She paused to take a sip of her coffee, the memory washing over her. "She was twenty years older than me and a successful pastry chef as well as an instructor at the school."

"Wow," Lily said. "How did it start?"

"Well, she was fairly butch, so it was a pretty safe guess that she was gay, although we'd never really talked much. So, and I still don't know why I did this, I just kissed her one day when she was teaching me to make filo dough after hours."

"That was so brave," Lily said, chin in hand, her coffee forgotten. "What happened after that?"

"It lasted for a few months, and was actually some of the best sex I've ever had," Sara said. "Then all of a sudden she just started freezing me out. She was always too busy to get together, didn't reply to my calls or texts, the usual. Only back then I didn't realize what was happening, so I was pretty devastated."

"Did you ever talk to her about it?"

"Well, after this had been going on for about two weeks, I got the courage up to go to her office after class. I was crazy nervous." Sara tapped her fingers against her coffee cup. "I shouldn't have bothered, though, because she was making out with another student when I opened the door."

"Did you ever get to talk to her about it?" Lily pushed her muffin aside, captivated by the drama.

"We did finally talk, but she just made me feel like it was all my fault she was fucking someone else, which of course I believed."

Lily looked down briefly, pulling a bite from her muffin. "Sam said after you left that this situation was all her fault, and she deserved it for not talking to both of us."

Sara sat back, surprised.

"And if it makes you feel any better, the first thing she said to me was to not ever touch her girlfriend again." Lily looked up. "She can be a little scary, and last night was definitely one of those times."

Sara's stomach dropped. "She didn't threaten you, did she?"

"Oh God no, not at all! She never gets angry, so it was just surprising." Lily paused. "Sam is a great person. She'd never hurt anyone, she just has a mafia quality to her sometimes."

"You're so right, that's exactly what it is!" Sara laughed. "I've been trying to wrap words around that for weeks!"

They giggled and chatted for a few more minutes before Sara had to leave to get to the diner for her interview. Lily stood and hugged her as she left.

"Thank you for being so kind to me. You didn't have to be," she said. "And if it helps, I've never seen Sam like this. She's definitely in love."

When Sara walked out into the late morning sunshine, she found herself thinking that if nothing else, Sam had good taste. Lily was a sweetheart.

❖

She got home late in the afternoon and dropped her bags by the door as she came through the cabin door. There, lying on the floor, was a white envelope with Sam's small, neat handwriting on the front. *Sara.*

Her heart raced as if she was suddenly sprinting up a mountain. She put the envelope on the table and walked into the kitchen, opening a better than usual bottle of Barolo. She poured it and sat down on the couch, looking at the envelope sitting there on the table.

There's no way she would have considered opening it if she hadn't spoken to Lily. Or maybe she would have. Or maybe she wouldn't open it at all. Her hands shook as she slipped her finger under the flap of the envelope. She sank down into one of the chairs and took out a small stained index card with dog-eared edges and yellowed paper. It was a recipe. At the bottom left corner, there was a date, 1979, and the initials G.D.

"Gus Draper." Sara said the words out loud, suddenly realizing how special this little piece of paper was.

It was the recipe for his Monte Cristo sandwich. A tear fell from her chin onto the table, and she read and reread every word, laying it carefully on the table to look again in the envelope, in case Sam had written a note too. She had.

I'm so sorry. You have every right to hate me. I hate myself for hurting you. Please forgive me.

Sara tucked the note back in the envelope and set it back down on the table.

CHAPTER FIFTEEN

L ater that evening, Sara called Jennifer to come over and they sat down with Sara's homemade salsa, guac, and chips. Sara poured Jen a margarita and sat down across from her.

"So," Sara said casually, handing her the glass, "Sam's been fucking her receptionist for the last few months."

Margarita sprayed everywhere as Jennifer choked on her drink. "Shut. Up," she said, her eyes wide with shock. "I didn't see that one coming."

"Yeah," Sara said, "I didn't either."

She slid the salt off the rim of her glass with her finger and let it drop onto the table. She always forgot she hated the salt. Sara filled Jennifer in on the details of the previous evening and her talk with Lily, and Jennifer listened with rapt attention, the chips forgotten in front of her.

"So what does she look like?"

Sara thought for a moment. "Very slender, dark hair, gorgeous blue eyes, hipster vibe."

"So, beautiful?" Jen was never one to mince words.

"Unfortunately, yes. Very."

Jennifer tapped her finger on the table, deep in thought.

"What?" Sara said.

"I totally understand why she was upset, but it's weird that she bonded with you so quickly afterward."

"Really?" Sara thought back to their conversation. "Why?"

"She seemed to feel bad about last night, right?" Sara nodded. "But did she say anything about sleeping with Sam when you two were together?"

Sara shook her head.

"I fault Sam, not her, if that's the case, but you were in and out of Sam's office a few times, right? So she knew when you came on the scene."

"Definitely," Sara said slowly, "and looking back, I think she knew something was up because she was always weird when I came in."

Jennifer made up for lost time with her margarita, then scooped the salt from the rim with her lime and squeezed it into her mouth.

"Are you *positive* they even had sex while you two were together?"

Sara shook her head and poured Jen another margarita. She shouldn't get her hopes up. Sam and Lily had probably had sex the night they came back from the road trip. Great. Why did she have to be so gorgeous? It just made it worse somehow.

"So," Sara said, redirecting her attention back to her sister and trying to sound cheerful, "I want details about this Murphy guy."

Jennifer ran to her bag and dug around, producing a wrinkled stack of papers that she plopped in front of Sara. "It's done."

"You're divorced?"

Jen nodded, smiling, and it struck Sara how much better she looked. She was still a bit too thin, but she looked fit and beautiful. And happy.

"Wait," Sara said. "So does this mean you and Brian can get together for real now?"

"Yes," Jen said. "We actually have a date tonight. He's cooking me dinner." She looked down at the table and Sara could tell something was on her mind. "And now that it's here, I feel like I'm going to be a disappointment or something."

"Why would you think that?" Sara scooped up a chip full of the green tomatillo salsa, dropping some on her shirt before it made it into her mouth.

"Well, it may not be tonight, but eventually we're going to sleep together. And Trevor's the only guy I've ever had sex with."

Sara waited, knowing there was more on her mind.

"And oh my God, if you laugh, I'll hit you..." Jen paused and dropped her voice to a whisper. "But I've never had an orgasm. What if that's important to him and I can't do it?"

"Oh, Jen," Sara said, instantly hating Trevor just a little bit more. "I had no idea."

The shatteringly intense climaxes she'd had with Sam flashed across her mind, but she quickly pushed those thoughts out of her head. If she wasn't going to go there again, there was no reason to make herself miserable thinking about it.

"You're thinking he's going to want to dump me, aren't you?"

Sara realized Jen was looking intently at her and she'd been lost in thought.

"God, no!" Sara reached out and covered Jen's hand with hers. "Trust me, it's going to be just the opposite."

"But…"

"Don't even waste your time worrying about it." Sara waved her hand and cut her off before she finished her sentence. "Just be honest and let him know it's just never happened for you. If anything, he'll feel special because he'll be the first person to give you that."

Sara thought for a moment, deciding whether to ask the next question or not, but finally curiosity won out. "So you've never had an orgasm ever? Not even with yourself?"

"No, and if you tell anyone that, I will literally kill you."

"Your secret's safe with me, but I know what I'm getting you for your birthday now." Sara ducked as Jen threw a chip at her, laughing and holding up her hands.

"You lesbians are big on vibrators, I know. I've seen what's in your bedside table."

Sam got home after work and walked into the house, grabbing a beer on the way out to the back deck. She sank down in the Adirondack chair and put her feet up on the railing, thinking back to when Sara had almost drowned on the dock at Montauk. Sam had never felt so desperate. She was normally a rock in a crisis, but the thought of losing Sara was too much—she hadn't taken a breath until Sara did. Now she'd give anything to go back and tell her about Lily before last night ever happened. But what was done was done, and she had to face facts; if Sara was going to come back to her, she'd have done it by now.

Sam left the beer on the railing and walked down to the barn beside the house. Gus had kept horses when Marcy was still alive—she'd loved them—but he couldn't deal with the memories after her death, so he let Sam fill it with gym equipment and a punching bag. The bag wasn't about fitness. She only used it when life got so shitty she had to punch something, and this definitely qualified. She took off her work shirt, leaving her in just the cargos and a white sports bra, then taped her wrists before she pulled on her gloves. Sam hit harder than she'd ever done with that first punch. She threw her fists into it over and over again until her arms ached and her knuckles started to blister under the gloves. She pounded until she couldn't tell anymore what was sweat and what was tears.

"Sam."

Sam spun around and looked at the barn door she'd left open. Sara was leaning against it. Sam was afraid to move; she didn't want her to disappear.

Sara locked her eyes onto Sam's. "I need to know the last time you slept with Lily."

Sam shook her head to clear it and thought for a second. That was not at all what she expected her to say.

"It was…" Sam paused. She needed to tell the truth, and she needed to get it right the first time. "Okay, do you remember the pancake breakfast?"

Sara nodded, a glimmer of hope starting to rise against her better judgment.

"And then the day after that we did your first boat lesson?"

"Yes, the first time you came over."

"It was that night. After the lesson."

Sara thought back. "When you said you had somewhere you needed to be."

"That's right," Sam said. "Then after we kissed for the first time, she came on to me a day or two later and I turned her down."

Sara looked down, pushing the hay around the concrete floor with her foot. "Why didn't you just tell me? Everyone has a past."

She looked into Sam's eyes until Sam broke her gaze, then stepped back and threw a hard last punch at the bag.

"Because I'm an idiot." Sam said, looking over at the bag to hide the tears still in her eyes. "There's no other way to say it. I was afraid I'd lose you and I didn't want to take that chance. So I took the easy way out."

Sara took a few seconds to think. She'd wanted honesty, and this was it. She looked up and held Sam's eyes. "Okay," she said. "That's good enough for me."

Sam stared at her for a few long seconds. "Wait…what did you say?"

"I said that's good enough for me. I believe you."

Sam walked over to Sara and pulled her into her arms, kissing her with more passion and relief than she ever knew she could feel. She didn't want to let her go, but finally she loosened her hold.

After a moment, Sara leaned back and looked at Sam, her eyes sparkling. "Did you really tell Lily I was your girlfriend?"

Sam paused, trying to think of what she'd said and how Sara could possibly know that. Clearly, there was only one way. "You talked to Lily, didn't you?"

"Yep," Sara said. "I ran into her at Moxie this morning and just asked if we could talk."

"I'm a little afraid to ask," Sam said, "but how did that go?"

"Actually," Sara said, "I can totally understand how she felt. I had a fling with one of my instructors in culinary school when I was about her age, so we bonded over that."

Sam shook her head, trying to take it all in. "So you guys bonded? Seriously?"

Sara nodded. "I wasn't really angry at her. I just had to know what happened, and I needed to figure out how I felt about you."

Sam pulled off her gloves and looked up. "And how do you feel?"

Sara reached for Sam's bloodied hand and held it to her heart. "Like I'm in love with you."

Sam pulled Sara back into her chest and wrapped her arms around her. She drew in the warm, familiar scent of her hair and whispered, "Good, because I've been in love with you since the day you threw a little fit about the boat license in my office."

"I did not throw a fit!" Sara leaned back with an indignant look on her face.

"You certainly did," Sam said. "And it was the cutest thing I'd ever seen."

Sara looked down, laughed, and caught a sudden glimpse of how filthy her white tank top was. Barn dust and sweat from Sam's workout streaked it.

"I look like I've gone a few rounds with that punching bag myself now." She pinched the front with two fingers and held it away from her body. "I may need a shower."

Sam laughed, pulling off her gloves and unwinding the tape around her wrists and knuckles. A stubborn piece of tape refused to let go of Sam's wrist and Sara paused to loosen it enough to slip it past the knuckles.

"What did you bring?" Sam said, nodding in the direction of a paper bag at the door.

"Just something for later tonight."

Sam walked over and looked into the bag. Brioche, ham, and raspberry jam.

She picked up the bag and held her hand out for Sara, closing the door behind them. "You'll make an amazing Monte Cristo."

❖

Later, after Sara had finished the beer Sam had left on the railing earlier, they watched the sunset from the deck, listening to the first of the night owls start to stir in the trees. The lake was shimmering and dark, reflecting the last of the bright gold sunset, framed by the mountains beyond. The deck lights turned on automatically and Sam started into the house to put away the ham that was still sitting in the bag on the deck.

"Will you turn on the shower for us?" Sara asked, leaning her head back from her chair to look at Sam.

Sam stopped to kiss her and push a stray lock of hair out of her face as she walked into the house, the screen door slapping shut behind her.

When Sara got to the bathroom a few minutes later, candles glowed from every surface, and the shower pounded like a hidden rainforest waterfall from around the corner. Sara stripped off her clothes and walked into the shower room to find Sam naked, warm water streaming in rivulets down her muscular body. Flickering gold light from the candles along the windowsill shone warm and hazy through the steam, and she turned around under the water to press her naked body against Sam. Sam opened her eyes and shook the water from her hair, then wrapped her hands around Sara's waist, sliding them up and across her nipples.

"Turn around." Her voice was as hot as the water, sultry and low.

Sara turned to face her and Sam picked her up, wrapping Sara's legs around her waist and pressing her back against the wet stone wall. Holding her eyes, she slid one hand down between their bodies, her fingers smooth and insistent against Sara's clit. Her rhythm was steady, building quick and strong until Sara threw her head back and moaned.

"Not yet, baby," Sam said, slowing her pace.

"Please?" Sara tightened her legs around Sam, her breath still hard and fast. "I can't take it."

"I know," Sam said, pausing and holding her eyes. "But I'm going to teach you."

Sam sat her gently on a teak bench built into the side of the stone shower wall, just out of the reach of the water, and sank slowly to her knees in front of her, lifting one of Sara's thighs over her shoulder. She teased her clit, sucking it lightly into her mouth then stroking it with her tongue. When she felt the heat building too fast, she softened her touch, biting lightly across the inside of her thighs or using just the tip of her tongue to brush the edges of her clit, ignoring Sara's attempts to pull her closer. Then just as she stilled, Sam drew it back into the warmth of her mouth, swirling around it slowly, rolling it under her tongue.

Sam waited until she felt Sara's nails dig into her arms to put Sara's other thigh over her shoulder, then buried her mouth into the heat of her, feeling her clit throb under her tongue as she got closer to the edge. She paused just once, to look up at Sara through the steam.

Sara's thighs started to shake as Sam pushed her over the edge into an orgasm so intense it exploded into her entire body. Sara held

Sam's head hard against her with both hands, her fingers tangled in her hair, the only anchor she had in this intense, spinning pleasure so deep it felt endless.

When she finally started to calm, Sam ran her hands up and down Sara's slick thighs and across her breasts. Sara jumped when her thumb started to massage Sara's swollen clit again. "It's too soon, I can't."

Sam lightened her touch and looked up at Sara. "Yes, you can."

Sara's voice trailed off as she felt Sam's tongue darting deep inside her while still working her clit. It seemed like only seconds until she heard herself cry out and arched into her second climax. Her body trembled as Sam continued to thrust her tongue inside and back across her clit, drawing out the last tremor of her orgasm.

Sam smiled and moved up her body, pulling Sara into her arms, and held her for a few minutes before she pulled her up and reached for a white towel from the cabinet in the shower room. Sara stood and held the towel to her body.

"I think my legs are shaky," she said.

Sam wrapped her up in her arms again, and Sara reached up and ran her hands through Sam's wet hair.

"What?" Sam asked, pulling the bath sheet tighter around her. "I can tell you're thinking about something."

Sara dropped her eyes, her voice low. "*How* do you make me come like that?"

Sam smiled, running her fingers through Sara's hair, then down her back, pulling her closer. "It only gets better."

"Okay," Sam said, looking at the disheveled mess that was Sara's first attempt at flipping a Monte Cristo sandwich. "I think what's going wrong here is just a tool issue."

She handed Sara another spatula. "After you have it put together and dip it in the egg mixture, it's really soft, so flipping it usually takes two of these."

"What?" Sara said, holding them both up together. "What do I do with the other one?"

Sam set the last attempt aside and built another sandwich, layering together the ham, bright raspberry jam, and cheese. She turned the sandwich over a few times in the egg and milk mixture and settled it back into the pan, where a large scoop of butter was melted to the perfect temperature.

"Now," Sam said, "What you want to do is slide one spatula underneath when you're ready to flip it, then put the other spatula on top."

"Ah, I get it." Sara took both spatulas and slid them into place. "Like this?"

"Perfect. Now flip it."

Sara held both spatulas firmly against the sides of the sandwich and turned her wrists smoothly, so that the golden brown side was facing up and the other side was frying.

"Genius," Sara said, "How have I not done this before now?"

"It's actually easier to do it at a diner where you have a deep fryer you can just plunge it into—it cooks the egg instantly and seals everything in. But this method works when there's no fryer."

"This was more complicated than it looked." Sara slid the sandwich from the pan to the cutting board and sliced it diagonally before she put it on two plates. "I bet this took some time to learn."

"All I wanted for my birthday one year was to learn how to make a Monte Cristo and serve it to someone in the diner." Sam smiled and caught the jam dripping from her sandwich onto her fingers. "Dad let me practice until I had it down pretty well. I still remember the huge stack of failed attempts on the counter when I was done. It was a disaster for a while there until I got the hang of it."

"Who did you serve it to?"

"I just picked someone at random and set it down on his table like I'd just won a Michelin star or something."

Sam laughed and looked over at Sara, who was licking jam from the tips of her fingers.

God, she's beautiful, Sam thought.

She looked tiny in the hoodie she'd given her, and her hair was still damp and falling around her face. She tucked it behind her ears just before she picked up her sandwich. A few freckles were scattered across her cheeks and the gold flecks in her green eyes sparkled as she looked at Sam, waiting for her to say what was on her mind.

Sam smiled. "Still going with that name on the window?"

Sara thought back to Sam walking into the final sale of the diner, all guns blazing, her eyes flashing fire about the *Alchemy Gastropub* logo Sara had hired someone to paint on the windows.

"Nope."

Sam smiled, and Sara took the opportunity to steal the last bite of her Monte Cristo.

❖

The next morning, they overslept and Sam drove Sara into town on her way to work.

"Will I see you tonight?" Sam traced Sara's chin with her finger, pulling her into a kiss.

"Definitely," Sara said. "Come over to the cabin after work. I'll cook."

"About seven?"

"Perfect. I have to meet Mary this morning, then train the kitchen staff this afternoon, but I should be home well before then."

Sara leaned over and kissed her again, then jumped out of Sam's truck and headed up the street from the station to the diner. Sam watched her in her rearview window until Murphy knocked on her window.

"Jesus, Murphy, you scared the shit out of me," she said, climbing out of her truck. She reached in for her bag and shut the door. "You're an idiot. I'm armed and I'm quicker than you."

He laughed, falling into step beside her as they walked into the station. Behind the front desk, there was an elderly woman in polyester pants and sensible shoes, with one pink curler stranded in her gray hair. It wasn't clear whether it was intentional or she'd just forgotten it was there.

"Good morning, gentlemen," she said, looking at Sam and Murphy. "How can I help you?"

Murphy coughed into his hand in a failed attempt at hiding a laugh, and Sam held out her hand to the new receptionist.

"Good morning," she said, stifling a completely inappropriate urge to laugh. "I'm Sam Draper, the captain."

"Oh!" She said, squinting her eyes and peering at Sam, "I thought the captain was a woman."

Murphy wasn't even trying to hide his laughter at this point. Sam shot him a look. "I assure you…" Sam paused as she looked for a name tag on the woman's shirt.

"Margene."

"I assure you, Margene," Sam said, "I am a woman."

Sam looked behind the desk and pressed the button that opened the security door to the hall.

"If there are any calls for me, can you just put them through to my office?"

Margene looked at the phone, pressing several of the function buttons at once. "How do I do that?"

"No worries," Sam said, smiling and opening the door, "Murphy here is going to spend as much time as it takes to show you everything you need to know."

Once in her office, Sam dropped her bag and jacket in the chair across from her desk and picked up a note. It was from the chief of police.

Found a replacement for Lily. Do me a favor and try to stay away from this one.

Sam groaned and balled it up in her hand, tossing it into the wastebasket at the end of her desk.

Sara hurried into the drugstore, ten minutes late to meet Mary. A cinnamon roll was on the counter for her already, and Mary handed her a coffee as she pulled a stool from behind the counter to the end and sat down.

"What's your rush?" Mary put a bite of her cinnamon roll into her mouth and looked at Sara.

Sara tried to catch her breath. "Sorry I'm late, I—"

"You were getting out of Samantha's truck," Mary said, pushing the sugar in her direction. "I saw that. And you're not leaving until I get details." Mary smiled at her and sat back in her stool.

"It's been in the works for a while," Sara said, "but it's official now. We're together."

"Well," Mary said, "Sam's a lucky girl. I was hoping that would happen."

"There's only one problem," Sara said.

"The diner?"

Sara nodded. "I was hoping you had some magic solution to make this go away," Sara said. "I can't just give up the diner, and honestly I shouldn't have to, but Sam won't step foot in it and refuses to talk about it."

"God, she's the most stubborn little thing, always has been." Mary paused. "Well, certainly not little anymore, but you know what I mean."

They both sat, sipping their coffee, trying to come up with the answer that wasn't there.

"Well," Mary said finally, "she's stubborn, but not stupid. She'll probably sort this out by herself."

"Hopefully sooner rather than later. I open in two weeks."

"Is it that soon?" Mary said, getting off her stool and gathering the cups to hide under the counter. "Then we'd better be getting over there. I'm not opening the store until noon, so we have some time."

"I'd love your company," Sara said. "But I thought you'd just gotten me some recipes?"

"Well," said Mary, locking the door to the drugstore behind them, "Maybe a little more than recipes."

It was a quick trip across the street, and Sara unlocked the door and turned on the lights, stepping aside for Mary.

"Wow…" Mary said, after a long few seconds. "I'm speechless."

Sara laughed. "Now that's saying something!"

Everything in the dining room gleamed. The walls were painted a pale blue with white trim, black and white checked vinyl booths surrounded white Formica tabletops, and new chrome tables and chairs sparkled under the lights. Sara had gone for a classic retro diner feel, but softened it somewhat with overstuffed hound-tooth sofas along two walls, each with its own floor lamp and coffee table, in addition to a large mirror on the wall encased in a vintage frame. Cheerful pillows in hot pink, orange, and lime brightened the sofas and the lamps cast a soft gold light down on each sitting area, instantly making it cozy and inviting.

"This is *beautiful*," Mary said, "How did you even do all this?"

"Actually, I decided what I wanted and had an interior designer contract out the labor, so I really didn't have to do anything but keep tabs on the progress over the last few months. The kitchen was easy, everything there was turnkey, but what took the longest was the outside."

Mary turned and looked back at the door they'd just opened and sidewalk beyond it. "No." Sara laughed. "Other direction. The deck in back."

They stepped out the side door of the dining room onto an expansive wood deck, built on two levels.

The lower deck had a gas fireplace set into a hand-laid stone hearth to the right, and a staircase to the left led to the covered upper deck. The tables were natural wood, and the chairs were a mishmash of antiques that mirrored Sara's kitchen.

"There are heaters along the floor in the upper level, and clear vinyl curtains that we'll pull to keep the heat in and the snow out in the winter."

"I don't know what to say," Mary said, still looking around and taking everything in, "except that you've done this place proud. Gus would have loved it."

"That's high praise," Sara said. "It was important to me that you like it."

"Like it?" Mary said, glancing at Sara, "No, I love it. And that girlfriend of yours is a horse's ass for not being here."

After Mary had looked around the deck, Sara opened the kitchen, and the second she walked through the doors, she smelled food in the oven.

Mary nodded toward the ovens in answer to Sara's unasked question.

"I asked around with some of the old regulars to the diner, and everyone was so excited about contributing a recipe that they sent along the actual dish as well as the recipe. Everything was already cooked and ready to go. I thought I'd put them in on a low temperature so we could taste them while we looked at the recipes."

When she opened the three ovens, eleven different dishes, all covered with foil, were warming on the shelves.

"I'm so excited!" Sara said, getting a stack of saucers and a pen and paper. "So that means I can skip the trial-and-error process and go straight to what we want on the menu."

"That should be your decision," Mary said, pulling out the first dish and setting it on the stainless steel prep table in front of them. "I don't know anything about restaurants."

"Mary, I love your cooking, and I need your help whether you like it or not. My restaurant was fussy fine dining. I've always loved more casual food, but I'm not exactly a diner expert."

"Well, if you insist," Mary said, looking very pleased with herself. "Let's taste the meatloaf first." She dished steaming squares of meatloaf onto two saucers and handed Sara a fork.

"What's the sauce on the top?" Sara said, getting a taste on her fork and touching it to her tongue. "Is it tomato based? I love how it's gotten darker around the edges, almost caramelized."

Mary smiled. "It's ketchup. Did you not eat meatloaf as a kid?"

"We had a cook when I was growing up, and this was definitely not in the dinner rotation."

They each took a bite, savoring in silence. Sara was the first to speak.

"Wow. This is really complex, the rosemary is wonderful with the meat, and the texture is perfect, which I didn't expect," she said, putting another bite into her mouth. "I love it."

"Do you know Karen Harvey that runs the hardware store?"

"Yep," said Sara, "I went to her for the pine siding I put in the cabin bathroom."

"Well, she sent that one, and she'll be excited it made the cut."

Mary took a stack of recipe cards out of her jacket pocket and dug through them until she found Karen's meatloaf, then handed it to Sara.

"It definitely makes it," Sara said, setting it aside to start the pile of keepers. "What's next?"

They went through every dish, including something called chess pie that Sara ate two pieces of before she went on to the next dish. Her favorite was a macaroni and cheese recipe from one of the police officer's wives—it was baked in a deep dish with Gruyère, cheddar, and Fontina cheeses, with a crispy topping of toasted breadcrumbs browned with bacon. Mary's cinnamon rolls, of course, went into the winners pile. Roasted short ribs with a homemade steak sauce was also a winner, and the owner of Moxie Java contributed a cherry pie with crust so flaky it nearly brought tears to her eyes. In the end, everything contributed by the locals made the cut.

"Well, that's the local favorites section done," Sara said, "And I think I have the rest of it nailed down as well. It's mostly comfort food like lasagna, and Southern fried chicken with biscuits. We'll have to see how it goes with the kitchen staff. I'm starting their training on the recipes this afternoon."

"It's all pretty straightforward, with the exception of that chess pie," Mary said. "Unless the rest of the menu is really complicated, I'd guess they'll pick it up pretty quick."

The afternoon flew by as Sara started training the kitchen staff. They turned out to be quick learners, and if everything continued to go well, Sara found herself thinking that she might not have to be in the kitchen much at all. At around seven, Sara sent them home and cleaned the kitchen, carefully putting away the rest of the local dishes to go back to later when she was breaking down the recipes in more detail for the staff. Just as she turned to leave, her phone pinged. It was Sam.

There were four accidents on the water today and I'm still dealing with the fallout. Any chance of dinner tomorrow instead?

It's a deal, Sara typed back. *I'm exhausted and just now leaving the diner.*

Sara gathered the rest of her things and headed out to her truck, excited to be going home until she remembered she didn't have her truck. Sam had dropped her off that morning.

"Great," Sara muttered as she locked the doors to the diner.

The streets were almost deserted and it was almost dark. It wasn't a long walk home, only a mile, but it suddenly felt like fifteen. She wondered if she could get Jen to give her a ride until she remembered Jen didn't have a car yet, and there was no way she was going to ask Sam to drop everything and drive her home, so she threw her bag over her shoulder and started toward the cabin. Her phone pinged before she was even past Moxie Java and Sara dug for it, finding it all the way in the bottom of her bag.

Meet me at the docks, gorgeous?

This is Sara, she texted back. *Did you mean to send this to Murphy?*

It was only about a second before Sam's reply lit up her screen. *Very funny.*

When she came down the hill, she saw Sam's patrol boat pulled up to the outside edge of the farthest dock. Sam jumped out and met her at the bottom of the hill, taking her bag off her shoulder and handing Sara her jacket.

"I thought we said tomorrow?" Sara said, slipping into Sam's patrol jacket.

"I'm just here to drive you home and kiss you good night."

"Wait," Sara said as they walked down the dock to the boat. "Isn't this my jacket?"

Sam raised an eyebrow and loosened the ropes tied to the dock rings. "If it is then you've been having my name embroidered on your clothes, which is classic stalker behavior, don't you think?"

Sara laughed. "No, this is the one you gave me the first time we met, then I said I was keeping it the next day when you were a jerk about the boat license."

"Yep, you left it on the chair when you stormed out."

"Well," Sara said, snuggling into it and setting into the passenger's seat, "thanks for returning it."

Sam leaned down to kiss her, lingering a moment to breathe in the scent of her skin. She'd never noticed the scent of someone's skin before, but Sara always smelled like warmth and fresh air.

She stood and started the engine, reversing slowly out and away from the dock, then accelerating toward the center of the lake. Summer was slowly starting to fade into fall, and the evenings were already colder. It was September first tomorrow, and all the campers and staff had been leaving McCall in stages over the last couple of weeks. Town was already quieter. Lake Patrol always slowed down in the fall, and they'd have a few weeks to rest before the skiers took over the town in late October.

Sara watched the water rush past the boat in white waves. The houses on the north shore came into view, the lights in the windows like squares of gold set into the darkness. The sound of a boat engine had become soothing, familiar, like she'd lived there all her life. As they rounded the corner of the shoreline, Sara's cabin came into view, with a new floodlight that illuminated her dock and parking slip.

"Sam," she said, tugging at her sleeve and pointing to the dock. "Where did that come from? I've never had a light on my dock."

Sam smiled, slowing gradually as she approached. "You've always had one. The switch is on your back deck. It just didn't have a bulb in it. I stopped by and replaced it this afternoon."

Sam pulled up to the side of the dock and cut the engine. She hopped up on the dock and wound the rope loosely to the dock ring, holding her hand out for Sara. They walked to the back of the cabin and Sara unlocked the door, reaching inside to switch on the lights.

"Thank you," she said. "You'd better be careful, a girl could get used to this kind of chivalry."

Sam pulled her into her arms and kissed her, holding her face gently with her hands. "Get used to it," she said, kissing her one last time and walking back to her boat.

The next morning was Saturday, and Sara woke to find Jen asleep on the couch below the loft.

"Hey, Jen," she said, coming down the stairs in a tank top and pajama pants. "Is this your way of telling me you want pancakes?"

Sunlight streamed through the windows and Jen stretched her arms toward the ceiling. "It was too late to bike back into town from the trails, so I just stopped here. What time is it?"

"It's almost noon, sleepyhead."

"And it's Saturday?"

Sara nodded as she started the coffee and pulled her hair into a bun. Jennifer leaned over the back of the couch.

"Hey," she said, "Guess who has an interview at the high school on Monday?"

Sara ran and jumped over the back of the couch and squarely onto her sister. "No way! To teach?"

"No," Jen said, with a completely straight face. "To landscape the grounds with bonsai trees."

Sara hit her with a couch pillow.

"Of course to teach," Jen said, "Advanced mathematics, as well as helping with the AP track students."

"Jen, that's amazing!"

"Amazing enough for pancakes?"

Sara smiled. "And I have blueberries in the fridge from the farmer's market last Thursday."

A truck rumbled down the driveway just then and came to a hurried stop. Jen looked out the window and called back to Sara. "Lake Patrol, Sam's here."

She'd just flopped back down on the couch when another Lake Patrol truck pulled up and parked, then Sara heard both doors slam. She looked at Jen, who was sitting up by now, and they both jumped at the loud knock at her door.

"What the hell?" Sara mouthed to Jen.

Jen shook her head and started for the door, but Sara pulled her back. She looked out the window before she opened the door.

"It's just Sam and Murphy," she whispered. "But what are they doing here?" Jen shrugged as Sara opened the door.

Murphy burst past her and pulled Jennifer into his arms. Sara looked at Sam after realizing she wouldn't be getting an answer from Jen, who was now kissing Murphy as if they hadn't seen each other for months.

"What the hell is going on?"

"Your guess is as good as mine," Sam said. "I just got a radio call from Murphy to meet him here ASAP, so I did."

They looked over at Jen again, her forehead pressed against his.

"Okay," Sam said. "Not that this isn't sweet, but I'm still not sure why we're here?"

Murphy answered, his arm still around Jennifer. "I got a call to get down to the Wilson dock."

"Wait," Sara said, looking at Jen. "Isn't that where you're renting a slip to dock your houseboat?"

Jen nodded as Murphy went on.

"And when I got there, Mrs. Wilson said she'd been hearing

banging in Jen's houseboat all night. When she went down to check on her, the door was locked, so she called us. I was the first one to answer, so I went down to the boat and looked in the window. The place looked trashed. Everything had been thrown around, even the canisters on the counters were tipped over onto the floor."

"Oh my God! Who was in there?" Jen looked suddenly pale.

"So I called for backup and tried to call Jen a thousand times, but it was just going to voicemail."

Jen reached for her phone and looked at the black screen. "It must have died after I got here. I usually plug it in, but I didn't have my charger."

"How long ago was this?" Sam said, pulling out her phone. "Did backup get there before you left?"

"Yeah, then I radioed you from the truck on the way over. I don't know what's happened since then."

Sam put the phone to her ear and walked outside, pulling her holster and firearm out of the truck and strapping them on as she talked.

Chapter Sixteen

"What the hell?" Sara said. "Who would want to rob a houseboat? I never even lock the cabin."

All three of them lined up at the cabin windows facing the truck and watched Sam as she paced back and forth in front of her truck. Just when Jennifer lost patience and started for the door, Sam finally clicked her phone off and walked back to the house.

"Well," she said as she came in, "there's good news and bad news."

"Spill it, Draper." Jen was in no mood for stalling.

"The short story is that someone did get into your boat and trash the inside, but the officers said that there was no major damage. Although I think you'll be spending some time cleaning your kitchen in the near future."

"What?" Sara asked. "What would they want so badly in the kitchen?"

"Do you leave your windows open?"

"The nights have been so cool that I open one in the main room and one in the bedroom," Jen said.

"Why?"

"Well, it looks like a little crew of raccoons decided to come in and make themselves a midnight snack."

Murphy looked at Sam, both of them suddenly trying not to laugh.

"That explains the almighty mess," Murphy said. "I just saw everything tipped over and thought something must have happened to Jen."

"I would have thought the same thing," Sam said. "If that was Sara's place, I'd be blazing down this road going ninety too."

"They won't hurt the raccoons, will they?" Jen's hands were on her hips. "It's my fault they were in there in the first place."

"They've already got them trapped and are headed back into the woods to release them," Sam said. "They'll be pissed off, but totally safe."

Sara headed back into the kitchen and started getting out the eggs and flour for the pancakes.

"I know Sam's not working," she said, looking back at them over her shoulder, "but are you on duty, Murphy?"

"No, ma'am," he said. "I was off at noon, I was just on my way home when I got the call."

"Perfect," Sara said, cracking eggs into a bowl. "Then both of you can stay for breakfast."

Murphy looked like he'd just won the lottery, then headed outside with Sam to put the guns away.

"Oh my God," Jen whispered as the door closed behind them. "Look at me! I can't believe he saw me with my hair all wild and no makeup." Jen pointed at the messy waves that had already escaped from her bun. "Something tells me he couldn't care less, but this isn't exactly my best look either."

They both thought to look down at the same moment. The sheer tank tops they were wearing didn't hide much, and they both burst into laughter at the same time.

"And we might as well be naked. Fabulous," Jennifer said, heading for the loft. "Can I borrow an actual shirt?"

"Only if you bring me one." Sara poured milk into the mix and whipped it with a whisk, turning on the heat under the pans on the stove.

❖

Sara had the pancakes done in record time, and they took their plates out to the back deck to eat in the sunshine. A late summer breeze was coming off the lake and swept through the tops of the trees, and a group of three canoes in the distance shouted back and forth across the water.

"Seriously the best pancakes I've ever had," Murphy said, pouring syrup onto a second stack and cutting into them. "I had no idea we even had a chef in McCall until that pancake breakfast you did for the Island Scramble."

"What's the Island Scramble?" Jen said, spearing another pancake and dragging it to her plate.

"It's a huge fundraising event for the high school here, and the Lake Patrol hires caterers to do a pancake breakfast for it every year," Murphy said. "There's news coverage from Boise and everything." He dipped some pancake in syrup and put it in his mouth, closing his eyes in bliss.

"And an hour and a half before the breakfast was supposed to start," Sam continued for him, "the catering company said they somehow double-booked themselves and weren't coming at all."

"So you had all those people expecting breakfast and no one to cook?"

"Until your sister saved the day," Murphy said, nodding at Sara and choosing another sausage from the serving plate. "Best pancakes I ever ate. Everybody was talking about how beautiful it was, too. It looked like a picture in a magazine."

Jen smiled over at Sara. "That doesn't surprise me at all."

"They're sweet, but they're actually making it sound way better than it was," Sara said, taking the orange juice pitcher back in to refill.

"No, we're not," Sam said to Sara, shaking her head. "She saved my ass. There's no other way to put it."

"That girl could run a country if she wanted to," Jennifer said, looking over at her through the kitchen window. "She's always been crazy talented."

Sara stuck her head back through the door from the kitchen. "I'm going to make some mimosas. Anybody up for it?"

"God, yes," Jen said, leaning back in her chair and looking out to the lake. "That's what has always pissed me off about my parents," Jen said quietly. "She's smarter than me and my brother put together, but they made her feel like there was something wrong with her until the day she left home because of the dyslexia."

"What?" Sam said, running her fingers through her hair and staring at Jennifer. "I didn't know she's dyslexic."

"Shit, sorry." Jen covered her mouth with her hand. "I thought she'd told you."

"No worries. I won't tell her it came from you," Sam said. "But is that why she said she almost failed out of high school?"

"I'll tell her I told you, she's used to my mouth," Jen said. "And yes, in middle school her teachers had her tested and told my parents, but they just pretended it didn't exist. They went on and on about how she just wasn't applying herself. I think they just didn't want anyone to know."

"How could I have been with her all this time and not known?"

"She covers it really well," Jen said. "Like in a restaurant, she'll point at the menu or she'll pick out one thing…"

Like the Monte Cristo, Sam thought.

"Then ask a question about it to figure out what it is, then that's what she orders. Anyway, that's why she went to culinary school, which mortified my parents. My brother and I both went to traditional colleges."

Sara came back through the door just then, carrying a pitcher in one hand and four champagne flutes in the other.

"What?" she said, looking around in the awkward silence. "Jennifer, what did you say?"

"Why do you always assume it's me?" Jen took the glasses from her and gave everyone one. "I may have mentioned the dyslexia thing."

"Jen!" Sara sighed and started pouring the mimosas into the glasses. She glanced at Sam, who got up to take over pouring. "Actually, I should have brought it up by now, so whatever." Sam set the pitcher back on the table and pulled Sara in to kiss her cheek.

"Hey, Murphy," Sara said, taking her glass and sitting down, "did you know that Jennifer still sucks her thumb in her sleep?"

Jennifer just put her head down on the table with a little moan.

Later, after Sam and Murphy did the dishes, Sam left to do errands, promising to return for dinner. "I'm taking you out, though," she said, kissing her gently at the door. "You cooked breakfast."

They said goodbye and Sara returned to the kitchen, where her sister and Murphy were still standing.

"Now," she said, "Let's get back to fun facts about Jennifer."

❖

As promised, Sam was back that evening to pick Sara up for dinner. She knew she'd still be getting ready, so she'd left the door open. When Sara finished and walked into the living room, she found Sam standing on the back deck, looking out over the water. Sara stepped out and locked the door, but when she turned around, she stopped in her tracks.

"Someone parked their boat at my dock," she said, turning to Sam. "Is that legal?"

Parking space at the community docks was a rare find on the weekends, even in late summer, and she'd heard some people just park at random docks and walk in to town. They walked down for a closer look. It didn't look like the boat that would belong to someone that would steal parking. It was gorgeous and looked straight out of a boating magazine. When they got there, Sam climbed in and held her hand out for Sara.

"Wait…This *your* boat?"

Sam handed Sara a pair of sunglasses. "Yeah. I thought we'd take mine this time."

"Wow," Sara said, turning around and taking it in, "It's beautiful."

The outside was a dark shimmering gray, with a polished mahogany control panel and steering wheel. The interior was covered in the softest pale gray leather and chrome, and there was a wide seat in the back with a built-in refrigerator.

"Do you want to drive?" Sam held out the keys.

"Absolutely not," Sara said, still running her hand over the buttery leather seat back. "Not even a little bit."

Sam smiled and backed up the ski boat, turning smoothly into the open water and putting on her sunglasses as they headed into the glare of the afternoon sun on the water. She headed to the western side of the lake, past town and the community docks, to a part of the lakeshore Sara had never seen. Sara got up from the passenger's seat and stepped in front of Sam at the wheel, sliding her hand under Sam's on the throttle. She wasn't learning how to drive a boat anymore, but it was her favorite place to be. Sam leaned down and kissed her neck, and Sara leaned back against her chest.

Sam slowed, then cut the engine as they got closer to a weathered gray dock, outstretched like a silver wing over the water. She pulled into a slip and tied her boat off, offering her hand to Sara as she got out.

"What is this place?" Sara asked, looking up the winding stone path beyond the docks.

A beautiful slate gray house with brilliant white shutters sat at the top of the path and seemed to have light spilling out of the windows, even in the late afternoon sun. Sam led her to the house and onto a deck. The deck overlooked the lake and sat above a natural stone fountain that splashed into a turquoise ceramic pool. Climbing freesia and fig vines were draped over an arbor overhead, and a lone weathered wood table was waiting, set with four chairs and simple terra-cotta plates.

"There's only one table here," said Sara, as Sam pulled her chair out for her. "Is this a restaurant?"

"Not exactly," Sam said, sitting across from her and pouring her a glass of Chardonnay from the bottle on the table.

"You are here!" A short round man with a heavy French accent and a white apron stepped onto the porch and greeted Sam with genuine affection, setting a cold beer on the table for her and pulling her into a tight hug. "Excellent! And this must be your Sara," he said, taking her in before kissing both of her cheeks and turning to Sam to whisper, "You are right, she is very beautiful."

He scurried off as quickly as he'd appeared, mumbling something about the oven.

"I'll introduce you when he comes back," Sam said. "His name is Maurice. He's a chef from Marseille in the south of France. His partner passed away years ago and he retired here early to be close to his daughter; who teaches at the elementary school in McCall."

"So this is his home? It's gorgeous," Sara said, looking around at the lush lavender wisteria and vines dripping from the arbor toward the deck. "And whatever he's cooking smells amazing."

"Well, I could hardly expect to impress you with my cooking, so I asked Maurice to lend a hand."

"Well, it worked, I'm officially impressed," she said, leaning in and lowering her voice to a whisper. "And he's adorable."

"Somehow he and my dad became instant best friends when Maurice moved to McCall years ago. They hung out in the diner every day for breakfast, and Dad and I ate here a lot too." Sam smiled at the memory, looking back to the door he'd disappeared into. "They'd usually get in the kitchen together and argue about the perfect way to cook this or that and forget to actually plate any food. Eventually I'd just have to come into the kitchen and start getting into things."

Just then, Maurice burst through the door again with a tiny dish in each hand.

"Sara," he said, in his charming French accent, "I make this especially for you. It is an *amuse bouche*, a foie gras bonbon with bitter chocolate, pistachios, and Rainier cherry."

He set a dish in front of each of them and smiled at Sara's excitement. "Samantha tells me you are a chef?"

"I am," Sara said. "I trained in Memphis and owned a restaurant in Savannah before I moved here."

"I'm *so* jealous!" Maurice said, closing his eyes and clasping a hand over his heart for emphasis. "All that beautiful seafood right at your door."

"Literally right at my door." Sara laughed. "They brought the live seafood delivery to the kitchen at seven every morning."

"You know, that is just how they do it on the Cote D'Azure," Maurice said, excited at the memory. "I worked there as an apprentice when I was a young boy, and I remember the boxes of squid on the doorstep every morning."

After that, it didn't take long for them to start chattering away about the French obsession with squid ink. Watching them, Sam realized how important it was to her that Maurice like Sara, which he clearly did. It was as close as she could get to introducing Sara to family.

Afternoon turned to evening, and course by course, a tasting menu of classic French cuisine appeared on the table. Maurice somehow managed not to venture too far from Sam's tastes while still appealing to Sara's more refined palate. He brought a traditional dessert plate of cheeses at the end of the meal, and Sara insisted he join them. He poured them both a glass of petite Syrah and pulled up a chair, chatting to Sara as if he'd known her forever. He spread some questionable-looking soft cheese on a baguette slice and handed it to Sam, who immediately passed it on to Sara. Maurice rolled his eyes.

"Not only does she turn up her nose at French wine, she has no appreciation for beautiful cheese."

"Is this D'affinois…with white truffles?" She brought it to her nose and closed her eyes. "Oh my God, I haven't had this in years. I'm in heaven!"

Maurice smiled, his round cheeks beaming with happiness at having someone to share his favorite things.

It was well into the evening before they finished, and Maurice hugged Sara goodbye with the promise of a wine and cheese evening the following week. She thanked him again and promised to bring him some special Malbec with a long French name that Sam didn't understand, but seemed to thrill Maurice. He held Sam in a long hug as well, whispering something in her ear that Sara didn't hear, but she caught the tears in Sam's eyes as they walked back to the boat.

"Thank you," Sara said as they walked back down the path to the dock. "This was beyond amazing."

"Thank you for being so sweet to him," Sam said, squeezing Sara's hand as she stepped into the boat.

"You made him so happy."

Sam started the boat and Sara stepped into her spot between her and the steering wheel, Sam's strong arms on either side of her.

"Where to?" Sam said into her ear as the boat picked up speed and the wind whipped the words from her mouth.

"Home," Sara said, "Yours."

Sam steered toward the north shore, holding Sara a little tighter than she ever had.

❖

When they arrived at Sam's house, Sara went inside to get the hoodie, which by now she'd claimed as her own, out of the bedroom while Sam got water, two glasses, and the bottle of scotch and went out to the deck. Sara walked outside to the deck barefoot, wrapped in the hoodie, and curled up in the chair beside her, looking out toward the dark, mirrored surface of the water. Sam handed her the scotch, which she downed in one gulp.

Sam refilled her glass and arched an eyebrow. "How are you feeling over there?"

"A tiny bit drunk," Sara said, "But I want to ask you something." She paused. "I've wanted to for a while, actually."

Sara turned toward Sam in her chair and stretched her legs out so her feet were in Sam's lap. Sam curled her fingers over Sara's toes to keep them warm and took a sip of her scotch.

"Is there anything…" Sara said, hesitating, "that you've wanted to do in bed that you haven't done yet?"

Sam put her glass down and laughed, pulling Sara's legs closer. "Where's this coming from?"

"I just…" Sara bit her lip and dropped her eyes, her voice trailing off.

"Tell me," Sam said, running her palm over Sara's leg. "I want to know everything about you."

"There's something I've always thought about, but it's never really been the right time. Or maybe it just wasn't the right person." Sara pulled the sleeves of her hoodie down over her fingers and tucked them in her lap. Sam just waited; Sara would tell her if she wanted her to know.

"Wait," Sara said suddenly, looking up. "I asked you first."

Sam paused. "There's not too much I haven't done, to be honest. Maybe one thing."

Sara nodded and reached for her scotch, which Sam lifted gracefully out of her grasp.

"I can tell this might be hard for you to talk about, but you're a little tipsy already, and I want to make sure I'm not taking advantage of you later."

"Okay." Sara took a deep breath and tucked her feet underneath her in the chair. "I've always wanted to do this but never found the person I trusted enough, I guess."

"Just tell me." Sam smiled, her hand on Sara's thigh. "I'm not exactly easy to shock."

Sara paused, trying to find the right words. "I've never had sex with someone that used a strap-on."

Now it was Sam's turn to be surprised. "Seriously?" she said. "Never?"

Sara shook her head. "I know it's weird, everybody does it, I just never felt comfortable enough until now."

"First of all," Sam said, "not everyone does it, not even close, and I'm honored you trust me enough to talk about it."

"What about you?' she asked, reaching for the water Sam brought out with the scotch.

Sam raised her glass and turned it to catch the moonlight. "I had a harness made for me about twenty years ago, when I first came out, by a lesbian leathersmith I knew in Boise."

"Wow," Sara said "She made it to fit just you?"

Sam nodded.

"And…what do you use with it?"

"Honestly, it depends who I'm with," Sam said, "and what they need. Everyone's different."

"What do you think I need?" Sara's voice was almost a whisper.

"Well," Sam said, "I'm in love with you, so this is new territory, but I think I have a pretty good idea."

"Will you show me?"

Sam got up and turned out the lights, then picked Sara up in her arms and walked into the house, kicking the door shut behind her.

"Not tonight," she said, her breath warm against Sara's ear. "I want to make sure we remember it."

"When?" Sara whispered back, melting into her arms.

"Soon, baby," Sam said, laying her back on her bed and pulling the duvet up over both of them.

Sam pulled Sara back against her body and wrapped her up in her arms.

"Sam?" Sara whispered into the dark, "Thank you for tonight, with Maurice. No one's ever done anything like that for me."

"Shhh," Sam soothed, stroking Sara's hair as she lay in her arms. "Someday you'll believe me. It only gets better."

CHAPTER SEVENTEEN

For the rest of that week, Sara was buried in work at the diner. The kitchen staff ended up doing an excellent job through training, which was a relief. Sara knew from experience they could make or break a restaurant. By the end, they knew the menu backward and forward, in addition to making every dish several times. Sara relished the thought of not having to be in the kitchen constantly, and with a good staff, that was possible.

By Friday, the new sign was finally applied to the front of the diner, promptly covered with paper by Sara to keep it under wraps for the opening. The new menus arrived next, and the framer delivered seventeen brown paper–wrapped pictures for the walls, all different sizes. Sara slowly peeled the paper from each when she was finally alone in the diner. She'd done an excellent job restoring and mounting all the pictures of Gus and the locals through the years that were left behind when Sara bought the building. She spent the rest of that afternoon on a ladder attempting to hang them so they looked straight from every angle, which proved to be impossible. Around five, she just gave up and went across the street to see if Mary could help her before she lost her mind.

It turned out Mary was closing up anyway and looking for an excuse not to mop the floors of the drugstore. Sara had left the diner unlocked, so they walked in and Mary turned slowly around, walking over to peer at some of the small photos and handwritten recipes.

"This is incredible, Sara," she said. "Where in the world did you get all this?"

"Most of them were actually already on the kitchen walls unframed, I saw them when you brought me over the first time, but when I was cleaning out the office, I found a stack of photos that hadn't made it onto the walls."

Mary continued to look, occasionally laughing out loud or stopping to tell a story about someone in one of the pictures.

"So what do you think?" Sara said, her hands on her hips. "I'm afraid it will upset Sam."

"Has she still not been in here?"

"No, but not for lack of trying. Every time I bring up even the smallest detail about the diner, she refuses to discuss it. I don't know what to do to make it easier if we can't talk."

"Sara," Mary said, hand on hip. "It's not your job to make anything easy. It's Samantha's job to pull her head out of her ass."

Sara laughed, thankful that she had at least one person to talk to about the diner. It opened in six days, and the person she loved most wouldn't be there to support her.

"And how are you feeling about all this?" Mary said. "It must be stressful."

Sara nodded and motioned her back to the kitchen, where she put on oven gloves and retrieved a pot roast surrounded by tender vegetables and the start of a beautiful brown gravy. When Sara pulled the meat lightly with a fork, it fell off the bone, so she turned the oven off and took off her gloves.

"How do I feel?" Sara said, going back to Mary's question. "I know it's selfish, but the fact that she's shutting herself out of this part of my life completely is frustrating. She won't even try."

"You couldn't be more right," Mary said, shaking her head, "and I don't blame you for being upset."

"I'm completely in love with her, so we have to find a way to work it out. Do you think she'll ever want to be a part of it?"

"I don't know," Mary said. "She's as stubborn as they come, and I wish I could say yes, but I just don't know."

Sara dished up two bowls of steaming pot roast and vegetables and tore some bread for each of them off a crusty loaf she'd made earlier that day.

"Oh my God," Mary said with her mouth full, "please tell me this is on your menu."

"It is," Sara said. "I'm planning on serving it on Sundays. I love it too."

Sara reached into the cooler and brought out two bottles of porter. "Want a beer?"

"Hell, yes," Mary said, the bottle opener on her key ring already in her hand.

❖

The next day was Saturday, and Sam went into the office around seven to get some paperwork done before she took off for the day. Sam had plans with Sara later that evening, but she had to get some of her paperwork off her desk. She'd been distracted lately, and if she let it build up any more she'd never catch up on Monday.

But, she thought, *first things first.*

Moxie Java opened at seven, and they made cream cheese muffins on Saturdays, so she parked her truck at the station and walked up the hill, following the scent of roasted coffee beans to the door.

Double espresso and muffin in hand, she was almost to the door when Mary walked in. She stopped Sam in her tracks and told her to have a seat, stopping at the counter to get whatever coffee goes with twelve packs of sugar. Mary slid into the booth with Sam and started ripping the tops off packets.

"Mary, what can I help you with?" Sam said, looking at her watch. "I don't mean to rush off, but I've got a stack of paperwork on my desk that's taller than you."

"You're not going anywhere, Samantha." Mary stared her down while she slowly stirred sugar into her coffee, one packet at a time. "You and I are going to have a little conversation about your dad's diner."

Sam leaned her head back on the back of the booth. "That's a little bit of a sore subject right now. Can it wait?" Sam knew as the words came out of her mouth she shouldn't have even bothered.

"Well, too bad, it's past time to get this shit sorted out, so you're not going anywhere."

Mary counted the empty packets in front of her and pushed the basket she'd emptied toward Sam, who sighed and grabbed her a new one off the next booth over. They looked at each other for a while in tense silence before Mary spoke.

"What the hell are you doing, Samantha?" She let her words sink in before she went on. "You're going to lose Sara because you're too proud to pull your head out of your ass?"

Sam looked down, running her keys through her fingers one by one. "Mary, you know it's not that easy."

Mary tapped her fingers on the table and looked at Sam, who sank back into her seat again, plans for escape looking more and more unlikely.

"I'm not saying it's easy," Mary said, "I'm saying it will cost you the love of your life unless you get it figured out."

"Geez, Mary," Sam said, shaking her head. "You don't mince words, do you?"

"I've lost two parents and a husband. I know you think if you just never go in there again, you'll never have to think about losing Gus, but we both know it doesn't work like that."

Sam shook her head. "It's not that I've consciously decided that. It just feels like too much."

"Listen, Samantha," Mary said, her voice softening. "Since the moment he laid eyes on you, Gus's life was all about making you happy, making sure you never had to feel scared or alone again." Mary put her hand over Sam's and squeezed. "Do you think this is what he'd want? You losing someone you love because you can't let him go?"

Sam swiped at a tear with the back of her hand.

"Honey," Mary said, "he's not in that diner anymore. It's just a building."

"Well, it doesn't feel like that."

"I know." Mary turned the gold wedding ring still on her left hand. "And you'll always have memories of your dad in that diner. But those are in your heart, not in the bricks of that place."

Sam nodded, and Mary wiped a tear from Sam's face with her thumb. "You know, Gus would have adored Sara."

"I know," Sam said, a smile finally breaking through. "I've thought that since the day I met her."

Mary pulled out her keys and pulled one off the ring. She slid it across the table toward Sam. "This is yours now, sweetheart," she said. "I hope you use it."

She stood and walked out, squeezing Sam's shoulder as she went.

Sam sat there for a few minutes, then walked out of Moxie Java, pulling her phone out of her pocket as she walked back toward the station.

"Jennifer?" she said, "I need your help with something."

❖

Later that evening, Sam knocked at Sara's door and she opened it with a toothbrush in her mouth, her nearly dry hair wild like a gold dandelion puff around her face. Sara was wearing just her underwear and Sam's jacket, looking at her wrist for her nonexistent watch.

"Oh no!" Sara said, stepping behind the door while attempting to pull the bottom of the jacket over her backside. "Is it that late?"

"Not really," Sam said, "I'm early."

Sam was right on time, of course. She stepped in, closing the door behind her and pulling Sara in for a kiss. Sara stood on her tiptoes to kiss her, then ran back toward the bathroom to finish getting ready.

"Ten minutes, max!" she called down the hall toward Sam as she disappeared.

Exactly fourteen minutes later, Sara emerged looking adorable in a navy sleeveless dress and leather flip-flops, her hair somehow transformed into shiny waves caught in a loose braid that fell over one shoulder.

"Wait," Sara said, looking suddenly confused. "Wasn't I supposed to meet you at your house?"

"I just came to walk over with you," Sam said, "It's getting dark."

They stepped out of the cabin and started down the road to Sam's house. Dusk had almost settled and the deer stared at them from the forest on each side of the road, their eyes soft and deep as they watched them pass. Sam took Sara's hand and held it so that her own covered it almost completely.

"Did you learn this stuff in the butch handbook?"

Sam laughed. "What stuff?"

"How to hold my hand so my fingers don't get cold when it's chilly."

"As a matter of fact," Sam said, "that is in the handbook. In the chapter titled *How to Melt a Femme*. I was reading that around the time we met."

Sara looked over at her with one eyebrow raised. "Hmm... you may have that chapter confused with *How to Give a Femme a Ticket*."

Sam threw her head back and laughed, squeezing her hand. "You may be right. That's still one of my favorites."

Sam's cabin came into view with the shimmering navy blue lake beyond. A velvet green lawn surrounded a winding path made of gray slate slabs, and to the right, a large labyrinth made of short stone walls sat at the edge of the trees.

"What's that?" Sara said. "I love it. It looks like the mazes they have in some of the gardens in England."

"It's a labyrinth," Sam said. "I've always loved them. Something about them is soothing. I was running out of things for the seniors to do, so I had them start on one a few years ago."

"The high school seniors?"

"Some of the junior and senior class come out and do landscaping for me. I don't know how it started really, but word got around, and I get new students every year that want to learn how to do it." Sam opened the door and stepped aside for Sara. "I pay them, of course, and keep track of what they've earned. If they can show me they've saved at least eighty percent at the end of the year for college, I match it."

Sara took off her jacket, laying it over the back of Sam's sofa. "Wow. That's amazing."

"It's not a big deal." Sam walked over to the kitchen and pulled out a bottle of Sauvignon Blanc. "I got lucky with my parents. I never had to worry about stuff like that. It's not like that for everyone."

She handed Sara a glass of the pale gold wine, chilled perfectly and already frosting the outside of the glass. They walked out on the back deck, and after Sara sat, Sam went back in to get the cheese and baguette she'd laid out on a raw cypress slab earlier, surrounded by olives, prosciutto, and baked garlic in olive oil. She put it on the table between their deck chairs and pulled a can of spray cheese out of her jacket pocket for Sara, who grabbed it immediately and kissed her cheek.

"You know," Sam said, "it was actually lucky that you were such a pain in my ass in the beginning."

"Oh really?" Sara smiled, baguette in one hand, spray cheese in the other. "And why is that?"

Sam took a swig of her beer and reached across to rest her hand on Sara's thigh. "Because the first time I met you, you were topless. Then when I busted you in the cove, you were literally wearing a soaked white tank top over a black lace bra and panties when you climbed into my boat."

"Oh really?" Sara teased. "I had no idea you even noticed."

"Right," Sam said. "Even as pissed off as I was, I don't think I hid it well."

Sara spread some soft baked garlic onto a piece of baguette, then topped it with prosciutto and handed it to Sam. "You didn't hide it all."

They watched the sun set over the lake, the air holding a chill that signaled the arrival of fall. The first of the leaves had painted themselves yellow and fiery copper, fading slowly into crimson as the days went by. The fact that the diner opening was in four days kept edging into Sara's mind as she talked to Sam, but she pushed it away every time. The diner would take up the majority of her life soon enough. She didn't want to waste the time she had left with Sam, worrying it would drive a wedge between them.

Sam stood up, offering her hand to Sara. "Bring your glass and follow me."

She left the food where it was and led Sara to the far end of the back deck and up a spiral staircase to the second level. Tucked into an alcove was a beautiful cedar-sided hot tub, already bubbling, the steam rising and hovering in the cool air. A bench beside it held a stack of fluffy towels and two robes, as well as a bucket of ice and a bottle of Sara's wine, already open and chilled.

"Wow," Sara said, leaning back into Sam's chest.

"Something tells me you haven't been treated like you should have been in the past," Sam said, unzipping the back of her dress. "Just a guess."

"That's putting it mildly." Sara stepped out of her dress and underwear, unhooking her strapless bra and folding everything neatly on the bench. "Although I hope you're serious about me because you're ruining me for anyone else in the future."

"I see you've discovered my plan," Sam teased, stepping into the water and holding her hand out for her.

Sara's nipples had hardened in the cool air, and the tight lines of her body were a contrast to the soft curves of the moving water as she lowered herself into it. Sam refilled her wineglass and handed it back to her, pulling Sara closer into her naked body.

"Is this your way of getting me naked, Draper?"

"Absolutely." She tilted her head to the side, seemingly in thought. "Although you've always seemed to lose your clothes around me pretty easily, starting that first day."

Sara splashed her in response and moved across from Sam so she could see her.

"Do you remember the conversation we had the last time you were here at the house?" Sam asked.

Sara nodded. "I asked you what you'd never done in bed and you said that there was one thing." She smiled, her eyes teasing. "Knowing you, I'm not sure I want to find out what it is."

Sam pulled her closer and held her eyes. "I've never slept with someone I was in love with, until you."

"Sam Draper," Sara said, "You're such an undercover romantic."

"Well, don't tell anyone, I've got a reputation to protect."

Sara laughed and moved into Sam's lap, wrapping her legs around Sam's waist.

"In fact, someday I might even buy you a hoodie that fits you to keep at my house," Sam said. "But no promises."

Sam's arm was stretched out along the edge of the hot tub, and Sara reached for her hand and brought it to her mouth. Sara slowly sucked one of her fingers into the warm wetness of her mouth, circling the tip of it with her tongue.

Sam's eyes were locked onto hers. "Jesus, Sara." She leaned

her head back and looked up at the night sky. "I'm not responsible for my actions if you keep doing that."

"I see now you've discovered my plan," whispered Sara, leaning into Sam's neck and running her tongue along the curve of her ear. Sam slid her hands from Sara's hips to her ass, pulling her hard into her body.

"We should take this inside now," Sam said, drawing one of Sara's nipples firmly into her mouth, then letting it go with the slightest scrape of her teeth. "Or we're doing this right here."

Sam got out first and handed Sara a thick white robe, then wrapped one around herself. "Just leave everything here, we'll get it in the morning."

"Oh," Sara said, looking up at Sam. "You think I'm staying the night?"

She kept a straight face for just a second before she laughed, and Sam swatted her ass as she held the door open for her. Sam stayed downstairs to build a fire while Sara showered, and she reemerged a few minutes later wearing Sam's enormous hoodie and a pair of sheer black panties.

"Not that I'm complaining," Sam said, "But where did those come from? I'm pretty sure they're not mine."

"I've claimed a drawer in your bedroom," said Sara, curling up on the couch. "And I brought some lingerie I think you'll like so you will let me keep it."

"Baby," Sam said, leaning over to kiss her, "you can have the whole damn dresser."

It was Sam's turn to shower, and she came back downstairs a few minutes later wearing faded jeans and a sweater, her dark hair damp and raked back with her hand. Sara was staring into the flames. Sam got them both a glass of scotch and settled into the couch beside her. "So what are you thinking about so hard over here?"

Sam passed Sara's glass to her.

"My plan to take over your dresser."

"You don't need one, but you might want to drink that scotch."

"Why is that?" Sara said.

Sam smiled. "You may need it."

"Hmm," Sara said, "I'm not sure if that's scary or hot." She smiled, pulling her sleeves down over her hands. "Which happens frequently, actually. Lily referred to it as your *mafia quality.*"

"I'm going to leave that completely alone," Sam said, laughing, "but I *would* kill anyone who tried to hurt you."

"See?" Sara teased. "There it is again." She walked over and sat by the hearth to warm her back.

"I can't believe you two were talking about me," Sam said. "I have a feeling this is going to come back and bite me in the ass."

"Totally possible." Sara agreed, trying not to smile.

Sam looked at her, with damp hair and bare legs, teasing her about her ex. The sexiest thing about Sara was her defiant little attitude, or maybe it was the contrast between that and the way she let Sam take her in bed.

"Come here, baby."

Sara sat down on the couch, the tension thick and hot between them. Sam sank to her knees in front of Sara, slowly spreading her legs, sliding her hands up the inside of her thighs. Sara pulled the hoodie off over her head, leaving only the sheer black panties. Sam looked at her for a moment, then ran a finger underneath the elastic. She was already deliciously wet.

"Fuck," Sara said, leaning her head back and closing her eyes. "How do you always do this to me?"

"Do what to you?" Sam whispered, leaning in and biting the thin silk layer between her and Sara's clit.

She felt how wet she was, and felt the heat that met her tongue as Sara moved her body down, trying to get closer. Sam edged the panties down her thighs, holding Sara's eyes while she slid two fingers deep inside her.

"Oh my God," Sara said, her breath deep and hard.

Her hips moved against Sam's hand, and Sam dipped her head between her thighs, dragging her tongue slowly across Sara's clit, curling her fingers up inside her to press the spot that she knew Sara craved, stroking it until she felt Sara's breathing quicken and the muscles in her thighs tense.

Sam paused, stroking Sara's thighs, then stood and held her hand out to Sara. Sam led her to the bedroom, turning out the lights downstairs and lighting a fire in her bedroom fireplace. Sara got into bed, pulling the sheets up over her and hugging her knees as she watched Sam blow gently on the dried kindling, coaxing it silently into bright yellow and orange flames, the crackling of the pine logs the only sound in the room. Sam stood by the fire, taking her in, then lay down and pulled Sara into her arms. Sara's eyes were just beginning to close when she felt Sam take her hand and place it just below the button of her jeans. She met Sam's eyes, then moved slowly closer, running her palm lightly over the hard length of it.

"Baby," Sam whispered, "I don't have to stay strapped on. You can change your mind anytime, just tell me and it's gone."

Sara looked at her and unbuttoned the top button of her jeans. "All you need to lose are the clothes."

Sam laughed, sliding them off in the firelight and getting back into bed. Sara ran her fingertips lightly over the harness. It was beautifully made, thick black leather with brass detail and a brass buckle that fastened at each hip. Her initials, *SD*, were stamped into the leather. Sam wrapped her hand around the back of Sara's neck, pulling her into a kiss. Her hands slid over Sara's body, smoothing over the curves of her hips and waist, then pulling Sara gently over on top of her.

"God," Sam said, taking her in. "You're so beautiful."

"I'm glad it's you," Sara whispered, grazing Sam's nipples with the flat of her palm, "that I'm doing this with."

Sam looked into her eyes. "I'm honored to be the one you trusted."

Sara leaned forward to kiss her, her breath quick with excitement, Sam's hands stroking her thighs as she started to lean slowly back. She felt the first touch and hesitated, then leaned farther back, slowly, until it was inside her and she felt Sam's hips between her thighs.

"Are you sure you want this, baby?" Sam reached up and tucked a stray lock of hair behind her ear.

Sara held Sam's eyes. "More than I want to breathe." She started to move gently, then gradually with more confidence, her body meeting Sam's with every stroke.

Sam held Sara's hips, her thumb sliding over Sara's clit, as Sara leaned back and closed her eyes, her hands braced on Sam's thighs behind her. Her hips moved in slow grinding circles, unknowingly moving the harness underneath just enough to put the perfect amount of friction on Sam's clit. Sara leaned forward long enough to whisper in her ear, then sat back up and braced her hands on Sam's. After a minute, she found what gave her the perfect pressure inside, her nipples hardening and a fine mist of sweat glistening on her skin. Her thighs gripped Sam's hips as she rocked back and forth, eyes closed and head thrown back in pleasure. Sam drank in the sight of her; she knew Sara was close to climax. Her breasts were flushed with arousal, her clit swollen and slick under Sam's touch. But she also knew either Sara had to stay still for a few seconds, or it would be her going over the edge.

She gripped Sara's thighs and closed her eyes, feeling it quickly building past the point of no return. Sweat started to slick over the hard lines of her body, her muscles tight.

"Fuck, baby, I'm coming…"

Sam arched hard under Sara, hands tight around her hips as her orgasm shook her, rocketing through every inch of her body with a blinding intensity she never knew was possible. She let out a guttural groan, just as another orgasm suddenly swept through her, taking her breath with it.

Sara couldn't take her eyes off Sam. When her breathing finally slowed, Sara bent down to whisper in her ear. "Seeing you come like that was the hottest moment of my life."

Sam smiled, still trying to catch her breath, and ran her hand through her damp hair. "Not by a long shot, baby," she said, flipping Sara underneath her with one smooth motion. "Turn over."

Sam's voice was husky with strength and arousal. Sara turned over and Sam pulled her up gently onto her knees in front of her.

"Remember when you asked me if I knew what you needed?" Sara nodded. Sam traced the curve of her hip with her palm. "Do you want me to show you?"

Sara nodded and Sam laid a hand gently between her shoulder blades. "Lean forward and give me both of your hands."

The quiet power in Sam's voice instantly brought Sara close to the edge. She leaned forward until her chest was on the bed as Sam took her hands and held them both in just one of hers at the small of Sara's back. Sam guided the shaft slowly inside Sara, and she moaned softly with pleasure.

"Jesus, Sam," Sara said, suddenly breathless.

Being inside her and watching the lush curves of Sara's ass press back against her hips was almost too much, but Sam focused and leaned into her, still holding Sara's hands behind her back. She reached around at Sara's waist and placed her other hand low on her tummy, exploring until she found where she needed to be. She pressed gently with her fingers and met that touch from the inside with perfect pressure and a slow, building rhythm.

"Oh my *God.*" Sara's voice trembled, her hands tensing underneath Sam's.

Sara had never felt anything like this, slow burning pleasure so shatteringly deep and intense that suddenly nothing else existed except Sam, deep inside her. As the intensity built, Sam slowed her pace and focused the pressure until she felt Sara's orgasm take over and heard her soft scream as she went over the edge. Sara trembled as the orgasm pulsed hard through her body, soaking Sam's thighs with the warm rush of her climax.

After, Sam wrapped her arms around Sara and laid her down, pulling her in, whispering for her to breathe. Sara melted instantly into her arms.

"Well," she whispered, her voice already falling into sleep, "you did it. You've ruined me for any other butch. Ever."

Sam smiled and pulled her closer, realizing suddenly how much she wanted that to be true.

Chapter Eighteen

Sara turned over lazily in bed and snuggled closer to Sam. She was deliciously sore and opened her eyes as the memory washed over her. Unfortunately, she also caught a glimpse of her watch.

"Shit!" she said softly, throwing back the covers. "I'm so late!"

She scrambled for her clothes before she realized she'd left them at the hot tub. She was just pulling on the jeans Sam had taken off the night before when Sam opened her eyes.

"Not that you don't look cute as hell in those," Sam said, "but where are you going?"

Sara pulled on Sam's T-shirt and stole her flip-flops, stopping to give her a hurried kiss on the way out the door.

"I have the menus being hand-delivered to the restaurant at nine and I have to sign for them or they go back," she said. "But I'd love to go to lunch later if you have time."

"You got it," Sam said. "I have to do some stuff at the station anyway. I'll call you around noon."

Sara ran back and jumped on top of her, covering her with kisses, then ran out the door.

Sam lay back on the bed, staring at the ceiling as a sinking feeling of fear settled into her chest.

❖

Sara ran to her cabin, raced through a shower, and threw herself into her truck, almost forgetting the diner keys. She'd had the menus completely redone, which had taken much longer than she'd expected, and the company offered to send someone to hand-deliver them today. She got into town and skidded into a parking space at five minutes after. A confused-looking guy with two boxes and a clipboard was waiting at the front door of the diner, looking at his watch.

"I'm Sara Brighton," she said, breathless, as she got to the door and unlocked it.

"I just need you to sign for these," he said, handing her the clipboard.

Sara signed it hurriedly and moved the boxes inside. She took one to the kitchen and set it on the prep table, slicing the top open with a paring knife. The menus were perfect; they were laminated, with a simple font and a vintage picture of Main Street from the 1950s with the lake in the distance on the top.

Local favorites, the dishes from the recipes she and Mary had sampled, were on the left, with each cook's name next to his or her dish. On the right were *Southern Comforts*, dishes that Sara had developed around her favorite Southern favorites, from buttermilk fried chicken with mac and cheese to skillet cornbread with bourbon honey butter. She'd put her heart and memories into these dishes, and she was nervous—there was no guarantee they'd be popular, and the memory of her last disastrous tasting loomed in her mind as a distinct possibility.

Mary had helped her refine the list and picked out her favorites, insisting that she'd have to take the pork chops and butterbeans home to really make up her mind about them, then poked her head back in the kitchen on her way out and grabbed the container of pulled pork BBQ with slaw and brioche buns.

"Just for research," she said, breathing in the aroma of the sweet, smoky BBQ sauce that Sara had made with blackstrap molasses.

It was a good sign that Mary loved her food. Maybe everyone would this time.

Sara spent the day setting up her computer system in her office and double-checking the food and linen orders. Everything was in place to open Thursday evening. It was a "soft" opening, only for locals, with no charge. She wouldn't open for regular business until the next weekend, but a soft opening was great practice for her staff and a way to thank everyone who'd helped her along the way. Maybe there had been a silver lining to Sam not setting foot inside the diner; she hadn't been there to lean on, so every time something happened with the construction, plumbing, or anything else she had no clue about, someone local had stepped up to help her. Word had started getting around town that she was putting a new diner where McCall's used to be, and some of them had even stopped by and poked their heads in the door when the lights were on just to meet her.

Mary had called Steve McCarthy, a retired electrician, when the lights above the counter inexplicably fizzled and died, and he'd somehow fixed the problem in less than ten minutes, including the walk out to his truck for a part. Sara sent him home with a huge chunk of pot roast and he'd shown up to check on her a couple of times in the next few weeks, just to see if everything was still okay. The morning her new gas fireplace arrived, she was struggling to get it through the door until Bart, the guy she'd bought her boat from, saw her from across the street and brought it inside for her. He'd stayed to unpack it, set it up, and even programmed the remote for her, despite her best efforts to convince him she could do it herself. She did get him to let her wrap up some roast chicken and garlic mashed potatoes for him, though, and by the time she'd gotten to Moxie Java the next morning, everyone seemed to be talking about the new diner going in up the street. When she asked him about it later, he'd just pulled the visor down on his cap. "That chicken was damn good," he muttered. "I might have told some people about it."

By the time the opening had rolled around, Sara felt like she'd met everyone in town, and the ones she hadn't met somehow seemed to know who she was and wished her luck when they saw her. She'd even hired some of the high school kids that had impressed her at the pancake breakfast, including Mara, who was turning out to have great ideas.

But now the opening was looming, and she had almost everything ready, which unfortunately only served to give Sara time to stew about what might go wrong. She realized just before noon that she was pacing back and forth in the kitchen, so she told herself to stop being ridiculous and do something constructive. The last box of cutlery was still on the counter from the delivery the previous week, so she set about unpacking it and washing them by hand. She turned the hot water on and waited for it to warm, then reached the cold water. The second she turned the handle it fell completely off, sending a wide stream of water ten feet into the air. She looked up, shocked, then reached for the handle to turn it off. Which of course was no longer there. The water showed no signs of letting up and actually now seemed to be shooting even higher, which hadn't seemed possible. In desperation, Sara covered it with a small saucepan, but that rocketed off in two seconds.

"Fuck!" she said, tossing the saucepan across the counter and trying to press the heel of her hand down over the exposed pipe.

The double doors to the kitchen opened and Sam ran over to the sink, opening the cabinet underneath and pulling out a huge pipe wrench. She reached back to the shutoff valve and tightened it down until the water stopped.

"You're my hero!" Sara said, jumping into her arms and wrapping her legs around Sam's waist. "How did you know I broke it?"

"I didn't," Sam said, putting her gently down on the counter beside the wrench and pulling her in for a kiss. "I opened the door and heard something major going down, so I ran in here."

"Wait," Sara said, the fact that Sam was finally in the diner slowly sinking in. "I can't believe you're here."

"I'm sorry it took me so long, baby," Sam said. "I should have been here for you a long time ago." Sam pulled Sara into her arms. "I don't have anything to say for myself. But will you forgive me?" she whispered.

"There's nothing to forgive." Sara snuggled into Sam's arms, her anxiety forgotten.

"So," Sam said, "what are the chances of me getting a personal guided tour?"

"Excellent," Sara said, hopping down off the counter. "You're the guest of honor." Sara took her hand and walked into the dining room.

"Wait," Sam said, pausing at the diner counter, looking at the stools, every one of their seats embroidered with the word *Reserved*. "What's this?"

"This counter is reserved for the over-fifty crowd," Sara said. "Everyone I talked to mentioned they used to know someone who'd sit here every morning, reading the paper. So I have four copies of the paper set to be delivered to the diner by six every morning, and those carafes"—Sara pointed to a group of five insulated coffee carafes at the end of the counter—"will hold complimentary coffee and remain on the counter all day."

"Wow," Sam said, laughing. "They might try to kiss you when they hear about this."

Sara laughed and Sam looked out the open rear door to the deck. "What in the world is out there?"

"Go look," Sara said, following her out the door, where Sam stopped in her tracks.

"This is incredible," she said, "Dad always said he was going to do something out here in the back but never got around to it."

"Do you like it?"

Sam just stared, taking it all in. "It's beautiful, baby," she said. "I love it."

She waited as Sam climbed the stairs to the second level and looked up at the heaters and the vinyl curtains that zipped closed to keep the warm air inside in the winter.

She turned and called down to Sara. "Now, this is just genius."

"Thanks," Sara said. "Obviously I didn't do this in Savannah, but I thought it might allow me to utilize the space year-round."

"Absolutely." Sam looked around, appreciating the comfortable details Sara put into the décor, including the hearth and fireplace at one end of the bottom deck.

"Just...wow," she said, shaking her head as she joined Sara on the lower deck.

"Ready to see the inside?" Sara asked.

Sam took a breath, and then Sara's hand. As they walked in, Sara went to click on the lights, including the warm gold lamps by the sofas. When she had finally gotten them all and had turned around, she knew what Sam was looking at. She was walking slowly up and down the walls, stopping to look at the framed photos of Gus with the McCall locals, and even the one of Sam behind the counter, barely taller than the surface, while Gus laughed with someone sitting on the other side, coffee cup in hand.

When Sam finally turned around to face Sara, her face was wet with tears. "Do you know how long I've felt guilty because I couldn't face preserving those pictures?"

Sara crossed the room and hugged her, holding her close.

"I'm sorry," Sam said finally, letting her go and wiping her eyes with the back of her hand. "I'm actually okay. They're mostly happy tears."

"You don't ever have to apologize to me for tears, happy or otherwise," Sara said. "I love all of you."

Sam tilted her face up to hers and kissed her gently. "I feel like a weight has been lifted off my shoulders," she said. "Thank you."

Sara smiled, looking over at a pulley system mounted on the wall. Sam's eyes followed the ropes to the ceiling, where a rough-hewn farm table, twelve feet long, was tucked snugly up to the rafters.

"Is that what it looks like?"

Sara walked over to the wall and pressed a button. The table started to descend from the rafters to the middle of the room, smoothly and slowly, until all the legs touched the ground. The details clicked into place for Sam. "That's why there's a space here with no tables."

"Yep, but we won't have to take the chairs from the other tables, check this out."

She ducked under the table and pulled down an iron lever, which let down the bench seats on each side that were stored, folded flush against the underside of the tabletop.

"That's the coolest thing I've ever seen," Sam said, shaking her head and running her hand over the smooth surface of the wide oak planks.

"Don't be too impressed. I designed it but I had someone build and install it for me," Sara said. "It's actually there primarily for Sunday night roast."

"Roast?"

"Our hours are short on Sundays—we shut down at two in the afternoon so the staff can clean up and get ready for locals' night. Every Sunday evening, I'll do a roast of some sort, and everyone who comes brings another dish, like sides or dessert. Totally free, kind of like a potluck."

"And it's just for locals?"

"Only locals, and everyone's invited. If it gets big, we have plenty of extra tables." Sara giggled at her own joke, instantly looking adorable.

Sam pulled her into her arms. "You have no idea how amazing all this is," she said. "The whole town lost something when the diner closed. You're giving it back."

Sam kissed her, holding her face in her hands, then sank down to one knee. She pulled a black velvet box out of her pocket and opened it. Inside was a two-carat yellow diamond, set on a classic white gold band.

"Sara," she said, her voice shaking just a bit, "I don't deserve you, but I'll spend the rest of my life making you happy if you'll let me." She cleared her throat, suddenly so nervous she forgot what she needed to say next. "Will you marry me?

Sara stood with her hand over her mouth, in shock, then raised her eyes to Sam's. "Yes," she said, smiling. "A thousand times yes."

Sam slid the ring on her finger, a perfect fit thanks to Jennifer, then jumped up and folded Sara into her arms as huge cheers erupted outside. Sam turned Sara toward the window to reveal everyone they knew crowded around it, trying to get a better view. Sam gave a thumbs-up sign and held Sara close while they poured in the door, most carrying bottles of champagne and everyone holding one of Mary's mason jars.

"Wait," said Sara, looking up at Sam. "If I'm married to Captain Draper, does that mean my boating license never expires?"

Sam laughed and held her close. "Never," she said. "It's yours forever."

Not too long after that, Lake Patrol officers pulled Sam away into congratulatory slaps on her shoulders from all of them and a cold beer from Murphy's secret stash. Maurice found Sara and kissed both her cheeks, tears in his eyes.

"Samantha has always been my daughter too," he said, looking over at Sam, smiling and laughing with her officers. "And I knew the moment I met you that you were the one." He pulled Sara into a tight hug. "*Félicitations, mon chérie.*"

Mary found Sara soon after and hugged her until she was in danger of looking mushy, and even Lily had written her a note and given it to Jennifer for Sara.

Congratulations to you both. Sam is a lucky woman.

Sara was touched. She tucked it in her pocket to show Sam later and smacked Jen's arm with the back of her hand.

"I can't believe you didn't tell me this was happening!"

"I only found out yesterday! Do you like it?" Jen said, holding Sara's hand up to the light.

"It couldn't be more perfect," Sara said honestly, mesmerized by the endless brilliant sparkle.

"Well," Jen said, her nose slightly in the air, "that's because I didn't let her pick it out unsupervised."

Sara laughed and hugged her sister, looking over at Murphy. "Don't worry," she whispered, "I'll return the favor."

Champagne flowed all afternoon and everyone laughed and drank, congratulating Sam and Sara and all gravitating toward the pictures on the walls. Sara's cheeks ached from laughing at the stories they told about each other, some true and some even better because they weren't.

As the sunlight started to fade, Sara found Sam and took her hand, leading her out the front door of the diner. Brown kraft paper was still taped across the top of the window, and Sara pointed up at it. Sam was just tall enough to reach the top edge and ripped it down in one motion. It was the diner's new sign. *Gus's Place.*

Keep reading for an excerpt from

RETURN TO MCCALL

available now from Bold Strokes Books

CHAPTER ONE

A spicy waft of cinnamon enveloped Sam Draper as she opened the door of Moxie Java, cradling the phone between her face and shoulder as she searched her jacket pocket for her wallet. "I'm here now, babe, and it smells like they have those amazing cinnamon rolls. Want me to drop one by the restaurant before I head back to the station?"

Sam pulled her wallet from her pocket as she said a quick good-bye to her wife, Sara, and dropped the phone back into her jacket. For once, there was no line at Moxie Java, the only coffee shop in the tiny mountain town of McCall, Idaho. Sam congratulated herself on her timing as she spied their famous cinnamon rolls dripping with cream cheese frosting on a cooling tray behind the counter.

"Good morning, Heather." Sam smiled at the teenager behind the counter, who stared back blankly, her face strangely pale and tense. "I'll take two of those beauties behind you and a large black coffee."

Heather bit her lip and stood stiffly in place, an unattended lock of bright teal hair falling across her face, her eyes locked over Sam's shoulder. The walls seemed to echo Sam's words, bouncing them across the café, then watching as they drifted slowly to the floor, reverberating in the hollow silence. The tension in the air settled onto Sam's shoulders as she instinctively shifted her focus. Her eyes flicked to Heather's hand, stiff and motionless by her side except for the single finger pointing to the left. Sam shifted her face into neutral and turned slowly where she stood, keeping her gaze soft and steady as it settled onto another thin teenage girl. This one held a Glock semiautomatic weapon, her hands shaking, her finger pulled tight against the trigger.

Sam studied the girl's red-rimmed eyes and uneven black hair haphazardly tucked behind one ear. She wore glasses with a crack down the center of the left lens and had a tense grip on the gun. Too tense.

"Hey there." Sam kept her voice soft and wished that she'd worn her service weapon while off duty for the first time in her career. "Take it easy. My name is Sam."

The girl shook her head slightly as if to discard Sam's words, then jerked her head toward the sound of a young boy coughing in one of the window seats. His mother pulled him closer and whispered in his ear, looking frantically out the window before wrapping him in her jacket.

Sam took a quick glance around at the situation. Moxie Java was at about half-capacity, about fifteen people in the building, including herself and the staff behind the counter. Everyone was staring, their eyes darting back and forth between her and the gun pointed in her direction, including a portly deputy in a beige Ada County Sheriff's Department uniform handcuffed to the back of his chair. His shiny bald head was slick with sweat, and his wrist strained against the metal rungs as he stared at the gun.

Sam turned back to the shooter and softened her gaze. "Look, why don't you tell me why you're doing this? There has to be a reason." She paused, watching the girl's eyes fill with tears that were quickly blinked back. "What's going on?"

"Stop talking!" Her words were sharp, staccato, and seemed to clatter and fall flat onto the floor in front of her. "I just need her—" The girl paused, then jerked her head toward Heather. "To go lock the damn door so no one else can get in."

Heather waited until Sam nodded, then walked with shaky steps around the counter to lock the door. She hesitated before she went back toward the counter, her eyes still locked on Sam.

"Why the hell is everyone watching *you*?" A touch of panic elevated the girl's voice, and her eyes spun wildly around the room. "I'm the one with the gun."

Silence settled between them. Out of the corner of her eye, Sam caught one of the employees starting to say something, so she jumped in first.

"The rumor is that I look like a tall Tom Cruise." Sam flashed her most charming smile, silently willing the McCall locals to take the hint and not reveal her status as law enforcement. "So that could be it."

"No." The girl studied her with the barest hint of a smile. "That's definitely not it."

One of the bussers behind the counter snorted, and she glared at him, the smile fading quickly from her face. The boy in the window seat started wheezing again as his mother dropped to her knees at the end of the booth, pulling him toward her.

Sam kept her eyes on the girl with the gun. "What's your name?"

"Why?" Her eyes snapped back to Sam. "So you can pretend to care?"

"Look, it sounds like that kid is having an asthma attack. And if he doesn't get out of here and get treatment, things could get real serious, real quick." Sam paused, locking eyes with the shooter. "And I can tell you don't want that to happen."

"Right, so they can go straight to the cops?" Her glance flitted to the ground, then back to the boy. "That's all I need. More police up in here." Her eyes flicked over to the handcuffed deputy, then back to Sam.

Another snort from the teenage busser, and this time, both Sam and the shooter turned to look at him.

"Um…" the busser said, trying not to look at the gun she now had pointed at his head. "Hate to burst your bubble here, but…" His voice trailed off as he nodded in Sam's direction.

"What?" The shooter haphazardly swung the gun back in Sam's direction. This time, it was close enough for Sam to see that the safety was off. "He's a cop?"

Sam was about to answer when several local voices behind them did it for her. In unison. "*She's* a cop."

The gun in her hand sagged slightly as she registered the information, then snapped back up.

"Listen," Sam said softly. "I'd love to return to this fascinating discussion on misgendering butch women, but I think something else is more important." She looked pointedly back to the boy struggling to breathe by the window. His breath had sunk to a low, audible scrape.

"Just go." The shooter's voice was low and soft as she caught his mother's pleading gaze. "Get him outside. But nobody else moves, and you…" She spun the gun toward Heather. "Lock the door behind her."

The mom scooped him up in her arms and carried him to the door, followed by a nauseated-looking Heather, who quickly unlocked the door to let them out, then locked it behind them. She walked back toward the counter, lifting her eyes to the girl only once. "She said to tell you thank you."

For just an instant, the girl's face softened before she pulled it back to stone.

"Look, unless you want me to start calling you Moxie, you need to tell me your name." Sam paused. "It's not too late to get out of this, but we're going to have to work together for that to happen."

The girl kept the gun trained on Sam but lowered one stiff hand and shook it out. The busser chose that moment to pick up one of the cinnamon rolls and leisurely fold half of it into his mouth, icing dripping onto the front of his apron.

"All right. Moxie it is." Sam turned her attention back

to the girl and took a slow breath. "You need to let the rest of these guys go. Whatever you want, they don't have it. So let's simplify things here."

The last of Sam's words were drowned out by sudden shouting from the deputy, who'd decided now was a good time to get up, wave his one free hand around, and act a damn fool. "Goddammit! I've *had* it!" He attempted to drag the chair toward the front of the restaurant, his face fury red and spitting with every word. "All I had to do was get one lousy delinquent from point A to point B, and I'll be damned if I'm going to let that little thieving Mexican bitch make me look like a—"

Moxie's face was expressionless as she trained the red laser sight at the deputy's head with a look serious enough to make everyone but the deputy duck under the nearest table. Dust floated in the wide beam of silent sunlight between them, and everyone watched the next move in the deputy's master plan, which was to stand in the middle of the floor and wet himself, apparently.

It was all Sam could do not to roll her eyes as she turned back to the girl. "Listen, Moxie." Soft sounds of crying and true panic had started from every direction as Sam paused, choosing her words carefully. "We've got to get everybody out of here. I'm not going to be able to help you fix this and get closer to what you want if that gun goes off."

"Why do you think I want something? Why does everybody always think that?" Moxie lowered her gun and swiped at a tear with the heel of her hand. "'Cause I don't. I just can't go to one more stupid house." She paused to draw in a shaky breath. "I can't. And I'm sure as hell not going to where that guy just tried to take me."

Sam looked out the expansive front windows of Moxie Java at the officers running up to the building in formation, guns in the low ready position. Her brother-in-law Murphy brought up the rear and signaled them to surround the building.

Sam caught his eye through the glare of the window as he held his hand to his face in the phone sign.

"Listen, if you put that gun down long enough for me get these people to safety, it'll be just you and me. We can figure out how to get past this."

"Yeah, right." Moxie glanced up, suddenly looking very young and completely exhausted. "How do I know you're not trying to trick me?"

Sam shook her head, her voice soft. "I don't trick people, Moxie. That's just not my style."

"Yep, that's true." The same busser finished the last of his cinnamon roll and swiped at the icing of the next one with his finger. "Draper's good people. Everyone knows that."

Sam turned back to Moxie and lifted an eyebrow in a silent question. Moxie slowly lowered her gun and stepped back as Sam stepped into action, informing the officers outside of the plan with a quick call and making the exit process as smooth as possible. Everyone but the deputy was out the door in under sixty seconds until the busboy stopped to swipe one of the chocolate muffins out of the display box.

"Oh, for the love of God, man." Sam signaled him out the door, trying not to laugh despite herself. "Step on it!"

His hair flopped into his face, and he grinned as he passed her, tucking a sugar cookie into the chest pocket of his shirt.

Finding the keys and unlocking the fuming deputy's handcuffs took forever, and Sam walked him to the door to put as much distance as possible between him and Moxie. He jerked from her grasp and out the door, shouting more of the same tone-deaf obscenities. It was all she could do to not slam the door behind him.

When she got back to the front of the shop, Moxie was sitting on the floor, the gun still cocked, but it was now lying quietly in her lap. Sam got a takeaway cup of water from behind the counter and set it on the floor a few feet away. When she raised her head to speak, Sam noticed a smattering of caramel freckles across her nose.

"Why are you being so nice to me?"

"I've been in law enforcement a long time. Long enough to know this isn't what you want to be doing." Sam steeled herself against the smile she felt forming on her face. "So tell me, how did you get away from the Deputy of the Year over there?"

Moxie's face melted into her first smile, at least until she saw the officers with their guns pointed at the glass door.

Sam's phone buzzed, and she checked it, then held it up. "It's the officers outside. They need an update. Is that okay?"

"Whatever." Exhaustion softened the edges of her words as she dragged a hand through her hair. "Just tell them to back the hell up."

Sam phoned one of the officers. The second Murphy picked up, he asked her if anyone was hurt. Sam said no, feeling the burn of Moxie's stare as she glanced in her direction. Murphy paused, then asked if Sam wanted the officers to hold their position until otherwise instructed. Sam hesitated before she said yes. She was betting on her ability to get through to this girl, but she was very aware that that's exactly what it was. A bet, one she could lose in a split second.

Sam slipped the phone back into her pocket. Moxie traced the lines of the gun with her finger, then tipped her face to the ceiling. A tear slipped off her chin and onto the black barrel in a silent splash.

Sam looked around until she found what she knew would be there. A rumpled black trash bag stuffed to the top and slumped against the table leg where the deputy had been cuffed. "So," she said, waiting until Moxie met her eyes. "Foster kid, huh?"

"What?" Her eyes locked onto Sam's in a look of delayed shock. "How'd you know that?"

Sam nodded at the limp bag leaning against the side of one of the tables. "Your fancy luggage kinda gave that away."

She nodded, swiping at another tear with the heel of her hand. "Yeah. I feel like I live out of those."

Sam nodded, noting the bruise on her cheekbone that had faded to a greenish-yellow outline. "So the deputy was taking you to your next placement?"

Moxie nodded, then reached for the water and drank it greedily with a shaking hand, as if she'd just remembered she was thirsty. Afterward, she crushed the cup, sinking it into the corner trash like a pro.

"You play?"

"I did. I was at my last place for my first two years of high school." Moxie shook her head, still staring at the trash where the cup had disappeared. "I made the varsity team, but who knows now? I don't even know where they're sending me."

"So just a sudden shift, huh?"

Moxie nodded, her eyes fluttering closed for just a second before she tightened her grip on the gun in her lap.

Sam nodded toward her. "Something to do with that bruise on your cheek?"

Moxie's fingers rose slowly to the side of her face. "How could you possibly know that?"

"It doesn't take a genius to figure out a shiner like that and a new foster placement at the same time means trouble." She softened her voice and met Moxie's eyes. "You get in a fight?"

"Nah. Not really." Moxie shook her head. "My foster mom caught her new man picking the lock on my bedroom door a couple of nights ago and decided she needed to remind me who he belonged to."

"Yeah, she doesn't want to lose that one." Sam rolled her eyes to the ceiling. "He sounds like a straight-up prize."

That made Moxie laugh, and the tears had cleared from her eyes by the time she looked up. "Hey, didn't I hear you tell someone that you were bringing them a cinnamon roll?"

"Yep, my wife, Sara." Sam smiled. "She owns the restaurant across the street."

Moxie nodded, clicking the safety back into place. "Gus's Place or something, right? I saw it as we came into town."

. "Exactly. Sara makes the most amazing food, but I've got to be honest, she'd trade me in a heartbeat for a Moxie Java cinnamon roll. And I'm not sure I blame her."

The girl glanced at the trash bag across the dining room. "What are they going to do with me out there? When we leave?"

Sam got up slowly, retrieved the bag, and set it down between them as she helped Moxie to her feet. "You're worried about your stuff, aren't you?"

She nodded. "Yeah, it's kinda everything I own."

Sam looked out the window at the officers, who lowered their guns slowly in response to her signal. "Listen, here's what's going to happen. First, I'm going to wrap up a cinnamon roll for Sara. Frankly, I'm scared of what'll happen if I don't, and then we'll walk out there together. But no matter what, I won't let anyone touch your stuff, okay?"

Moxie looked up, worry fading from her eyes as she carefully handed Sam the gun. "Thanks for being so nice to me. You didn't have to be, especially with me threatening to shoot the place up and everything."

"So how old are you? Really?" Sam laid a ten-dollar bill on the counter and dropped the only cinnamon roll the busboy hadn't touched into a bag.

"Fifteen." She hesitated, starting to say something twice before it fell out in a rush. "And you're a real cop? No offense, but you don't seem like one."

"Well, you got me there, Moxie." Sam sent a quick text to the officers outside to let them know the suspect had been disarmed, and they were on the way out. "I'm not a cop. I'm McCall's Chief of Police."

About the Author

Patricia Evans is currently writing your new favorite novel in her hand-built tiny house, nestled deep in the forest, where she's surrounded by a bevy of raccoons and a sleepy brown bear named Waddles.

She travels to Ireland and Scotland several times a year in search of the perfect whiskey and cigar combination and spends most of her time trying to ignore the characters from her books that boss her around as she writes by the fire.

Follow her adventures:
www.tomboyinkslinger.com
@tomboyinkslinger on Instagram
patricia@tomboyinkslinger.com

Books Available From Bold Strokes Books

And Then There Was One by Michele Castleman. Plagued by strange memories and drowning in the guilt she tried to leave behind, Lyla Smith escapes her small Ohio town to work as a nanny and becomes trapped with an unknown killer. (978-1-63679-688-8)

Digging for Destiny by Jenna Jarvis. The war between nations forces Litz to make a choice. Her country, career, and family, or the chance of making a better world with the woman she can't forget. (978-1-63679-575-1)

Hot Hires by Nan Campbell, Alaina Erdell, and Jesse J. Thoma. In these three romance novellas, when business turns to pleasure, romance ignites. (978-1-63679-651-2)

McCall by Patricia Evans. Sam and Sara found love on the water, but can they build a future amid the ghosts of the past that surround them on dry land? (978-1-63679-769-4)

Promises to Protect by Jo Hemmingwood. Park ranger Maxine Ward's commitment to protect Tree City is put to the test when social worker Skylar Austen takes a special interest in the commune and in Max. (978-1-63679-626-0)

Sacred Ground by Missouri Vaun. Jordan Price, a conflicted demon hunter, falls for Grace Jameson, who has no idea she's been bitten by a vampire. (978-1-63679-485-3)

The Land of Death and Devil's Club by Bailey Bridgewater. Special Liaison to the FBI Louisa Linebach may have defied all odds by identifying the bodies of three missing men in the Kenai Peninsula, but she won't be satisfied until the man she's sure is responsible for their murders is behind bars. (978-1-63679-659-8)

When You Smile by Melissa Brayden. Taryn Ross never thought the babysitter she once crushed on would show up as a grad student at the same university she attends. (978-1-63679-671-0)

A Heart Divided by Angie Williams. Emmaline is the most beautiful woman Jack has ever seen, but being a veteran of the Confederate army that killed her husband isn't the only thing keeping them apart. (978-1-63679-537-9)

Adrift by Sam Ledel. Two women whose lives are anchored by guilt and obligation find romance amidst the tumultuous Prohibition movement in 1920s California. (978-1-63679-577-5)

Cabin Fever by Tagan Shepard. The longer Morgan and Shelby are stranded together, the more their feelings grow, but is it real, or just cabin fever? (978-1-63679-632-1)

Clean Kill by Anne Laughlin. When someone starts killing people she knows in the recovery world, former detective Nicky Sullivan must race to stop the killer and keep herself from being arrested for the crimes. (978-1-63679-634-5)

Only a Bridesmaid by Haley Donnell. A fake bridesmaid, a socially anxious bride, and an unexpected love—what could go wrong? (978-1-63679-642-0)

Primal Hunt by L.L. Raand. Anya, a young wolf warrior, finds herself paired with Rafe, one of the most powerful Vampires in the Americas, in an erotic union of blood and sex.(978-1-63679-561-4)

Snake Charming by Genevieve McCluer. Playgirl vampire Freddie is on the run and a chance encounter with lamia Phoebe makes them both realize that they may have found the love they'd given up on. (978-1-63679-628-4)

Spirits and Sirens by Kelly and Tana Fireside. When rumored ghost whisperer Elena Murphy and very skeptical assistant fire chief Allison Jones have to work together to solve a 70-year old mystery, sparks fly—will it be enough to melt the ice between them and let love ignite? (978-1-63679-607-9)

Aubrey McFadden Is Never Getting Married by Georgia Beers. Aubrey McFadden is never getting married, but she does have five weddings to attend, and she'll be avoiding Monica Wallace, the woman who ruined her happily ever after, at every single one. (978-1-63679-613-0)